Readers are gripped by Kathleen McGurl's novels:

'A rollercoaster of a novel, full of twists and turns . . . An immersive read that I cannot recommend enough. I inhaled it in two days'
RACHEL BURTON

'An absolute page turner, it had me gripped and in its spell . . . From the first page I was absolutely hooked'
READER REVIEW

'Atmospheric and captivating . . . A well-paced and gripping story with a satisfying conclusion. Highly recommended'
JANE BETTANY

'Once you start reading you cannot put it down'
READER REVIEW

'Captivating . . . a sparkling gem of a story'
DAISY WOOD

'The story has lots of twists and turns, but the best part of it all are the incredible characters who feel as though they come to life on the page'
READER REVIEW

'A richly textured, poignant story that swept me away'
ADRIENNE CHINN

'Very addictive'
READER REVIEW

KATHLEEN McGURL lives in Christchurch with her husband. She has two sons who have both now left home. She always wanted to write, and for many years was waiting until she had the time. Eventually, she came to the bitter realisation that no one would pay her for a year off work to write a book, so she sat down and started to write one anyway. Since then, she has published several novels with HQ and self-published another. She has also sold dozens of short stories to women's magazines, and written three How To books for writers. After a long career in the IT industry, she became a full-time writer in 2019. When she's not writing, she's often out running, slowly.

Also by Kathleen McGurl

The Emerald Comb
The Pearl Locket
The Daughters of Red Hill Hall
The Girl from Ballymor
The Drowned Village
The Forgotten Secret
The Stationmaster's Daughter
The Secret of the Château
The Forgotten Gift
The Lost Sister
The Girl from Bletchley Park
The Storm Girl
The Girl with the Emerald Flag
The Lost Child
The Lost Diamond

The Vanished Girl

KATHLEEN MCGURL

ONE PLACE. MANY STORIES

HQ
An imprint of HarperCollins*Publishers* Ltd
1 London Bridge Street
London SE1 9GF

www.harpercollins.co.uk

HarperCollins*Publishers*
Macken House, 39/40 Mayor Street Upper,
Dublin 1 D01 C9W8
This edition 2026

1

First published in Great Britain by HQ,
an imprint of HarperCollins*Publishers* Ltd 2026

Copyright © Kathleen McGurl 2026

Kathleen McGurl asserts the moral right to be identified as the author of this work.
A catalogue record for this book is available from the British Library.

ISBN: 9780008591731

This novel is entirely a work of fiction. The names, characters and incidents portrayed in it are the work of the author's imagination. Any resemblance to actual persons, living or dead, events or localities is entirely coincidental.

All rights reserved. No part of this publication may be reproduced, stored in a retrieval system, or transmitted, in any form or by any means, electronic, mechanical, photocopying, recording or otherwise, without the prior written permission of the publishers.

Without limiting the exclusive rights of any author, contributor or the publisher of this publication, any unauthorized use of this publication to train generative artificial intelligence (AI) technologies is expressly prohibited. HarperCollins also exercise their rights under Article 4(3) of the Digital Single Market Directive 2019/790 and expressly reserve this publication from the text and data mining exception.

Printed and bound in the UK using 100% Renewable
Electricity by CPI Group (UK) Ltd

This book contains FSC™ certified paper and other controlled sources
to ensure responsible forest management.

For more information visit: www.harpercollins.co.uk/green

For Jo, Lu and Ali – who've been my friends forever

Prologue

Pippa, 7 August 1976

Pippa's mum had told her to go to play with Lynne, who lived up the road, but Lynne wasn't at home and her mum said she'd gone out with Jo somewhere on their bikes. Pippa had run back home, got her bike out of the shed, and pedalled off in search of them. They were probably with those boys that they hung around with. One of the boys was Jo's brother, but Pippa didn't really know the other one.

They were all a few years old than her, and Pippa sometimes felt awkward when she was with them. She was only eight. It was all right if it was just Lynne and Jo, who were twelve, but not the boys, who were older still.

Pippa pedalled her bike hard through the estate and out into the countryside. She had a good idea of where the girls might be – she'd heard them talking about an old broken-down farmyard they'd been playing in. The sun was hot on her back. It had been hot for weeks now. There had been no rain since April, and the grown-ups were all complaining about the brown grass and the lack of water. Sometimes the water went off, and her mum would put jugs of water on the kitchen table with a tea towel over them, and that's all they had to drink until the water came back on.

'What if we run out of water completely?' Pippa had asked. Mum had laughed and said that would never happen. But what if it did? If she found Lynne and Jo today, and they weren't with the boys, Pippa would ask them. They'd probably give a better answer. Grown-ups didn't like answering eight-year-olds. Twelve-year-olds knew lots of things, but they could also remember what it was like to be eight.

Pippa was sweating and puffing hard by the time she reached the farm. The entrance was all locked up, but there was a gap in the hedge – just to the right side of a padlocked gate. She leaned her bike against the gate and went through the gap. There were no other bikes out there, but maybe the other kids had somehow hauled their bikes through the gap.

Inside the farmyard all was quiet. That wasn't a good sign, Pippa thought. She'd imagined as soon as she got there she'd hear sounds of them playing, shouting, talking, laughing. But there was nothing.

'Lynne! Jo? Are you here?' she called out, but her voice sounded small and lost, and no one answered.

The big farmhouse stood to the left of the yard, closed up because no one had lived there for years. On the right was the old hay barn where Lynne and Jo said they played – games of 999-In and hide-and-seek, and make-believe games in which the bales of straw were moved around to form pirate ships or castles or magical kingdoms. Pippa headed over to the barn – maybe the kids were in there, doing something quietly. She pictured them huddled around a board game like Ludo or Snakes and Ladders. Lynne had Mousetrap at her house – that was Pippa's favourite game, and she loved it when she was invited to play with the older girls.

'Hello?' she called as she entered the dark space. Her voice sounded tiny under the high roof. It was a little bit cooler inside, out of the sun, but not much. There were gaps in the roof that let the light in. 'It's only me, Pippa.'

But there was no answer. She felt suddenly scared, too nervous to search any further inside the dark barn. It was hard to see properly after being out in the sunshine, and there could be all kinds of monsters hiding behind the hay bales.

Maybe the girls were back at Lynne's house now. That's where she would go next, and if they weren't she'd just ask Lynne's mum if she could stay there anyway. If she promised to be quiet and keep out of the way, perhaps she'd even be given an ice pop.

Pippa turned to leave the barn and immediately noticed someone by the gates. They must have come while she was inside, because she hadn't heard them arrive. She would have to go right past them to get to the gap in the hedge but somehow she didn't want to. She wasn't supposed to be there. She was going to get told off. She stepped back, wondering if she could run back into the barn and hide in the hay until they went away.

'Hello, you! Come over here.'

Still Pippa held her ground, feeling uncertain, but not for any reason she could put her finger on. It wasn't as though they were strangers. It was just . . . something felt wrong.

'There are kittens inside the house. Do you want to play with them?'

Well, that changed things. Pippa adored kittens, so she skipped over happily towards the house. She knew she'd been right all along to come to the farmhouse. Now she'd have a fun afternoon after all.

Chapter 1

Jo, March 2024

It's hard to explain precisely why I decided to move back to the little village of Hareton Wick in Hampshire. The village is bounded on one side by the New Forest – that's now a national park – and on the other by rolling arable farmland. It's a pleasant, bucolic little spot. These days you can drive to Southampton in under an hour, but back in the mid-seventies, when I last lived here, the roads weren't as good and my dad had to drive an hour and fifteen minutes each day to reach Southampton university where he worked.

It's funny to think I am so much older now than my parents were then. I have so many memories of that time. Some good, but not all of them.

When people have asked me: *Why move there?* I've given various explanations. I've told them I like country living; that I want to be settled in a place where I'll be happy to retire in a few years' time. That I work from home, creating online training material, and can live anywhere, so why not pick a pretty village, and it might as well be one I already know? And it has the advantage of being close to Dad, in Southampton. He's getting to that stage in life where he needs more support. Obviously supporting him is going to fall to me, the one who stayed in England. My brother David won't do a thing, just like he didn't when Mum needed care. David moved to Australia, and when I'm feeling uncharitable, I'm sure he did it to get out of needing to take any responsibility for our ageing parents.

He escaped; I didn't. And now I'm back where I started.

I'm not one given to much self-analysis. But if I had to dig deep and work out exactly why, after nearly fifty years, I've actually moved back to the place where I spent my early childhood, it's probably because this is where I was happiest, in that long, hot, last summer, before my world fell apart. And because, in an odd sort of way, it feels like there's unfinished business for me in Hareton Wick. We left so suddenly when everything went wrong.

There's also, I should admit to myself at least, a more recent reason. Something I can't put out of my mind. Something that caused a descent into the bottle, from which it's been a long haul out. Something that my subconscious is associating with this place, with what happened just before we moved away. At least that's what my therapist suggested.

The upshot of it all is that I ended up moving back here last week, buying myself a two-bed bungalow in an estate which didn't exist back in 1976. It would have been too weird by far to move to our old estate or the street where my old best friend, Lynne, had lived. She'd messaged me, in reply to the change of address email I'd sent her. *Hey, Jo, when you're settled, let's meet up for a coffee and a chat about old times. It's been far too long.*

She was right. We'd kept in touch after my family moved away and we'd met up sporadically for a while, but eventually contact had dwindled to Christmas cards with a few words scrawled in them. At some point, we'd added email addresses to those Christmas cards, and when I'd emailed about my change of address, I'd provided my mobile number. Lynne had remained living in the area, though not in the village itself, all these years. It would be good to catch up and reminisce. I didn't yet know how much I wanted to tell her of my recent problems, however.

But that wouldn't happen just yet. I had a thousand boxes to unpack. I wanted to meet my new neighbours, but so far I'd been too shy to knock on their doors. I wanted to be living here, I wanted to meet with Lynne and reminisce, but at the same time, I didn't want to meet anyone else from back then. At least not yet. I needed a new start, a new beginning in a place I felt safe.

And I needed to lay the demons from the past to rest.

I glanced out of the patio doors of my sitting room. It was at the back of the bungalow, overlooking a small garden that badly needed neatening up. It was March and the daffodils were just beginning to poke their heads out here and there between the corpses of last year's weeds.

It was one of those blustery days, where the sun came out every now and again but then the wind blew clouds across it and the temperature dipped. I rather like those changeable days, when the weather can't make up its mind what it's doing. I feel like it understands me, it matches the way my life's been lately – up and down and unpredictable. So, I donned a puffer jacket and woolly hat, shoved a pair of gloves in my pocket and set off on a walk around the village. I'd been meaning to do this since moving in, but there'd been other priorities – making the house liveable, buying groceries, visiting Dad, and then of course I'd had to work, at home, for the last few days. Boring, but it stopped me brooding. Also, it paid the bills. Which was just as well, because since I split up with Colin, I needed the income.

So today was the first day I'd properly ventured out. 'Keys, phone, purse,' I muttered to myself, patting my pockets, as I opened the front door and stepped out. Across the road, a man was just getting into his car. He lifted a hand in a kind of cautious wave, which I reciprocated, then drove off. One of my new neighbours,

I supposed. He looked about forty-five, white, balding – pretty average, really. I promised myself that soon, very soon, I'd call round to everyone to introduce myself. *Better do it sooner rather than later, Jo*, I told myself. It'd be embarrassing to leave it too long and have to say to everyone, 'I really should have called round sooner.' Mind you, none of them had called on me to say hello, yet. Perhaps they were just allowing me time to settle.

I turned left, towards the village centre. My route would take me across my estate and into the parts of the village I hoped I'd recognise. I'd driven round it all, of course, when I came house-hunting, but it's different in a car. You don't really look at what's around you. My home was on the main road of the estate, near the top of the hill. I walked down the slight hill, that curved around to the left and then the right. Leading off it were numerous short cul-de-sacs of five or six houses each.

If my house had an upstairs, there would probably have been a view across the countryside – not the open heather-clad moorland of the New Forest but the farmland on the other side of the village – fields of wheat and rape, winding lanes bordered by ancient high hedgerows, farm buildings dotted here and there.

At the bottom of the hill I turned into what became the village High Street a little further along. I passed the church that hadn't changed a bit over the last fifty years. Next to the church was a pub. I remembered it as The Stag's Head, a place my parents never visited. Mum turned her nose up at it, saying it was where 'working men' went for their pint after work. I used to say, 'But isn't Dad a working man?' After all, he had a job he went to every day.

'That's different,' Mum would answer. 'Your father's a white-collar worker. A university lecturer. Not that you'd guess, he's supposed to be so clever.' This last bit would be said in a half-whisper, accompanied by a roll of her eyes. I was young, just ten or twelve years old, and wasn't supposed to notice. But I did. I always noticed whenever she said anything against Dad, or he muttered criticisms of Mum. And it happened a lot.

The Stag's Head was no more. It was now a smartened-up gastropub named 'Julio's'. I peered at the menu displayed in the window. It looked good, so I made a mental note of its opening hours. One to try later. For today, I hoped there'd be a café somewhere in the village. A cup of coffee and maybe a cake would be lovely on a cold day like this.

Down the street a bit further was a row of shops, just as there had been in 1976. They'd changed, though. The greengrocer, butcher, and Spar grocery store I remembered had been knocked through to make one small Tesco supermarket. Next to it, the newsagent-cum-post office I recalled, where I'd spent most of my weekly pocket money on sweets and comics, was still there. I popped in to take a look. Gone was the long, wooden counter with piles of newspapers at one end and huge jars of sweets behind. In its place was a rack of greetings cards and selection of discounted books. At the end, the post office counter was partitioned off behind glass. A photo booth stood in a corner, with an 'Out of Order' sign sellotaped to it.

Outside again, I continued walking up the street. A turn to the left led to Brookhill Comprehensive – the last school in the area that I'd attended. Across the road were two charity shops, side by side. They'd been a haberdasher's and a children's clothes shop, if I remembered correctly. Mum had bought me white cotton knee socks from there.

Beside them was a café, as I'd hoped. I crossed the road and went in, ordering an Americano and a toasted teacake.

'One black coffee, one teacake,' the woman repeated, giving me a look that suggested she didn't like all the nonsense of modern fancy coffees. I should have ordered tea.

As I glanced around the café deciding which table to take, I noticed a man of about my age who was just about to leave. He was shrugging on a jacket and bringing his used cup back to the counter. Something about him looked familiar, although I couldn't quite place him. As I walked past him to an empty table he stopped me. 'Jo Salway, isn't it? Gosh, it must be . . . decades!'

'Yes, I'm Jo . . . Atkinson these days. I'm sorry . . . I can't quite . . .'

'Charlie Willis.' He put out a hand to shake mine. The name rang a bell, but I still couldn't quite work out how he knew me. I smiled anyway and hoped it'd come to me. 'Charlie, hello. You're right – I haven't been here for nearly fifty years. Hard to believe it's that long, eh?'

'Fifty years! Yes, I suppose it must be.' He smiled at me, and I was struck by the warmth in his eyes. He was a nice-looking man, it had to be said. 'You might remember my father more than me. Crispin Willis. He was friends with your parents, I think.'

'Crispin! Ah, yes, of course! Dad knew him quite well from the school's Board of Governors. Oh, and I do remember you too.' Once or twice the school governors had met at our house, and I remembered Crispin bringing his son round. 'Didn't you, me and my brother play *Escape from Colditz* one evening while our parents were in a meeting downstairs?'

'We did, but we renamed it *Escape from Brookhill*, as I recall.' Charlie laughed. 'Not that I was even at the school. How are you, Jo? And your brother, and parents?'

'Mum died a long time ago. Dad's still around – frail now, but OK. Lives in Southampton. David's in Australia with his wife, kids and grandkids.'

'And you?'

I shrugged. 'Divorced, one son who's a teacher, no grandchildren yet. Just moved back to the village. How about you?'

'On my own now, four grown-up kids. Lost my mum, and Dad's got dementia, so I need to take care of him and his assets.'

'Oh, I'm sorry to hear that. I always liked your dad.' A memory bubbled up of Mr Willis calling at our house and handing me a packet of sweets, with a wink and a whisper, 'Don't tell your parents!'

'Yes, he's a good man,' Charlie said. There was sadness in his voice. I couldn't imagine what it must be like to lose a parent to dementia. I was lucky, in that Dad showed no signs of it at all. He was physically frail but mentally as sharp as ever.

At that moment the waitress emerged from behind the counter with my coffee and teacake. 'Where're you sitting, love?' she asked.

'Oh, there,' I said, pointing to the nearest vacant table.

'Well, I won't keep you any longer,' Charlie said. 'Good to see you. Look, here's my number. Maybe we should meet and have a proper catch-up sometime?'

'I'd like that,' I said, taking the business card he handed me. 'I'll text you so you have my number too.'

We said our goodbyes and I sat down by the window to send the text and drink my coffee. I rather liked the idea of seeing Charlie again. Having a friend in the village could only be a good thing.

I watched as village life passed by outside the window. A couple of teenage boys cycled past, laughing at something. They reminded me of my brother David and his best mate Rick as they'd been during our last summer, before it all went wrong. Cycling everywhere with Lynne and me tagging along if we were allowed. Running wild from a young age. Kids didn't do that so much these days, preferring to stay home with PlayStations and computers. Or did their parents prefer them to stay home where they could be watched over, where they were safe?

They had a point. Back then we never gave a second thought to whether we were safe or not, as we roamed the lanes and fields around the village. We just took it for granted that the streets, the village and the countryside were there for our enjoyment. Right up until that day in the long hot summer of 1976 when little Pippa Jenkins went missing.

Chapter 2

Jo, 21 July 1976
Seventeen days before.

The story starts, I suppose, on the last day of the summer term that year. I was twelve years old, at the end of my first year at secondary school, and I was walking home as usual with Lynne. We'd removed our ties; we'd sung all the verses of 'No More Days of School' that we could remember, and we were already well into holiday mode.

'My dad says this is the longest period without rain we've ever had, since records began or something,' I said, trying to sound knowledgeable. It was yet another day when the sun had blazed down upon us all day. All I could think about was whether Mum would have been shopping and stocked up the freezer compartment in our fridge with ice pops or not. I dearly hoped so. If not, I'd have to go to the village shop with my pocket money and buy myself a Rocket or maybe an Orange Maid. Anything frozen.

Lynne nodded. 'Yeah, my mum says it's terrible they're turning off the water. Water is for everyone and they shouldn't turn it off.'

'But if there isn't enough water to go round, I suppose they have to. Thing is, everyone just fills up jugs and the bath when the water's on, to last when it's off. So surely, we all use the same amount in the end anyway?' That was what I couldn't understand. It made no sense. Plus, I hated having to drink the warm water that had been sitting in jugs on the kitchen counter all day. I hated too the smell of the toilet that hadn't been flushed since the morning.

'I can't believe we'll be second years when we go back in September,' Lynne said. 'This year's gone fast, don't you think?'

'Yes, it has! And you'll be a teenager next birthday. Really old!' I widened my eyes at my friend in mock horror.

'So will you!'

'Yes, but your birthday is way before mine. You'll be a teenager in November, but I'll still be twelve until May.'

'You're just a baby!'

I dodged the play-punch Lynne threw at me, giggling. 'Better a baby than an old woman!'

'Hmm. So, what will we do tomorrow then? Shall I come to you, or you to me?'

'I'll come to yours,' I said, decisively. 'Dad's at home, because the university term ended ages ago.'

'Are your parents still fighting?'

'Yes.'

'I'm sorry, Jo. I wish there was something I could do to help.'

I blinked back the tears that formed at my friend's kind words and forced myself to smile. 'Just letting me come round a lot helps. Anything to be away from them when they start shouting at each other.'

Lynne caught my arm and pulled me close. 'Mum said you can come round any day. For tea too, sometimes. But if you come at lunch time we must make our own cheese on toast or sandwiches or whatever.'

'Thanks. I like your mum. I wish I was your sister.'

'Wish you were too.'

We'd reached the zebra crossing on the village High Street. 'Have you got any money on you? Fancy going to get an ice cream or something?' I said, as we passed the newsagents.

Lynne shook her head. 'No. Anyway, that place is expensive, Mum says.'

'Yes, it is.' We walked on past the newsagents and the other shops in the small precinct and turned into a narrow passage that led into the scruffy recreation ground. Cutting through that was the quickest way to our estate. 'So, what'll we do tomorrow?' I asked.

'Let's go out to play. Otherwise we'll end up babysitting Pippa Jenkins. Her mum often dumps her at our house if she's working.'

'Why doesn't she stay with kids her own age?' I asked.

Lynne shrugged. 'You know they only moved to our road in May. She didn't change schools – kept on at her old school. I don't think they know anyone else in the village yet. She's all right, but she's a kid. Gets in the way. What's your brother planning to do tomorrow?'

I shrugged. 'I don't know. He'll be out somewhere with Rick, I reckon.'

'Think they'll let us tag along if they're out on their bikes? It was a good laugh at half term when we cycled out for that picnic in the woods.'

'When we ended up splashing around in the stream and got soaking wet!' I chuckled at the memory. If I recalled correctly, it was my brother David who'd started it – filling his bottle from the stream then flicking water at me. I'd flicked back of course, but Rick had been in the way and caught the spray. Then he'd waded into the stream in his plimsolls and kicked water all over both me and Lynne. Before we knew it we were all in the stream, laughing and splashing, and not caring in the slightest that our clothes and shoes were soaking. It was absolute bliss to cool down.

'That was fun!' Lynne laughed too. 'Wonder if there's any water in that stream now or if it's all dried up?'

'Maybe we could ask if David and Rick want to go there again?'

I looked questioningly at Lynne. Was she blushing? I sometimes thought that perhaps Lynne fancied David. I hoped not. If David fancied Lynne too, and they started going out together, where would that leave me? I didn't feel ready for that kind of thing. Not yet. I liked the way things were – playing out, just being kids, enjoying life and having fun. No need for all that boyfriend–girlfriend stuff. There'd be time enough when we were thirteen.

The boys were both already thirteen. David would be fourteen in October. But so far, he was still a kid, liking the same things I liked, wanting to do the same kind of stuff he always had. I was lucky to have him as a brother, close in age, similar in temperament. Lynne's sister was seven years older and never spent any time with her – Kate was always out with her boyfriend or her bitchy girlfriends. She was on the point of leaving home, and I sometimes fantasised about Lynne's mum asking me to move in and take Kate's bedroom when she left.

'Yeah, we could go there. But wasn't David going on about some old farmhouse he and Rick wanted to explore?'

I frowned. 'When did he say that?'

'Yesterday, break time. When your maths class was kept in late.'

'I haven't heard anything about a farmhouse.'

'Ask him at home tonight? Let's start the summer holidays as we mean to go on, with an adventure!'

I laughed at Lynne's excitement. 'OK, I will.' We'd reached the recreation ground, and were passing beneath the trees that ran along one side of it. It was a bit cooler, being out of the direct sunlight. 'Race you to the climbing tree!' I broke into a sprint with my school bag banging against my hip. Behind me I heard Lynne running too, laughing and panting.

She was, as always, faster than me and reached the tree just before I did, slapping her hand against its trunk. 'I win!'

'You always do. First up it?' I dumped my bag by the tree's roots and climbed up. The tree was a pollarded oak with plenty of low branches spreading outwards from its trunk. It was easy to climb to a spot in the middle from where you could settle yourself comfortably and watch the world go by. There was space for two and it was a favourite place for us ever since David had shown us it.

In a minute we were both there, nestled in the arms of the tree, sheltered from the relentless sun. We shuffled around until we were sitting back-to-back, acting as each other's back rests. 'Young ladies don't climb trees,' Lynne said, in a mock authoritarian voice, mimicking one of our teachers who'd once passed by and had looked up to see us giggling. We giggled again now at the memory.

'Do you think we'll ever feel too old to climb up here?' Lynne asked.

'Probably. When we're as old as Kate, maybe. She doesn't climb trees, does she?'

'I don't think she ever did. She'd be too concerned about chipping her nail varnish. Her latest favourite colour is blue.'

'Blue nails?' I'd never seen nail varnish in any colours other than shades of pink and red.

'Yep. Mum had a fit first time she saw it. Kate said she's getting green next.'

'Green!' I tried to imagine Kate with green nails. 'That'd look witchy.'

'I'll tell her you said that,' Lynne replied playfully.

'Don't! She'll kill me!'

'She would! Hey, who's that waving at us?' Lynne pointed to a boy a few years older than us who was crossing the rec.

'Ah, that's Mr Willis's son. Charles, his name is.' I recognised him, though I didn't know him very well. His dad was friends with my parents.

'Mr Willis?'

'Chair of the school governors. You know how last winter they had a meeting at our house, when the school staffroom was being repainted? Well, Mr Willis brought him round.'

'Oh, yes. He's not at Brookhill though?'

'Think he goes to school somewhere else. His parents are rich. Dad said really the meeting should have been at Mr Willis's house, but they had building work going on so it ended up being at ours.'

'What's he like?'

'Mr Willis? I like him.'

'No, idiot. Him.' Lynne waved a hand in the direction of the boy who was just disappearing from our view as he entered the cut-through to the High Street.

'Oh. Yeah, he's all right. We played a board game, him and me and David. Think I won.'

Lynne chuckled. 'D'you fancy him?'

'No, I do not!' I'd have playfully thumped her only we were sitting in a tree and I didn't want to risk knocking her out of it. 'You know I only have eyes for David Cassidy!'

We stayed up in the tree until our bums went numb. As long as we were home by teatime our mums didn't care how long we stayed out. My mum, I knew, preferred to have the house to herself as much as she could. Dad's term had ended weeks ago and he was at home most of the time now. Which meant I wanted to stay away from home as much as possible. Not because I didn't love Dad – I did, I loved both of them – but because the atmosphere in the house when they were both at home was strained to say the least.

At last, we climbed down, walked up the hill into our estate and parted at the point where I needed to turn left into Heather Avenue and Lynne would turn right to Beechwood Road.

'See you tomorrow, then?' she said.

'Yeah. I'll ring you later when I've talked to David.'

I must have sounded a bit down at the prospect of going home, because she suddenly hugged me. 'It'll be all right, Jo. They'll work things out over the summer holidays, I bet.'

I nodded but didn't answer. I wasn't so sure.

*

I let myself in through the back door as usual. No one I knew used their front doors, unless someone rang the doorbell. Our back door opened straight into the kitchen, where Mum was angrily stirring a pot of something for our tea.

'Hi, Mum,' I said, closing the door behind me.

'Leave that open. It's too darned hot.'

'All right.' I opened the back door again, but of course there was no breeze coming in and probably it was cooler inside than out. Mum didn't look like she was going to say anything more to me, no 'How was the last day?' or 'What are your plans for tomorrow?' So I went on through to the living room. Dad was sitting on the sofa with a pile of books beside him, reading grumpily. *How can a person read grumpily?*, I thought, but he was. His eyebrows were knotted together, his mouth was set in a thin line, and he kept flicking a page back and forth. I suspected he wasn't taking anything in.

He looked up when I said hello. 'Last day of term, right, Joanne?'

'Yes. Wish we had holidays as long as yours.'

'Wish I had longer terms! Or a research project for this summer. Remember, Joanne, I'm not paid over the summer break.'

I wasn't sure what I was supposed to say to that, especially given that he'd said it crossly, as though it was my fault. So I shrugged and went upstairs to get out of my school uniform. There were marks on the back of my skirt from the tree. Mum wouldn't be happy. But it was getting too short for me, and I'd almost certainly need a new one next term, so who cared anyway? I dumped it and my blouse into the clothes basket in the bathroom and pulled on a pair of shorts and a T-shirt. I went to splash cold water on my face but nothing came out of the tap. Water was off, again.

'Mum! Is there any water to wash my face?' I yelled down the stairs. Usually she put the plug in the bath and filled it if she knew it was going off for a few hours.

'No. Only some here in a jug if you want a drink. It'll come back on soon though. You can just wait.'

Another parent grumpy with me for no reason, so I decided to stay upstairs until I was called down for tea. I'd been planning to look in the freezer compartment for an ice pop but decided against it. I'd only get moaned at.

'Don't worry, Sis. Give them another half hour and they'll be all right again. You came home at the wrong moment.' David stuck his head out of his bedroom door and spoke in a whisper. He was still in his school uniform, though his tie was around his head, bandana-style. He beckoned me into his room, where I sat on the bed and lay back, trying not to cry. I hated it so much when Mum and Dad were like this.

'What happened? What are they sulking about this time?'

'Dad forgot to put the dustbin out, and it stinks. He said Mum could have done it as easily as him, if she'd remembered. She said it's his job and doesn't she already do enough round here while he sits about reading books all summer? And that it's not as if he's earning any money right now. And he said he earns enough—' David broke off, spotting my expression. 'Ah well, you know how it goes from there. Usual argument about nothing much.'

'I hate it when they argue.'

'So do I. Grown-ups are stupid sometimes, Jo. Don't let it get to you.'

I nodded and sniffed. 'What're you up to tomorrow?'

He shrugged. 'Not sure yet. Probably go somewhere with Rick.'

'Can me and Lynne come too?'

David regarded me seriously, then nodded. 'Sure. Back in half term we had fun, the four of us. And you need to be out of this bloody house, don't you?'

I winced slightly at his use of 'bloody' – if Mum heard either of us say that word, she'd have a fit. But everyone swore at school, and we knew words much worse than that.

'Will we go to the stream again?'

He shook his head. 'Nah. Rick was there last weekend and said it's more or less dried up. He's got another idea. Some old farmhouse out on Hawthorn Lane. No one lives there, and he reckons we'd be able to get in, or at least go into the barn.'

'An old house?' It didn't sound as much fun as mucking about in a stream.

'Yeah. We could explore. Might be haunted!'

I squealed, as he knew I would. He grinned. 'You and Lynne up for that? You little girls won't be frightened of ghosts?'

''Course we won't be! Yes, I'm up for it, and I bet she will be too. I said I'd ring her and tell her the plans.'

'I'm calling for Rick at ten. We can pick up Lynne on the way if she's ready.'

'Right. I'll tell her.'

All seemed quiet downstairs so I went down to the hallway by the front door where the telephone was fixed to the wall. Stupid place for it, I always thought, as we never used the hallway and there was nowhere to sit. The curly wire wasn't even long enough to let you sit on the floor. You had to lean against the wall when using the phone. 'It means you won't stay on the phone too long,' Dad always said whenever someone complained about it.

I dialled Lynne's number. Her mum answered and put Lynne on, and I told her the plan.

'Haunted? Ooh-er! Mum said she'd do us all a picnic, so I'll bring that. Ten o'clock is good. See you then!'

I hung up feeling so much happier. Me, Lynne, David and Rick, out on our bikes, with a plan and a picnic. On the first day of the school holidays. There was no sign of the weather changing so our only problem would be being too hot. But the best thing about cycling rather than walking was that you created your own breeze as you went along. It would be a great start to the holidays and if this old farmhouse turned out to be a fun place to play, perhaps we'd go there lots of times. I began fantasising that the four of us would move in and live there, sleeping on discarded mattresses on the floor, eating picnics brought by Lynne's mum. It would be like something out of a Famous Five book.

Chapter 3

Jo, 2024

My walk up the High Street had given me a taste for nostalgia. I'd enjoyed checking out what had changed in the village since the seventies. After leaving the café I took the little cut-through to the recreation ground, the route Lynne and I used to take walking home from school. The rec, as we'd called it back then, had been tarted up. Gone were the creaking swings and rusty slide, and in their place stood an adventure playground, on some sort of cushioned ground surface. Kids these days are pampered, I thought with a wry smile. In our day we had to fall onto hard ground and put up with it. How we survived without broken arms and heads, I don't know.

Except, some of us didn't survive, did we? The thought popped into my head, followed immediately by an image of *her*, but I dismissed it. Today wasn't a day for dwelling on bad memories, whether old or recent.

I walked the route that took me past my old house in Heather Avenue. It looked smarter than I remembered, and a side extension had been built where the garage used to stand. This meant there was no side access anymore, no more going round to the back door to get in. The current owners would have to use the front door all the time now. I smiled, imagining what Mum would have made of that. Giving the kids front door keys at the age of ten or twelve? She'd have hated the idea. Though she'd have hated even more having to answer the doorbell to us when we came home from school.

The wind was picking up and it was becoming cold, so I decided to head home. I'd done enough for one day. It was time I started looking forward rather than back; time I began to build myself a new life here in Hareton Wick. I needed local friends, and the best place to start would be to contact Lynne. It had been far too long since I saw her last.

I sent Lynne a message and we arranged to meet the following day for lunch at her house. She lived in a large old house within the New Forest National Park, tucked away on a quiet lane along with three or four others. It was exactly the kind of place my mother had aspired to but never reached: an imposing red-brick building with pointed gables and ancient roses climbing its walls.

I hadn't seen Lynne since we were in our twenties, but somehow, thirty-five years on, she looked exactly the same when she answered the door. Older, certainly, with more lines, but still the same old Lynne. The same sparkling blue eyes and cheeky smile, although her long grey hair was bundled on top of her head in a messy bun rather than in the obligatory ponytail we'd worn as kids.

'Jo! Oh, my God, Jo!' She pulled me into a squeeze. 'I can't believe you're here! You're looking amazing!' She held me at arms' length and looked me up and down, grinning broadly.

'You look amazing yourself, Lynne! I'm so glad to be here.' And I was. It felt like the years were rolling back just by being in her presence. We'd always had that close kind of friendship where you knew nothing could ever really come between you. Somehow, the years, our families, distance and personal circumstances had got in the way and we drifted apart. But now there were no excuses.

'Come on through. I thought we'd sit in the conservatory. There's only about five days a year when it isn't either too hot or too cold in there, and today's one of them, so we'd better make use of it. Malcolm's not joining us for lunch, though he said he'll stick his head in and say hello later. Can I take your coat?'

I shrugged off my fleece jacket, then followed her through the house, which was tastefully decorated. Here and there I spotted items of furniture, pictures or ornaments I thought I recognised from her parents' home. 'Yep,' Lynne said, noticing me staring at a painting of a shy deer, looking back over its shoulder at the viewer, 'that was Mum's. I'm not sure I like it, but I've put it up for sentimental reasons.'

'Has your mum . . .?'

'Died? Yes, three years ago. Dad too, four years before that. You?'

'You probably remember that my Mum died ages ago when I was twenty-three. Dad's still around. He lives in Southampton, but he's becoming frail and needs more support. That's one of the reasons I've moved here, I guess.'

'I do remember about your mum. I'm sorry. That's so young to lose a mother. Glad you'll get to spend more time with your dad, though. I remember him as being a lovely man. Very clever, wasn't he? I was sometimes a bit intimidated by that.' She laughed, and I joined in, though it was hard to imagine Dad intimidating anyone. 'Take a seat and I'll fetch some coffee. Lunch in about an hour, if that's OK?'

'Perfect.' I sat on a pretty little sofa in a glass conservatory that looked out onto a well-kept garden. There was a greenhouse tucked into a corner that suggested one of them was a keen gardener. Would it be Lynne? I couldn't remember her being interested in gardening, but then at twelve who was? Maybe it was her husband Malcolm, who I only vaguely remembered. I'd met him at their wedding but not since.

Lynne returned with a tray holding coffee cups and a plate of cookies. 'So, how's David?' she asked.

'Happy, as far as I know. Married, three grown-up kids, two grandchildren so far.'

'Nice! Do you see much of him?'

I shook my head. 'No, he lives in Australia. He went out there on a gap year, working in bars. Met Giselle and decided to stay with her.'

'Next time you speak to him, pass him my regards.'

I smiled as if to say sure, I'd do that. But actually, I rarely spoke to David. Between the time difference and, well, *our* differences, we'd drifted apart. We'd been so close as kids. But he'd done something that last summer, that I'd found hard to forgive.

'I had a bit of a thing for him, when I was very young,' Lynne admitted.

I grinned. 'I knew it! I used to be terrified you two would run off together and leave me on my own.'

'You'd have had Rick!' For some reason that idea made Lynne dissolve into peals of laughter.

'I liked Rick.'

'So did I. He's married to a lovely man called Anton now, and they run a little bistro together in Lymington. I went for dinner there, oh, last year some time. We could go for lunch one day, you and I.'

'I'd love to. But wait – he's gay?'

'Yep. We never guessed, did we, back then? To be honest, I'm not sure I even knew homosexuality existed.'

'I definitely didn't. But twelve-year olds now would, and would probably know half a dozen gay people.'

'Better that way, eh?'

'Definitely.' I took a sip of my coffee. 'Oh, I bumped into Charlie Willis the other day.'

'Who?' Lynne frowned.

'He's the son of a friend of my parents. I only knew him slightly back then.'

'Willis . . . Oh, yes, there was a Willis on the parish council for years.'

I nodded. 'That'll be Charlie's father, Crispin. Who else do you still know from those days?'

'Well, Tricia works in the chemist's, and she married Pete Hargreaves from school, if you remember him? And there's Anna Palmer who worked as a nurse but now she's looking after her mum.'

'Anna was in our class, I think?' I recalled a gaunt, shy girl who always sat at the back.

'Yes, that's her. She never married. Now and again I call her and we go out for an Italian. Sometimes I think that's the only social occasion she has.'

'Ah, sad.'

'She doesn't seem too sad. It's how she's chosen to live. Oh, and then there's Natasha Woods and her brother.'

'Natasha?' I frowned, wracking my brain to think who Lynne was referring to.

'Natasha Thompson, as she was. Her family had the farm up on Marsh Lane.'

'The one where we used to play?' I was sure that was Hawthorn Lane.

Lynne shook her head. 'Not that one – that's Four Oaks Farm, the derelict one. Marsh Farm is further on. Natasha married Jeff Woods and they still farm there. They took over from Natasha's parents. She runs the farm shop, and her brother – Horace, you remember him? – helps her.'

Horace. Long-buried memories surfaced in my mind – a young man, a boy really, not that much older than ourselves. He was what, back then, we rather cruelly called 'simple'.

'Horace? Yes, I remember him. He's . . . out, then?'

'Yes. They released him after about ten years. He's living with

Natasha now. He's still the same.' She gave a lopsided smile.

'He was—' Gentle, I'd been going to say. But then I remembered that last summer, and what people said he did – the reason he'd been locked away – and that hadn't been gentle at all.

'Yes, he was. Whatever you were going to say. Natasha looks after him well, keeps him close. People round here remember too clearly what happened.'

'Do they still . . . persecute him?' A sudden, vivid and horrific memory had popped into my mind.

'They would, I think, if he wandered down to the village. Older people – those who remember it all – think he should still be in Broadmoor. Natasha makes him stay up at the farm, poor lamb. But if you go up to her farm shop, and I recommend you do because her produce is the best around, you'll no doubt see him.'

Poor lamb, Lynne had called him. The Horace I remember had been looked on with sympathy before that last summer but with suspicion after. My mum had certainly never considered him to be a 'poor lamb'. Dangerous nutter was her verdict.

'Did they ever find Pippa Jenkins?' I asked.

We'd talked about this when we'd met up in our teens and twenties. But I wondered if anything more had surfaced in the thirty-odd years since.

'No, not that I ever heard. There was all that drama and searching back in the summer of '76, then it all gradually died away, after Horace was sent to Broadmoor. Pippa's mum tried for a while to keep the police investigation going, and on paper it *was* still open, but in practice they'd given up. Mrs Jenkins then moved out of the area. Mum kept in touch with her for a while; she married again and had another baby, maybe two. Then we lost touch as well. I don't think Mrs Jenkins wanted to be reminded anymore of all that had happened.'

'If she's still alive she must wonder what happened to Pippa.' It was hard to contemplate someone living nearly fifty years without knowing what happened to their child.

'Yes. And I always wondered why poor Horace got blamed for it all.'

I didn't. I knew exactly why. And I'd spent my entire life since that last summer feeling guilty that I hadn't stopped it.

We sat in silence for a moment, each lost in our own memories of that summer. And then a distant beeper alerted Lynne to something in the oven being ready. She jumped up, looking relieved to have a reason to end our rather morbid conversation. 'Well, that'll be lunch. Quiche and a salad. I'll put it on a tray and we can eat out here.'

I was left looking out at the garden once more, wondering exactly what had happened to poor little Pippa Jenkins. And whether I could have done anything that might have changed what happened. All my life, there's been that nagging feeling of guilt that somehow whatever happened to her was partly *our* fault.

I couldn't have kept *her* safe – the other one. If I'd tried, maybe it would have happened to me, in her place. But afterwards, I'd done the right thing. Not like with Pippa.

'Here we are,' Lynne said brightly, returning with a tray of food.

I smiled and helped her arrange it on a little bistro table in the corner of the conservatory. 'Looks lovely, thank you.'

She'd also brought an open bottle of white wine out, with two glasses. 'A sauvignon, is that all right?'

'Er, thank you, but I'm driving,' I muttered.

Lynne shot me a look as though she was going to suggest just a small glass, but then went to the kitchen and came back with a bottle of sparkling elderflower instead. I was glad she hadn't pushed me into explaining the real reason why I didn't want alcohol.

The rest of my visit passed pleasantly, chatting about this and that: my amicable divorce from Colin, what my son Ryan and Lynne's kids were up to these days, how her sister Kate was doing, and what I planned to do to my new bungalow. I invited Lynne to come over and see it one day soon. Now that we'd regained contact and lived so close, I was looking forward to hanging out with her, as the younger generation would say, on a regular basis.

But I didn't mention *her*. Not at this first reunion.

It was almost five years ago now. Hard to believe so much time has passed since that day. Ryan was away at university and I lived alone with Goldie, my unimaginatively named golden spaniel that I'd adopted after Colin and I split up. Goldie was an old girl at that point, and we were out walking in our usual place – some woodland, a short drive away from where I lived, where Goldie could ferret about in the undergrowth and sniff at things to her heart's content, without having to walk too far on her arthritic legs. I liked the scents of damp woodland, the way the sun filtered between the trees, the clumps of bluebells. As always, I followed Goldie off the path, letting her go where she pleased, picking my way around fallen trees and thick undergrowth, kicking up last autumn's leaves with my boots.

We were later than normal on that day's walk. I'd meant to take Goldie out as soon as I'd finished work, as I usually did. But a neighbour came to the door to pick up a package I'd taken in for her and we chatted for fifteen minutes before Goldie whined to hurry me along.

If I'd been fifteen minutes earlier . . . well it might all have been very different.

I'd been in my own little world, trudging after Goldie through the woods. I hadn't noticed anyone else, any noise beyond the usual sighing of the wind in the trees and rustling of small creatures beneath. And then Goldie gave a little whine, and looked back at me, as if to say *Come and look at this*. I went to see what she'd found, expecting at worst a dead fox, and saw *her*.

She was nineteen, as I learned later. A student from a nearby university. She'd been strangled – right there where she'd been left in the woods. Her killer had made some attempt to hide her, pulling undergrowth and leaves over her. Anyone who'd stuck to the path would not have seen her.

I stood and stared for a moment, aware of Goldie at my side looking up at me, waiting for me to take charge. And then I sank to my knees beside her and reached out . . . just in case she somehow wasn't dead, despite the bruises and the dirt and the lack of clothing.

I touched her shoulder, steeling myself ready to feel cold, clammy skin.

But she was warm. I gasped and pulled at her shoulder to try to turn her over, thinking perhaps there was a chance for her. Maybe there was something I could *do*, this time. Her long, dark hair was draped across her face. As I tugged at her the hair fell away and I saw her lifeless eyes staring at infinity, and I knew then it was too late for her. I pulled out my phone and called the emergency services.

They told me afterwards she'd probably only been dead for around fifteen minutes. If I'd left with Goldie on time, I might have been able to help her.

'If you'd been earlier,' one policeman said later, 'you might have been a victim too. The killer can't have left the scene long before you arrived. Possibly even hearing you and your dog approaching might have scared him off.'

Despite that, and despite the scores of police officers who arrived over the following hour, it took them until the following day to find him. Only after they'd brought in dogs to help search. He was found hiding in someone's garden shed, in a housing estate that backed onto the woodland.

I'd given a detailed statement, of course. Detective Shine kept me informed of progress over the next few days.

The killer was quickly charged and convicted. And the victim was buried a fortnight later. I didn't go. Everything was neatly wrapped up.

Her family would never forget her, of course. And neither would I.

At night I'd close my eyes and I'd see her lying there. My

fingertips would tingle with the memory of the lingering warmth of her skin when I touched her. I'd agonise for hours over what might have happened if that neighbour hadn't called, if I'd been there just minutes earlier.

And then, because when it rains it pours, Goldie's heart gave out and I withdrew into my grief – for my beloved dog who'd been such a great companion, for Stephanie Cross who'd had her life cut short in such a terrible way.

I withdrew into alcohol as well. And it was a long, tough climb out. To be honest, I'm still climbing.

Somehow, Stephanie Cross and Pippa Jenkins are the same person, in my nightmares, in my tortured waking dreams. If I'd been able to help Stephanie, I think it would have felt like atonement for not having done more for Pippa back then.

But Pippa's story is unresolved, she was never found. In some strange, twisted logic I wonder if moving back here, opening up about what I know of the events in 1976, might finally help me heal.

Leaving Lynne's house I decided to drive a different way home – a route that took me along an all-too-familiar lane, one we'd cycled along so many times. The hedges were still there, sporting hawthorn blossom at this time of year. I rounded the corner, up the little hill and there on the left was the old farm where we'd played a few times that summer. I pulled in beside the rusted, padlocked gate.

'I can't believe you haven't been developed yet,' I told the house. It was in a sorry state, and I climbed out of the car to take a closer look through the gates. The roof on the main house had huge holes in it, where slates had come off. The old barn was closed up but looked in at least as bad a shape as the house. It would only be a few more years before it collapsed completely. The land around the house and barn was full of brambles. You wouldn't be able to reach anywhere near the doors to get inside to explore. We'd definitely had the best of it fifty years ago.

As I returned to my car I saw, walking up the hill towards the farm, a figure I recognised from all those years ago. Older, of course, his face deeply lined under his flat cap, his body heavier than when he was a young man. But nevertheless instantly recognisable.

'Horace,' I whispered, wondering if I should get out to say hello. Would he remember me? Would he remember the group of kids he'd hung around with a few times, fifty years before? Would he know what one of them did that changed his life?

He was smiling as he approached, and he lifted a hand to wave awkwardly at me. I smiled and waved back. I then put my car into gear and turned it around, to head home. One day I'd need to talk to Horace. Apologise to him. But not yet. Not today.

Chapter 4

Jo, 22 July 1976
Sixteen days before.

I woke up on the first day of the school holidays in a mixed mood. Mum and Dad were arguing again. They were trying to keep their voices down, but their angry hissing carried up the stairs. I turned over, pulled the pillow up against my ears to block out the sound, and stared at the ceiling, trying not to cry. There was, as David had told me so many times, nothing I could do.

As I lay there, I remembered it was the holidays, and that I was going out for the day on my bike with my best friends. Lynne's mum was going to make us a picnic, and we were going to explore the old farm on Hawthorn Lane. And it wouldn't rain, because it hadn't rained for weeks and wasn't likely to start now. Everything would be all right, as long as I was with my friends.

David poked his head around my door. 'Leaving at quarter to ten, all right, Smudge?'

'Yeah, Rabid David, I'll be ready.'

He grinned at my feeble attempt at a new nickname for him. He'd called me Smudge ever since I'd spent an entire day with an ink smudge on my nose without realising it. I'd been trying to find something to call him that would catch on, but everyone resolutely called him David. Not even Dave.

I pulled on shorts and a T-shirt and went downstairs. The arguing had stopped. Probably because Dad had already gone out to the garage to do some car maintenance. It would be too hot there later in the day. Mum was clattering around in the kitchen, hauling the old twin-tub washing machine out from under the counter. I supposed she'd need to fill it before the water got turned off again.

'Morning, Jo,' she said, all bright and breezy as though there'd been no fighting. 'You off out today with David?'

'Yeah. And the others.' I picked up the box of Rice Krispies and poured myself a bowl, turning the packet around and placing it in front of me so I could read the back of it while I ate. There was an ad for a Barbie doll. You had to cut the coupon out and save tokens from five other packets then send them off for a free doll. There'd been a time when I would have been very excited about this offer. But these days my Barbie dolls stayed packed away in an old shoe box of Dad's. David's Action Man dolls had met the same fate.

Even though I'd read it every morning since we'd started that packet, still I read the back of the box while I ate my cereal. David came down and grabbed the box to pour himself a bowl. 'I was reading that!' I snapped at him, trying to snatch it back.

'Kids, please. Don't argue.' Mum put a hand to her forehead as though she had a headache. It was on the tip of my tongue to point out that the only real argument there'd been in the house that morning had been between her and Dad. But David gave me a look that told me to keep quiet.

Anyway, we weren't arguing. We were just following the morning ritual that we always did – pretending to fight over who got first dibs on the bathroom, who would have the cereal box in front of them to read at breakfast, whether or not it was fair that one of us had cleared more of the table than the other. We were siblings. You were supposed to bicker and argue like this. It's in the rules.

That day it was clear Mum wasn't tolerating anything from us, so we ate breakfast in silence, then cleared the table without being told to, and went back to our rooms to get ready for the day out. There wasn't really anything I needed to do, other than tie my hair back with a bobble and put on a pair of sandals. I went out to the garage where Dad was tinkering with something on his workbench and wheeled my bike out to the driveway. David was right behind me.

'Have a good day, kids,' Dad said, without looking up at either of us. I guessed he knew we'd heard the argument and was embarrassed.

'Yeah, thanks, Dad. See you at teatime,' David replied.

I simply said, 'Bye.'

We headed off. It wasn't yet quarter to ten but without even saying a word to each other we both knew it was better to get out of the house early. I looked back as I began pedalling up the street and saw Dad going back inside. Their row would start up again within minutes, probably.

'Let's go and get Rick first,' David said, and I nodded. It made sense. He lived at the other end of our road. From his house we would then loop around the block and along Lynne's road.

Rick wasn't ready when we arrived. He was in the kitchen washing his family's breakfast dishes with a scowl on his face. David and I sat at his kitchen table sniggering while he worked. 'I'm not allowed to go out until I've done a household job. Every blinking day, Mum says! Bet you don't have to.'

'No, we don't,' David said, and beneath the words I heard the unspoken part: *We'd rather have to wash up than put up with our parents fighting all the time.*

'You could help, then we'd get out sooner,' Rick grumbled, scrubbing furiously at a pan that looked like it'd had scrambled egg in it.

David laughed. 'Not likely, mate. It's your house, your job.'

'I'll remember that next time I'm at yours and your dad asks us to cut the lawn.'

'Can't imagine the lawn will ever need cutting again,' I said. We didn't have one anymore. Just a patch of bare brown earth with a few sticks of dry straw where once grass had grown. I missed the smell of newly mown grass.

'It'll come back when it rains,' Rick said, sounding knowledgeable.

'How do you know? We've never had a drought like this, Dad says.' David sounded a little petulant. He always hated it if someone else knew more than he did about something. He was too used to being the older sibling, I thought. I always tended to ask him questions and accept whatever he said, and he hated it if some other kid took that role.

Rick grinned and flicked a wet dishcloth in David's direction. 'I'm the wise one here, remember?' He knew exactly how to wind David up.

I grinned too, watching David's expression as he debated whether or not to rise to the bait. But then he got up from where he'd been sitting, pulled a tea towel from where it hung on the oven rail and began drying up.

'Thanks, mate.' Rick looked surprised but grateful.

'I want to get out on the bikes, not sit here listening to you being a know-it-all,' David said, and Rick nodded graciously, accepting defeat in this little battle of superiority.

I looked for a second tea towel but there wasn't one out. Suited me – I hated having to help with the washing-up. Jobs like dusting and hoovering were all right, but I didn't like dealing with dirty dishes.

Soon it was all done. Rick's mum came to check and gave him permission to go out. 'Now, boys, you'll look after Jo, won't you?' she said, with an indulgent smile in my direction.

I rolled my eyes. 'I don't need looking after, Aunty Pam.'

She chuckled. 'All right then. You and Lynne had better look after the boys, keep them out of trouble, eh?'

'We will.' I enjoyed the look of indignation on David's face as we headed out.

Next stop was Lynne's, where her mum, whom I called Aunty Margaret, had prepared a picnic for us all as promised. She was generous like that. 'She loves feeding people,' Lynne had often explained to me. 'Nothing makes her happier.'

Well, we had no objections, and neither did my mum nor Aunty Pam, who were both excused from having to provide food. That day we had sandwiches, little sausage rolls, a pack of Jammy Dodger biscuits to share and a bottle of orange squash each.

'Mum, can't we have Penguin biscuits instead?' Lynne whined.

Her mum shook her head. 'They'll only melt. I'm keeping them in the fridge. You can have one when you get back. Or have an ice pop if you prefer.'

'Thanks, Aunty Margaret,' I said. Got to keep her onside this early in the school holidays. I was hoping for many more days with picnics like this. I knew my mum was unlikely to provide one for all of us.

'You're welcome, pet.' She smiled and ruffled my hair, the way she always used to when I was little. At twelve I wasn't so keen on being treated like a kid and resolved to tell Lynne to ask her to stop. I thought Lynne probably would anyway, catching a look of embarrassment at her mother's action.

'Come on. Let's get going.' David was divvying up the picnic into the rucksacks the boys were carrying, and the baskets Lynne and I had on the fronts of our bikes. A few minutes later we were off.

We felt giddy with freedom and endless possibilities. Friends, a picnic, our bikes – the world was our oyster. We could go anywhere. But we'd already decided to go to Four Oaks Farm to explore.

'It's been empty for years,' Rick told everyone as we cycled through our estate and out of the village. 'The old people – Willis was their name – who owned the farm died, and their son isn't interested in running a farm, so he's just left it to rot.'

'We know him!' David and I said at the same time and laughed. I nodded to David to continue. 'He's a friend of our parents, kind of. Didn't know he was a farmer. I thought he ran a business renting out office space or something like that.'

'Well, he doesn't farm,' Rick said. 'Dad says he's sold off all the fields to other farms, and sooner or later he'll sell the house and yard to a developer.'

'What will a developer do?' I asked, as we turned left up the lane that led towards the farm.

Rick shrugged. 'Knock it all down and build a new housing estate, I bet. Or build just one or two really posh houses.'

'I wish they'd build a cinema,' Lynne said. 'It's the one thing we don't have in the village, and we really really need.'

'The *one* thing!' David laughed. 'We've got sod all in this village. We've no decent shops, no youth club, no amusements. Nothing to do.'

'We've got the countryside,' I said.

'Oh, yeah. But, you know, compare it to kids our age living in Southampton or even London. They've got loads of places to go and things to do.'

'We have to make our own fun.' That was how Dad always put it when David moaned about the lack of stuff for young people locally.

'Anyway, we're here, so let's make that fun!' Rick said, as we arrived at the entrance to the farmyard and got off our bikes.

'Gate's padlocked,' Lynne said, sounding dismayed.

'It is, yes, but there's a gap in the hedge,' Rick said. He leaned his bike against the gate and pushed back some dry foliage, revealing a gap between two bushes. It'd be easy to crawl through.

'What about our bikes?'

'They'll be all right here. Just get them off the lane.'

We piled our bikes together, leaning them against the gate, and one by one crawled through the hedge. David was last, waiting until he'd passed the picnic things over the gate to the rest of us.

'Let's put this stuff in the barn, out of the sun,' Rick said, pointing to the right where a large barn stood. Its door was open, hanging off its hinges. We all picked the stuff up and went over. I felt a little nervous. What if Mr Willis came? What if he was already here? Maybe at any moment a developer would turn up with a bulldozer and start knocking everything down? I didn't dare say anything to the others though. They'd have laughed at me and called me a baby. I was the youngest of the group, even if only by a few months.

Inside the barn it was pretty dark, though the sun shone in through a few cracks in the roof. I'd hoped it'd be cool in there, and although it was a bit cooler than outside, it felt warm and stuffy. There were stacks of hay bales against the back wall and a few more lay dotted around the rest of the barn. Rick put the rucksacks down on one of those, and Lynne and I added the bottles of squash we'd carried.

'Look at me!' David yelled. He'd climbed up the stack of bales and was right up near the roof of the barn. *Careful!* I wanted to call to him, but I'd sound like a parent, so I kept quiet.

'Bet I can get higher!' Rick said, charging over and clambering up. It looked pretty easy to do. Lynne and I looked at each other. She grinned, I nodded, and then we were over there too, climbing up the uneven stack of hay bales.

'They won't collapse, will they?' Lynne said, when we reached the top layer and sat with our legs dangling.

'No, they're safe enough,' David said. He was grinning with delight at being the first up there, the one with the idea. Rick had already climbed back down and was now pulling some of the loose bales around on the floor.

'We could build something with these, come and help!'

'Like what?' David said.

'A den, or something.' Rick was trying to pick up one bale to put on top of another, but it was too big for one person to lift. 'Come and help!'

'I like it up here!' David shouted down, sounding miffed that Rick had come up with a new, better idea than simply climbing up the bales. Lynne and I made our way down, and soon we'd helped Rick shift a few, stacking them three high, and forming a small den.

The straw made me sneeze. It was surprisingly dusty and scratchy. I looked at my forearms, which were covered with faint scratches. 'What'll we do with the den?'

'Use it as the "home" post for a game of 999-In!' David had climbed down to join us at last.

'Yeah!' We all shouted at once, and it was quickly decided that Rick would be 'It' for the first round. He went inside the little den, covered his eyes and began counting while the rest of us charged off to hide. I couldn't stop myself laughing. It was a kids' game, one I probably hadn't played since I was about eight years old, but here at the farm, with its enticing barns and hay bales, its overgrown garden and even the house itself, the game took on a whole new dimension. We couldn't get into the house, but I saw David run around to the far side to hide, while Lynne stayed in the barn and squeezed in behind a wall of hay bales. She was relying on keeping quiet, which wasn't going to work for me as I kept giggling. I found a hiding place in another shed that was unlocked and contained a few pieces of rusted farm equipment. I edged in and pulled the door behind me but didn't close the latch. In one corner there were some barrels so I tucked myself behind them, squatting down and keeping as quiet as I could.

Soon I heard the shout from Rick, 'Coming, ready or not!' and his footsteps running out of the barn into the yard. It wasn't long before he must have spotted David, and then there were two sets of footsteps running at full pelt back to the den.

'Yes!' David shouted, and I guessed he'd made it there first.

Which meant Rick was still looking for me and Lynne.

'What's going on here?' a man's voice shouted, and I froze. We weren't supposed to be in the farmyard, were we? Was it Mr Willis? If so, we were about to be told off. That would be the end of it. David and I would be kept home all summer if Mum and Dad heard of it. I said a swear word under my breath. We should have been more careful.

Chapter 5

Jo, 2024

It takes time to settle into a new home, especially when you're on your own. I'd bought a bungalow that had been recently done up by a developer – it had all the rooms painted white, a lovely wood-effect vinyl flooring throughout, a new bathroom and kitchen. The kitchen units weren't what I would have chosen but they were inoffensive and perfectly serviceable. The garden was small and easy to maintain. It was the perfect place to retire to, and best of all, it held no memories of that day five years ago.

This place was a blank canvas; somewhere I could build a future for myself. Where I could start over. Moving was the first step, but I knew it would be a long journey.

Although I'd done this on purpose to confront it head on, choosing Hareton Wick might have been a mistake. There were too many memories around every corner of that last summer, and of Pippa. I was wondering if it was the right decision after all. Maybe I should have left all that buried in the past.

But I was here now. I needed to make the house right for me and some of my old furniture didn't work at all. I needed a new sofa, a sofa-bed for the spare room so it could double as a study, and a better TV. Ryan was due to visit soon, so I needed to get on otherwise he'd have to use an ancient camp bed. He was tall, my Ryan, and on family camping trips he'd complained he'd outgrown that camp bed since the age of fourteen. Now he was definitely too big for it.

It's nothing that a trip to Ikea won't fix, I told myself. There was one in Southampton, and I could combine a furniture shopping trip with visiting Dad. I phoned him and arranged to call in on Saturday afternoon.

Dad's flat was near Southampton Common, a short drive out of the centre of the city. I parked in the spot outside where his battered old Rover used to sit. He'd had that car for forty years. I missed it still, but Dad was no longer fit enough to drive so he'd reluctantly parted with it.

I dug Dad's key out from the depths of my handbag and then tapped on his flat's door and called out, before letting myself in.

'Hey, Dad. How are you today?' He was sitting in his usual chair where he had a view over the communal gardens and could also watch TV, though today it was not switched on.

'Ah, Jo. I'm fine, thank you. Shall I put the kettle on?'

'Please.' I watched as he levered himself up from his chair and shuffled into his small kitchen. I could make the tea myself of course, but I knew he liked to do it himself, to prove he still could.

'You sit yourself down, Jo. You must be tired after traipsing all round the shops. Get what you wanted?' he called from the kitchen.

'I did, thanks, Dad. It'll be delivered Wednesday.'

'In time for Ryan's visit. Make sure that boy comes to see me too.'

'We'll both come, next weekend.'

'Haven't seen him for ages. Getting as bad as David.' I could hear a note of regret in his voice when he mentioned my brother.

'Ah, Dad, no. Ryan came about two months ago, didn't he? Took you out for dinner somewhere. David's not been near for years.' It annoyed me so much that David came home to England so rarely. I knew he could afford it. He just chose not to. Which meant caring for Dad as he grew older had been left to me. Just like nursing Mum through her cancer had been left to me too.

When David and I were teens, after the split, we'd lived with Mum. David had spent more time with Dad than I did – he was that bit older that he could travel by train on his own, and so he decided to spend every weekend with Dad. I only went every two months or so, in the school holidays, when Dad would drive up to Northampton to collect me. David sided more with Dad, whereas I took Mum's side, and I suppose that had added to the rift between us. 'Mum was always nagging him,' David had said. 'Always saying he never did anything around the house.'

'Because he didn't!' I'd replied. 'Never lifted a finger to help with housework or anything else.'

'And Mum never attempted to get a job, even when we were older and didn't need looking after as much.' David had a point, I supposed, now. Marriage should be teamwork, with each partner taking on a fair share of work and responsibility, whether they stuck to traditional roles or not. But back when we were still kids, I could only see Mum's point of view, and I had plenty of arguments with David about it.

Then David went off backpacking around the world, made it as far as Australia where he met and married Giselle, and never came back. When Mum got sick, I was the one who became her nurse, her carer, and dealt with all the 'sadmin' after she died. And I resented David for leaving it all to me, for not coming home to see Mum and help with her end days.

We'd drifted apart, with contact between us lessening year on year, down to just Christmas cards. I hated that we'd allowed it to happen. Sometimes I wished we could rewind to when we were kids, when we were best mates who did everything together.

Before it all went wrong that summer. I supposed those kids were still there, deep down, buried beneath the layers of adult life. I just didn't know how to reach them.

'Anyway, pet, here's your tea. And I saved a packet of Hobnobs for you. Not easy. I so nearly broke into them last night, then I remembered they're your favourites and I stopped myself.'

'Ooh, thanks, Dad!' I'd brought a packet of posh cookies but decided to leave them in my bag. Dad enjoyed treating me in these little ways.

'So how are you getting on, with the new house and all?' Dad asked when we were settled with our cuppas.

'Pretty good. I'll bring you over to see it soon. I was waiting to get the new sofa.'

But Dad shook his head. 'Ah, no. No point you driving all the way here and back twice in one day. I'm happy just seeing your photos of it.'

'Honestly, Dad, it's no bother—' I began, but Dad cut me off.

'Besides, I've no desire to spend much time in that village. I know you wanted to move back, but . . . well . . . I don't have happy memories of my last weeks or months there.'

I reached out and squeezed his hand. 'I know, Dad.'

'Not just what was happening with your mum and me. But all that . . . terrible bother . . . over that poor child.' He took a sip of his tea. 'I wonder about her sometimes. Did they ever find her?'

'Lynne says they never did.' I tensed, not really wanting to talk about it. An image of Horace smiling and waving at me the other day passed through my mind.

'It's so sad. Nice that you're able to catch up with Lynne again, though. And you're better? In yourself? After all that—' He waved his hand vaguely, to encompass everything that had happened over the last few years. Finding *her*, becoming ill, needing therapy.

I smiled. 'It's a long process, but I am so much better than I was, and I think being in the New Forest, in the country, will be good for me. Did I tell you I'm thinking of buying a bicycle?'

'No!' He chuckled. 'It's like you're going back to how you were at twelve. Living in Hareton Wick, seeing Lynne, cycling around the New Forest lanes! Next you'll be restarting school at Brookhill. You'll be in the second year, I suppose, though they'd call it year eight now. I'll have to nag you to do your homework, like the old days.'

I laughed. 'I was very good at doing my homework on time, I'll have you know. It was David who needed nagging.'

'And he still does,' Dad said with a chuckle.

He was right. I made a mental note to nag David about coming over to visit. Even though David and I rarely spoke, I'd need to call him. Dad was getting frailer by the day and who knew how long he'd have left? David should get a trip planned. Something Dad could look forward to.

I suddenly remembered something I wanted to ask him. 'Dad, are you still in touch with Crispin Willis?'

'Who? Oh, yes. I remember him. No, I'm not. We weren't close friends but our paths crossed a few times when we lived in the village. After we left there was no need to stay in touch. Why do you ask?'

'Oh, because I met his son the other day. Charlie.'

'I remember he had a son. Always thought it odd that Crispin was on the school's Board of Governors and yet he sent his son away to boarding school. He must have thought he was a cut above the rest of us.'

'Maybe. But he was always nice to me, I thought.'

'Hmm. You had a house-warming party yet?' Dad asked, in an abrupt change of subject.

'Er, no. I probably should. I've said hello to a couple of neighbours.'

'Invite them round. Just for a drink or a coffee morning. You never know when you might need them.'

I nodded. It was a good idea. Perhaps I'd do it at the weekend when Ryan was visiting. He'd be my support when I got older so it'd be good for him to meet my neighbours too. And I could invite Charlie as well. We'd swapped numbers and promised to meet again. It was a nice thought.

Ryan arrived on Friday evening, in time for a late dinner as planned. I had a pot of bolognese on the hob that only needed heating up. The table was set, a candle lit, and a bottle of wine stood open. For him, not me. There. Everything was ready. This would be the first time Ryan had visited me in a house that had not been his home, and I wanted it all to be perfect. He'd returned to live with me for a year after graduating from university, while he did his teacher training course. That was when I was at my worst. Now I wanted him to see I was moving on, that I was in a far better place mentally. I didn't want him to worry.

It was gone eight by the time I heard his car pull up outside. I opened the door and stood on the threshold ready to greet him. My son, my tall, well-built son, with his big bushy beard, purple polo shirt, and blue-framed specs. He looked exactly like what he was – a chemistry teacher with a reputation among the schoolkids for being cool. At least that's what he told me.

'Ryan!' I threw my arms around him as he entered the house carrying a rucksack with his things for the weekend.

'Hey, Mum. Good to see you.' He gave me a bear hug back, holding me tight until I gasped for breath. 'So, this is the place, eh?'

'Yes, this is it. That's your room.' I pointed to the first door on the left. He dumped his rucksack on the bed.

'Nice! Looks cosy. Anything to eat? I'm starving.'

'Give me five minutes and dinner will be served. Help yourself to a glass of that . . .' I indicated the bottle of wine, '. . . while you wait.'

'Wine?' Ryan looked at me with concern in his eyes.

'It's for you. Not me. I'm still off it, don't worry.'

'I do worry, Mum. Honestly, they say you shouldn't even have alcohol in the house.'

'Ryan, it's OK. I'm not one of those people who can never resist a drink. I got dependent on it for a short while, as a result of . . . you know. Now I'm off it. I don't usually have it in the house, but I bought it for you.'

'Thanks. I guess I'd better drink it then!' Ryan poured himself a glass of wine and sat at the table while I began boiling water for the pasta and turned on the heat under the sauce.

'So, how was your journey down?' I asked.

'Awful. Traffic on the M3 was horrendous.' He took a big gulp of the wine. 'Ah. That's better.'

I remembered that feeling. The way that first mouthful ran through you and began the process of making everything seem easier to deal with. My problem was that I didn't seem to know when to stop. I drank myself into oblivion night after night, after finding *her* and losing Goldie.

I'd gone to Alcoholics Anonymous in the end. Ryan had helped – insisting I went each week, driving me to the meetings if necessary. Those meetings, combined with my therapy sessions, had gradually brought my drinking under control and helped me begin the process of putting myself back together again.

'So what's it like living back here, where you grew up?' Ryan asked. There was a touch of uncertainty in his tone. I knew he didn't fully understand why I'd chosen to come here.

'It's good. My old friend Lynne lives nearby still and it was lovely to reconnect with her. Plus your granddad's only forty minutes' drive away. He wants to see you.'

'I'll pop over tomorrow.'

'Can you do it on Sunday? On your way home? Because I've invited a handful of neighbours, plus Lynne, for tea and cake in the afternoon. Sort of a house-warming party.'

'OK, sure. Meeting the neighbours early on is a great idea. Can I help you with the dinner?'

'No, it's all right. Almost done.' I drained the pasta, dished it up and brought the plates to the table. 'Tagliatelle bolognese. Your favourite.'

Ryan grinned. 'Well remembered! Thanks, Mum.'

I wondered if it still was his favourite, or if perhaps his tastes had changed over the last few years. It was hard sometimes, with adult kids, remembering to move on from treating them the way you did when they were teens. I imagined how I'd feel now if Dad pulled an ice pop out of the freezer for me, as a treat.

But Ryan certainly seemed to enjoy the meal, wolfing down every last bit of it and all the leftovers, just as he used to. It was a good evening, as we sat on my new sofa and caught up with each other's lives while he drank most of the bottle of wine. I loved having my boy back with me, even if it was only for a short weekend visit. Bringing together elements of my current life and my past life helped me find a new path.

But it made me remember how Stephanie Cross's parents had asked to meet with me, some months after her funeral. They were still grieving, of course, and I was at my lowest. But I'd agreed, and somehow I'd cleaned myself up and stayed sober enough to handle the meeting.

We were in the Cross family's living room. The mantelpiece was filled with photographs of Stephanie throughout her life, from sunny smiling toddler to the attractive young adult I recognised. Mrs Cross had made us all cups of tea, but no one was drinking them.

'You were there with her,' her mother said, clutching a sodden handkerchief. 'You sat with her. You could have left her alone after calling 999, but you didn't.'

'I didn't want anyone else to stumble upon her,' I said. God knows I'd been traumatised enough by finding her. There was no need to put anyone else through that.

'Detective Shine said you were kneeling beside her, guarding her.' Stephanie's father leaned forward as he spoke. 'We wanted to thank you for that.'

'We should have seen you sooner, but we were . . . caught up,' Mrs Cross said.

I nodded. *Caught up* – yes, I too had been caught up in my own misery since that day. But I couldn't find any words for them.

'We're glad she wasn't alone any longer, in those woods,' Mr Cross said. He too had tears streaming down his face. 'If you hadn't gone by, it might have been hours . . . days, even. They might never have found the killer. If you hadn't been there, he might have had time to hide her better, and we might never have known what happened to her.'

'The not knowing – that would have been worse.' Mrs Cross shuddered.

'If the killer hadn't been caught,' Mr Cross put in, 'I'd have found that very hard to deal with.'

'It was my dog who found her.' Goldie, sniffing, whining, calling me over to investigate.

'Thank her too, for us.' Mrs Cross smiled at me.

'She's . . . gone. She was old.' And now I was choking up, crying tears for a dog while they cried for their daughter.

'I'm so sorry.'

But I should have been the sorry one. If I'd been in the woods earlier, at my usual time, I might have saved her.

I wasn't with them for long – the whole meeting took only about twenty minutes. And when I got home I'd drunk an entire bottle of wine, glass after glass, straight down.

Not knowing would have been worse, Mrs Cross had said.

And they'd been grateful to me for simply being there, finding her, calling it in and then staying with her. Speaking out, doing what little I could for Stephanie.

That meeting had been the start of my healing process. The realisation that I had done the right thing at that time for Stephanie. It was a process that was still going on. Sometimes it felt as though I'd never fully heal, never be able to move on, until little Pippa

Jenkins was finally laid to rest. Because for her, I had never done the right thing.

Chapter 6

Jo, 22 July 1976
Sixteen days before.

'We're playing 999-In,' I heard Rick say to the unknown man. Here we go, I thought. We're in trouble. But the next words I heard the man say made me gasp.

'Can I join in?'

'Sure, why not?' Rick replied.

The man laughed, a joyous, deep sound as though it was the funniest thing he'd ever heard. And I thought I heard footsteps as though he was running around already.

'You've got to hide, and if I find you, run as fast as you can back here, all right?' Rick was explaining the game to whoever it was. It sounded to me as though he knew the man. I was torn – I wanted to look out and see who was there, but I also wanted to stay hidden and win the game.

While I was still dithering the door to my shed banged open. 'Bet you girls are in here!' Rick called out, and I suppressed a snigger. He turned my way but couldn't see me crouched behind the barrels. As he ventured further into the shed I picked my moment and darted out from my hiding place. I made it to the door just before Rick, and then sprinted back to the hay barn. It was touch and go – he grabbed me just as I reached the den, but fell over, panting with the exertion.

'Jo wins!' David said.

'No, I got her first!'

'Anyway, you've still got to find Lynne and Horace,' David said.

'Horace?'

A deep chuckle came from the corner of the barn. I looked around and saw a boy, who was just a few years older than David and Rick, peek out from where he was badly concealed behind some hay bales. Rick was carefully pretending not to have noticed him and jogged off, looking around the barn. Soon he'd spotted Lynne, whom he easily caught before she made it back.

'Just one more to find,' he said loudly. 'I wonder where Horace could be?'

Again, that deep chuckle. Rick headed up to the end of the barn, making a big show of hunting for someone.

'Who's Horace?' I whispered to David.

'He's . . . just Horace,' David whispered back. 'Lives near here.'

'Seen you, Horace!' Rick called. 'Now you've got to try to beat me back to the den!'

I watched as he jogged slowly to the area where Horace was hiding. 'Come on, Horace, run! Run to us!' David yelled, and Lynne and I joined in. Horace looked uncertainly from Rick to the rest of us and back. Then his face broke into a broad lopsided grin and he began a shambling run over to the den, reaching it just before Rick sauntered up.

'Well done, you beat me!' Rick said, clapping a proud-looking Horace on the back.

I recognised Horace now. I'd seen him around the village a few times, ambling from shop to shop, sometimes buying something small like a bag of penny chews or a bar of chocolate. Usually he was with his mum, brought along for an outing or to help carry bags. I'd never heard his name before. It was an oddly old-fashioned name, I thought, but somehow it seemed to suit him.

'Horace, do you know everyone?' Rick asked, and Horace shook his head. 'This is David, and his sister, Jo. And this is Lynne. Lynne's the only one who didn't make it to the den before me, so she's "It" now, all right?'

Horace nodded, and shuffled off to hide again, in the same place as last time.

'Hey, I haven't started the count . . .' Lynne protested, but Rick held up a hand to stop her.

'It's all right. Count now, and the rest of us'll play it properly,' he whispered.

Lynne began the count and we ran off. This time I went into the back garden of the house. Tucked into a corner, beside a rusted swing, was an old wooden Wendy house. It was half rotted but I managed to crawl inside and sat with my arms wrapped round my knees. While I waited to be found I thought about Horace. Was he going to be part of our gang now? I knew we should be nice to him, as it wasn't his fault he was like he was. But it was the same when Pippa hung around with me and Lynne. She spoilt things without meaning to. It just wasn't the same when you had to be responsible for a younger child. And from what I'd seen of Horace, he was just like a younger child. Younger than Pippa, even though he was fully grown. Were we going to have to put up with him hanging around us all summer? I couldn't help but hope not.

'Did you have a good time playing out today, kids?' Dad asked, as we gathered round the table for our tea. Mum had cooked sausages, chips and baked beans – David's favourite food. I preferred spaghetti bolognese, but Dad always said he didn't like 'that Italian muck'.

'Yeah, it was a good day,' David replied, and I nodded.

'Where did you go?'

'Just, you know. Out of the village, to a . . . spot where we played games and then had the picnic Mrs Richards made for us.' We'd decided that we wouldn't admit to having been at the old farm. The grown-ups would probably say we shouldn't have gone there, that even though it was abandoned and unlived in it still belonged to Mr Willis.

'That was good of her to feed all you kids. Mary, I hope you'll repay her by doing the same a few times over the school break?' Dad looked meaningfully at Mum, who bristled.

'Of course, Alan. I don't need you to tell me what to do.'

Dad looked as though he was going to say something more, but then he glanced at me and David. Something in our fearful expressions must have told him to hold his tongue, because he shrugged slightly and turned his attention to cutting up his sausages.

'So, who was there? You two, Lynne and Rick?' Mum asked, brightly.

'Yes,' I replied, 'and for part of the time there was Horace.' We'd had to share our lunch with him, but thankfully Aunty Margaret had provided more than enough.

'Horace?' Mum frowned.

'Horace Thompson,' David explained. 'I think his parents own a farm not too far from where we were.'

'Who's Horace Thompson?' Dad asked.

But Mum knew. She was in the village shops often enough. She was also a member of the village Women's Institute, so she knew everyone. She'd certainly know Mrs Thompson and therefore Horace. 'You know the Thompsons, Alan. That couple with the . . . odd son. They've got a younger daughter too. But Horace is older, I think he's about eighteen.'

'Odd?' Now Dad was frowning.

'Yes, I mean, I think these days you're supposed to call them educationally challenged. Something like that. He's simple, anyway.'

'You make it sound like there's something wrong with him,'

David said. 'Just because he's not the same as us, doesn't mean he's bad.' I loved my brother for sticking up for Horace.

'And you two were playing with him? Playing what?' Dad put down his knife and fork and stared across the table at us.

'999-In, mostly. We had to let him win, though,' David said.

A glance passed between Mum and Dad.

Dad coughed. 'I'm not sure you should play with him. He's not like you kids.'

'They definitely shouldn't be around him,' Mum said firmly.

'Why not? Rick knows him quite well. Says he's harmless.' David jutted his chin in the air as he spoke.

'I'm not so sure. People like that . . . well, you never can tell. I think it's best if you both stay away from him. Especially you, Jo.'

'I look after her!'

I suppressed a snigger. David didn't look after me. He knew all too well that I didn't need looking after and wouldn't accept it from him anyway. But I wondered why Dad was so concerned about Horace. From what I'd seen of him today, Rick was right. He was harmless, really.

'He's bigger than you,' Mum said. 'You just don't know what he might do, especially to . . . the girls. He might not mean to hurt anyone, but he might not even understand that he's hurting them. Best to keep well clear.'

I wasn't sure whether Horace was capable of hurting us – I doubted it, but Mum's words worried me.

David waved his fork in the air. 'Mum, don't you think Horace will only learn what's good behaviour by being around other people?'

I looked at David with respect. I'd never have guessed he'd stick up for Horace like this.

'He can learn good behaviour from someone else. Not from my kids,' Mum muttered, and began eating again, not looking at David or me. It was a sign the matter was closed.

David looked at Dad and opened his mouth to say something

more, but Dad shook his head. 'You do what your mother tells you. Both of you.'

For once they were presenting a united front. Well, I thought, that was something at least. There was no point arguing with them any further. David must have thought so too, for he glanced at me and gave a little shrug. Even if we did decide to hang out with Horace more over the summer, Mum and Dad didn't need to know. Just as we hadn't been specific about where we'd been today, we didn't need to be specific about who we'd been with.

Earlier I'd been hoping we wouldn't spend too much time with Horace over the coming weeks. Now I felt sorry for him, and was kind of hoping we would see him again. Maybe being with us would be good for him. He'd certainly seemed to enjoy himself today. He'd loved the picnic, and when it was time for us to go home he'd looked with envy at our bikes and told us he couldn't ride one but he'd like to. Rick had suggested, as we all cycled back to the village, that perhaps we could teach him to ride a bike. I'd quite liked that idea.

But it was clear there was no point discussing it anymore with Mum and Dad. We ate the rest of the meal in silence. Silence was at least better than having Mum and Dad snipe at each other.

Mum went out later that evening to a WI meeting, so there was just Dad and us kids in the house. After Mum had left he called us to the garden. We sat on deckchairs eating ice pops, and then he suggested a game of Scrabble sitting outside.

'It's too warm an evening to sit inside watching TV,' he said. 'Nice to get some fresh air when it's not quite so hot.'

David and I had been out in the fresh air, the heat, all day but we didn't point this out to Dad. Instead, David fetched the Scrabble game, which lived in a cupboard in his room, and we set it up on the old camping table. It had been a while since we went camping, though we used to go every summer. Those were the good days – when Mum and Dad still liked each other, when they would take us to the beach, or for bike rides, or to ruined castles to explore. When school summer holidays seemed endless, and we did everything together, the four of us as a family.

There was to be no camping trip this summer – our parents had already made that clear. No money, they'd said. Though I suspected it was because they hadn't been able to avoid arguments for long enough to book anything.

Anyway, Scrabble was fun, and Dad let us have two ice pops each as well as Penguin biscuits that had been kept in the fridge. We stayed up playing and then just chatting, the three of us, until the sun went down.

When the stars came out, Dad suggested he set up his telescope so we could all take a look. Normally we only did this on autumn evenings when it was dark much earlier. But it was so warm and too nice to go in, and Mum was still out, so why not?

Dad loved astronomy and had built a telescope stand at the bottom of the garden, using an axle from an old Ford Anglia mounted on a couple of brick towers. He attached his large telescope to this at an angle, counter-weighted by an old paint tin filled with concrete. It meant the whole thing could be easily swivelled and pointed towards any part of the sky. He'd even rigged up a small motor to it, that would counteract the Earth's rotation, keeping whatever you were looking at in your field of vision. We looked at Jupiter that night, and its larger moons, which were easily visible. Saturn with its rings showed clearly through the telescope. My favourite was always to look at the craters on the moon. It was a half-moon that night, and the craters along the line that marked the dark side of the moon from the light were crystal clear.

'They're sending two spacecraft to fly past Jupiter and Saturn, you know,' Dad told us. 'I read it in the *New Scientist*. They're called the Voyagers, and they'll be launched next year. Imagine, kids, that we can send probes made on Earth all that way!'

'Will they land on Jupiter?' I asked.

'No, they'll fly past and take photographs and send images back to Earth,' Dad answered patiently. Astronomy was his hobby. He was a leading member of a local astronomical society and loved everything to do with space. I'd been able to reel off the names of the planets in order since I was five years old.

'Cool!' David said. 'That'll be amazing!'

'It'll take years for them to reach the outer planets and send back data,' Dad said. 'But if it all goes to plan, they'll tell us so much more about our solar system.'

'When will they come back to Earth?' David asked.

'They won't. They'll fly past the outer planets and eventually leave the solar system. Maybe one day some other life forms will come across them. They'll be carrying some information about us – our biology, our culture, our technology – in case that happens.'

'Wow!' Both David and I gasped at this.

'A kind of time capsule,' David said, and I grinned. Those words had sparked an idea in my mind, one I couldn't wait to put into action.

Chapter 7

Jo, 2024

I took Ryan for a walk around the village the next morning, pointing out where I used to live, where I'd gone to school, the tree I used to climb with Lynne. He'd never been to Hareton Wick before.

'I love seeing where you grew up, Mum,' he said, as we walked along Heather Avenue. 'Gives you more of a backstory.'

'You mean I'm just a two-dimensional character without this place?' I said with mock indignation.

'I mean, this place shaped you, at least partially. And you shaped me. So, in a sense, this village is part of me too.'

I hadn't thought of it like that. He was right, though. Hareton Wick, and what happened that last summer here, had definitely shaped me.

We walked to the High Street and bought a selection of cakes and biscuits in the little Tesco for my house-warming tea party. I'd vaguely thought I'd bake a few items but that would have meant cooking all morning rather than going out with Ryan.

'Do you think I should offer alcohol this afternoon, as well as tea or coffee?' I asked Ryan. 'I could buy some wine or—'

He shook his head. 'No, Mum. Stick to the tea. No one wants a drink at three o'clock in the afternoon.'

I didn't answer. Back at my lowest point, I'd have been a bottle and a half in by three o'clock, every day.

So, tea and cakes it was. Lynne arrived first, then Mr and Mrs Simpson from next door, an old, widowed fellow named Peter from across the road, and the Rogers family – mum, dad and three children all under the age of eight – from next door the other side. I made mental notes of everyone's names, wondering if it'd be rude to write them all down.

'We won't stay long,' Mrs Rogers said, glancing at her boisterous children. 'These three will be well behaved if you let them out in the garden. They're like puppies, really. Nice to meet you.'

'You too,' I replied, opening the patio door for the children. It was a blustery day, but they seemed happy chasing each other around, with their mum keeping an eye on them through the window. In a safe, enclosed garden they were more closely watched than poor Pippa Jenkins had been fifty years ago.

'Ryan, how you've grown!' Lynne said with a laugh. 'Think I only ever saw you in one photo from your childhood. You were about two years old!'

'Well, I'm glad I've grown since then. You must be Lynne. Pleased to meet you,' he replied.

'Can I get you some tea? Or coffee?'

'Tea's great. Or if you happen to have any wine . . . I got dropped off by Malcolm so I'm not driving.'

'Er, Mum doesn't keep alcohol in the house. Not since . . .'

'Since?' Lynne looked from Ryan to me, frowning.

'Ah, nothing much, all over now. But he's right: I don't drink.' I poured Lynne a cup of tea and handed it to her, trying to catch Ryan's eye to warn him off saying anything more.

'Great selection of cakes!' Lynne said, as she picked up a plate and helped herself to a slice of lemon drizzle. I loved her for changing the subject and not pushing me to tell her more now.

'Peter, can I tempt you with any cake?' I said to the old man, who'd settled himself on the sofa, chatting to the Simpsons.

'Ah, no thanks love, I'm diabetic,' he replied.

'We're not,' said Mrs Simpson, jumping to her feet to choose some.

I answered the door to a few more neighbours from further along, and soon the little bungalow was buzzing with conversation. Someone brought a small dog, which was sent into the back garden with the children and became an instant hit.

'You seem to have landed on your feet, they're a decent set of neighbours,' Lynne said, catching me during a lull of hosting duties. 'I was chatting to Peter. He's lived in the village all his life. Used to live on your old road, believe it or not!'

'Really? I must ask him! Peter, Lynne says you used to live on Heather Avenue. What number? I lived there, at number twenty-seven until 1976.'

'Did you now?' His eyes lit up with interest. 'I was at number four. But you must have been a very tiny child in 1976.'

'I was twelve. My parents were Mary and Alan Salway.'

'Mary and Alan Salway . . .' Peter had a distant look in his eyes as he tried to remember. 'Ah, yes, I do remember them. Your father was a university professor, was he not?'

'Lecturer, not actually a professor. But yes. He lives in Southampton now.'

'I remember him. We paired up, he and I, searching for that poor lost child. Must have been the same year you moved away.'

'It was. I'll ask him if he remembers you.'

'Yes, do. We got along well that day, as I recall. Nice to hear he's still alive and well. So many aren't.'

Someone across the room said something that caught my attention, and I tuned into the conversation. It was Mr Simpson, chatting with Simon Rogers. 'A notice is up on the gate. Going to be quite a large development, by the looks of things. Don't know why it wasn't sold long ago.'

'Four Oaks Farm? Not entirely sure where that one is,' Simon said.

'Up Hawthorn Lane, at the top of the hill before it goes round the bend. You'd pass it going out to Marsh Farm shop,' Mr Simpson told him.

'Oh, that old place! Been derelict as long as we've lived here.'

'It was derelict fifty years ago,' I put in. 'I used to live in the village as a child. We used to play in the barn there, didn't we, Lynne?'

'Four Oaks? Yes. Loved playing there. So it's finally sold, has it?'

'To a big development company. There's an artist's impression of what they're going to build, stuck onto the gate there. They're going to call it Four Oaks Way. Nothing started yet, other than putting up the board.' Mr Simpson seemed to be enjoying being the one with all the information. 'It's outside the national park boundaries so there should be no problem with planning permission.'

The doorbell buzzed again and I went to answer it. This time it was Charlie bearing a large bunch of assorted-coloured roses. My stomach gave a little flip as I accepted them.

'So sorry I'm late,' he said. 'Got held up visiting Dad.'

'No problem. These are beautiful, thank you. Go on through – I'll put these in water.'

I must have been blushing too, for Lynne waggled her eyebrows at me in the kitchen while I found a vase for the flowers. 'Is that Charlie?' she whispered. I nodded. 'He looks nice!'

She went to offer him a cup of tea while I finished the flower arranging and composed myself. When I went back through to the living room Charlie had joined the conversation about Four Oaks Farm.

'Yes, I finally sold it,' he was saying to Mr Simpson. 'Dad never got round to it. He owned so much property, but now I have power of attorney I'm gradually getting rid of some of it.'

'It'll be interesting to see what they build there,' Lynne said. 'It's been crumbling away a bit more every year. It still looked habitable back when we were kids, didn't it, Jo?'

'Yes, though I remember the windows being boarded up at some point.' Around the time I'd moved away, I thought.

'That was because Dad was always moaning about kids trespassing in the farmyard,' Charlie said with a laugh. Lynne caught my eye and raised an eyebrow, and we shared a smile, both remembering those long summer days from years gone by.

The little party had been a success. Lynne, Ryan and I decided after everyone had left, and Lynne was helping me clear up. At her suggestion I'd written down the names and house numbers of everyone I'd met while they were still fresh in my mind. Charlie had given me a kiss on the cheek and promised to call and arrange 'a proper catch-up'. I was pleased – there hadn't been much chance to talk to him with so many other people in the room. Now, with the dishwasher on and the uneaten cake packaged up for me to take round for the Rogers' kids tomorrow, Lynne too said her farewells.

'We'll have lunch together soon,' she said.

'Sure. It's my turn.'

'Or we could book a table at Rick's bistro in Lymington. Whatever you prefer.'

'It'd be great to see him again.'

'Well, we must get something planned. We've still so much to talk about.' She hugged me and then she was gone.

'I'll do us a light dinner later,' I said to Ryan. 'I'm too full of cake to think about cooking and eating right now.'

'Me too. I'll help you make a salad or something.'

'Perfect.'

'Lynne's nice,' he said, slumping down on the sofa.

'She is, yes. I'm lucky to have an old friend still in the area.'

'Mum, why didn't she know about everything that's happened? Didn't you have lunch with her? Don't you think it's a good idea to make sure your friends know that you can't drink?'

'I do, yes, but . . . I was driving when I went to see her, and that was a good enough reason not to drink.'

'Still, you ought to tell her, Mum. And anyone else you're likely to see. Charlie, for example.'

'I barely know Charlie.'

'Barely know him . . . yet.'

I glanced at Ryan. There was a little smirk on his face. Clearly, like Lynne, he thought there was something between us, even though we'd only just met after fifty years.

'I will tell Lynne, some day. And Charlie, if I find we're meeting regularly. Right now, I just don't want to . . . burden them.' Telling them about my drinking would lead into what had caused it, and I didn't feel ready to talk about Stephanie yet. The brief mentions of Pippa's disappearance were all right. I could handle that. Pippa's story was so long ago. But the other was still too recent.

'Oh, Mum.' Ryan got up from where he was sitting and crossed over to sit beside me, wrapping his arms around me. 'I'm sorry. I can't imagine what it was like. But look, you *should* talk to Lynne about it all. That way if ever you're tempted – you know, to have a drink – you'll have someone nearby who understands and can help. Or just to listen – whatever you need. I wish I was closer then I could do it. You can always call me, or even Dad, if you need.' Ryan gave me another squeeze.

As well as Ryan it had been my ex-husband Colin and, oddly, his new wife Marion who'd been most supportive. It was Marion who'd recommended my therapist. And Colin who'd sorted out the AA meetings. We'd been divorced a long time and had managed to remain good friends. I was lucky in that respect. He'd been a good husband, and then a good ex-husband.

'Oh, love. Thank you. But you have your own life to live. Yes,

I will talk to Lynne, when I feel ready. Remember we've only just reconnected after a long time. In the meantime, I think as long as there's no stress in my life, I'll be all right.'

Chapter 8

Jo, 29 July 1976
Nine days before.

We spent the next few days doing other things. We didn't want to go back to the farm, didn't want to 'use it up', as Rick put it. So I held back on telling them all the idea I'd had after Dad had told us about the Voyager spacecrafts. Instead, we went to the recreation ground to play frisbee, and to the stream which was now just a track of dried-up mud. One day we took a bus into Southampton, and went to the swimming baths, where David scared us all by jumping from the highest diving board. Afterwards Lynne and I went to the shops, coming home with a new T-shirt each (mine was yellow, hers was orange) and a pair of little teddy bears that said 'Friends Forever' on their tummies. One each. I bought Lynne's and she bought mine.

On the way home on the bus, David and Rick took the mickey out of us for buying what they called toys.

'It's an expression of our friendship,' Lynne said defiantly. I just ignored them. They were cute, and it was good to know there was always someone there who cared for me, who'd listen to me.

And we *would* be friends forever. I knew it.

I fell silent as the bus approached Hareton Wick. We'd soon be home, and who knew what kind of atmosphere there'd be in our house. Lynne must have sensed something, for she butted my face with her 'Friends' bear. 'Your parents still arguing all the time?'

I nodded. 'Pretty much, yes. Over stupid little things. It's like they're always out to pick fights with each other.'

'So sorry to hear that. Grown-ups can be so stupid. But it'll be OK, Jo. And remember, you can always come round mine. Mum said you're welcome any time.'

I smiled my thanks. I couldn't speak, as I felt too choked up by her kindness.

Rick got off the bus at the stop before the rest of us. 'I'm tied up tomorrow with the parents, but shall we go to the farm the day after?' he said, as he stepped off.

'Yeah!' David punched the air, and Lynne and I nodded. As long as there was something to look forward to, some reason to leave the house, everything *would* be OK, as Lynne had promised.

As David and I let ourselves in the house that afternoon, by the back door as usual, we were greeted by Mum and Dad who were sitting at the kitchen table, each with a mug of tea. A notepad with some scribbles lay in front of them, and a map and some leaflets were open in front of Dad. My stomach gave a lurch – they looked like they were about to announce something important. The first thought that surged through my mind was that they were going to tell us they were splitting up.

'Hello, kids. Had a good day?' Mum said brightly.

'Yes, it was good.' I dropped my bag of shopping on a chair and went to deal with my other bag containing wet swimming things.

'Leave that, I'll do it later,' Mum said. 'Sit down, we've something to tell you.'

I glanced at David who looked as nervous as I felt. Here we go. We took our places at the table and waited expectantly.

'So,' Dad began, 'we know things haven't been great round

here lately. Your mum and I . . . not always seeing eye to eye.'

'We're sorry,' Mum put in, but Dad gave her a look as if to say, *Please shut up, and leave this to me.*

'We are sorry if it's been tough for you, but I want you to know that everything is all right. Your mum and I . . . well, it's just how grown-ups are, sometimes. It doesn't mean anything.'

Mum shot Dad a look at that last bit, a look I couldn't interpret. But Dad didn't acknowledge it and went on talking. 'Anyway, we want to make it up to you. So, I've booked us a spot at a campsite. Just for a week, but it'll be good to get away, eh? It'll be like the old days. The campsite is right by a beach so we can spend the whole time on the sand, or in the sea. What do you say to that?' He sat back, looking pleased with himself.

I felt a wave of relief wash over me. They weren't about to get divorced and throw our lives into upheaval.

David let out a little cheer. 'Sounds great, Dad, thank you!'

I smiled, trying to look happy about it, but actually I was torn. On the one hand, I loved camping trips and a week by the sea would be fantastic. On the other hand, it would be a week where it'd be very hard to get away from Mum and Dad for long, and I feared they might simply take their fights with them on the holiday.

'Jo, you're excited too, aren't you?' Mum put a hand on my arm.

'Yes, it'll be great.' I picked up the nearest leaflet which was for a campsite on a cliff top in Cornwall. The photo on the front looked fabulous. 'Is it this one?'

'Ah, no. That one was fully booked. It's here.' Dad pushed over a less glossy leaflet, for a campsite on the edge of the village of Croyde, in Devon.

I must have looked a little disappointed, because Dad smiled at me. 'It's just as good as the other one, believe me. You'll love it. We were lucky to get a place. Someone else had cancelled.'

'When are we going?' David asked.

'Sunday, for a week.'

That was just three days away! In the past our family holidays had been planned months in advance – campsites booked, camping gear brought down from the loft, checked and cleaned at least a week before.

'I know,' Dad said, 'it's short notice! But we can do it.'

'Any clothes you need for the holiday must be in the clothes basket tonight,' Mum said, 'so I can wash them tomorrow.'

Dad nodded. 'And, David, you can help me get the camping gear from the loft tomorrow so I can check through it all.'

'Sure. I'm free tomorrow, Rick's not around, so I can help all day.'

'Thank you, son. Then you can see your friends on Saturday for the last time before we go away.' Dad smiled indulgently. I was relieved. I was looking forward to going to the farmyard again. And now I could make the suggestion I'd been sitting on for a few days.

I told David first, when I found him alone in his room. 'What do you think about us burying a kind of time capsule at the farm? We could put stuff from 1976 in it, that'll remind us of this hot summer when we reopen it in the future.'

David grinned. 'Great idea, Smudge!'

I was delighted he'd so quickly taken to the idea. 'What shall we use as the capsule?'

David scratched his head, then held up a finger. 'I have the exact thing.' He opened his wardrobe and rummaged around, finally pulling out an old plastic ice-cream tub. It contained his old toy soldiers, something I thought he'd have got rid of years before. He tipped those out and pushed them aside, and waved the box at me. 'This'll be perfect.'

'I think we should use a plastic bag too, to be certain it's waterproof.'

'Yes, all right. So – we can't do it tomorrow because Rick's got to visit his granny and I'm helping Dad. Saturday, then. We'll phone the others and gather together some things. Better take a trowel too so we can bury it deep enough that it won't be disturbed. It'll be so cool digging it up again in the future!'

The next day, David was hard at work helping Dad bring the camping gear down from the stifling hot loft and into the garage to be checked. I stood and watched for a bit but there was nothing they needed me for, so I went back inside where Mum was busy with the twin tub.

'Can I go round Lynne's?' I asked.

Mum nodded. 'Sure. Be back for tea.'

'Will do.'

I rang Lynne first, to check she hadn't gone out somewhere, then set off. I walked there, but soon wished I'd used my bike. It was cooler cycling. When I arrived at Lynne's there was a small pink bicycle leaning against the side of the house. I went straight through to the garden, where Lynne had said she would be. I was hot and sweaty and couldn't wait to get in the pool in her garden.

It was a tiny circular pool – barely bigger than a paddling pool. We'd been about seven when her parents first installed it, and at that age we thought it was brilliant. The water came up to our chests and we were able to swim across it, or around the edge. Now it was barely waist height and a single stroke took you from one side to the other, so it wasn't much use as a swimming pool. But it was definitely a great way to cool off on a hot day, so I'd put my bikini on under my shorts and brought a towel.

'Hi, Jo,' Lynne called as I made my way across the garden. She was already in the pool, leaning against the side, her arms stretched along the edge. She wasn't alone. 'Pippa's here today.'

'Hi, Pippa,' I said, as I dumped my bag on the parched grass and began pulling off my T-shirt and shorts. That explained the bike. It must be hers.

The little girl grinned at me. 'Lynne's taught me handstands,' she said, as she pulled a pair of goggles over her eyes then ducked under the water. A moment later a pair of skinny legs broke the surface, toes neatly pointed heavenward. The feet wiggled a few times as if waving at us, which made us laugh, and then Pippa surfaced again. 'Was that good?'

'Brilliant!' I said, as I climbed the couple of steps and hopped over the side into the pool, making a splash. The water was warm but cooler than the air, and it was utterly delicious to bend my knees and sink under it, tipping my head back to wet my hair too.

'Does that feel better?' Lynne asked, and I nodded.

'Brilliant!' There was a large sycamore tree in the garden, and at this time of day it began to cast some shade over the pool. I scooted over to the shady side and lay back, floating.

Pippa ducked down and swam underneath me, bobbing up again by my armpit, giggling.

'Oi, don't do that,' I said. 'I just want to lie here quietly and cool down.'

'Sorry.' She wasn't though, she was still giggling. 'Lynne, can I have another ice pop?' Pippa asked.

'Mum said one each, and you've had yours,' Lynne said. 'I'll get one for Jo, though. Orange or red?'

'Orange,' I replied, and Lynne climbed out of the pool and jogged across to the garage where her family kept their freezer.

'I prefer the red ones,' Pippa said solemnly.

I didn't answer. She was a cute kid but to tell the truth I didn't want her there. I wanted to talk with Lynne without anyone else listening. We'd spent so much time with David and Rick, which was fun, but sometimes I wanted it to be just us girls. I wanted to sound Lynne out on whether or not she fancied David. She might not want to admit to fancying him, me being his sister, but I'd be able to tell if I was careful in how I questioned her.

Lynne arrived back with the ice pop for me, the top already cut off. I squeezed it up the polythene tube and sucked on it gratefully. It was only flavoured, coloured ice but it was a great way to cool down on days like this, and every day had been 'like this' lately.

'Better?' Lynne said. I nodded, and noted Pippa scowling

because she didn't have one. I glanced her way then looked back at Lynne and rolled my eyes, and she did the same. She felt as I did about having Pippa hanging round. But we were stuck with her for today anyway.

'Hey, Pippa,' Lynne said, 'somewhere in the garden there's one of my old Barbie dolls hidden. If you can find her, you can keep her.'

'Really?' Pippa's eyes lit up. She was obviously still young enough to want to play with dolls. I felt a pang of nostalgia for the days when Lynne and I would spend hours playing with our Barbies, requisitioning one of David's Action Men to act as Ken.

'Yes, really. But you're going to have to search hard to find her.'

Pippa didn't need telling twice. She jumped out of the pool and began running off, looking under bushes, up the tree, in all the corners of the garden.

'Is there really a Barbie somewhere?' I whispered.

Lynne grinned. 'In a box of old stuff in the shed. Which is technically in the garden. I'll get it out later to give to her. We're stuck with her today. Kate babysat her yesterday and Mum's gone shopping. I guess we ought to feel sorry for her, with her parents divorced and her mum leaving her alone all day.'

I nodded. I knew I'd hate it if my parents divorced, and it'd be even worse if you were as young as Pippa when it happened.

We had about fifteen minutes, I think, just the two of us wallowing in the coolness of the pool, me sucking on the ice pop, chatting about TV, popstars, books and music. Elton John and Kiki Dee's 'Don't Go Breaking My Heart' was number one in the charts, and we both loved that song. We performed a giggly rendition of it in the pool, stopping only when Pippa came over to see what we were laughing about.

'Nothing, Pips. Have you found the Barbie yet? Maybe behind the shed?' Lynne said, and the little girl ran off to continue searching.

'I feel a bit guilty,' I said, and Lynne pulled a face. 'Poor kid.'

'I know. But she's having fun, and she'll get the doll. Anyway, tell me, Donny Osmond or David Cassidy?'

I laughed. We'd asked each other this question periodically for about two years. 'David Cassidy. Got to be.'

She made a shocked face. 'But you were always a Donny Osmond fan, apart from briefly being a Bay City Rollers girl!'

'I know.' I grimaced, remembering the tartan scarves I used to tie around my wrists. 'I've changed. Actually, I fancy David Essex above all of them. Those eyes!' I put the back of my hand to my forehead in a mock swoon. 'Seriously though, do you fancy anyone closer to home?'

She tipped her head on one side. 'You're asking do I fancy David or Rick? Neither is the answer. Though I think Rick fancies you.'

'He does not!' I felt myself blushing. I'd never thought of it . . . Rick was just one of the gang, my brother's mate. Not someone I could ever imagine in a romantic way. Or could I?

'You like him!' Lynne's tone was gleeful as if she'd just unearthed my deepest secret.

'Only as a friend! Not as . . . you know.'

'At the farm, you and him, sitting next to each other on the hay bales, never taking your eyes off each other . . .' Lynne chuckled as she teased me.

'That's not true!'

'What farm?' We hadn't noticed Pippa come back from searching behind the shed.

'Oh . . . just that empty farmhouse up Hawthorn Lane. Four Oaks Farm. We've been hanging out there sometimes.' Lynne smiled kindly at Pippa. 'I've just had a thought. I think my mum might have put the Barbie in the shed. Shall we go and look?' She climbed out of the pool, wrapped a towel round her and took the little girl's hand to lead her back across the garden.

A moment later they were back, and Pippa was clutching the doll. It was one I remembered, the one that had suffered a little when Lynne went through her phase of wanting to be a hairdresser. She'd cut the doll's hair and coloured it with felt-tip pens. It was a mess. But Pippa looked pleased to have it and set about taking the doll's dress off so she could take it into the pool.

While Pippa was occupied again I told Lynne about the upcoming camping trip.

'That'll be fun,' Lynne said, looking at me warily.

'It will if my parents manage not to kill each other, after being together for a week in a small tent,' I replied. 'Anyway, tomorrow we're going back to the farm. And David and I have a plan.' Then I told her about the time capsule idea.

'Love it! It's almost like time travel – we're reaching forward to our future selves, and they're reaching back to us. I'll dig out some stuff for it this evening.'

The afternoon passed quickly. At four o'clock Pippa announced that it was time for her to go as her mother would soon be home from work. 'All right,' Lynne said. 'Nice to see you.'

'Bye, Lynne! Bye, Jo!' Pippa called as she skipped down the side of the house to where she'd left her bike.

I needed to leave soon after, and Lynne walked with me to the front gate. As we passed through it, I spotted something shiny on the ground and picked it up. 'What's this?'

Lynne took it from me and examined it. 'Looks like the top of a bicycle bell. Must have fallen off Pippa's bike.'

I had an idea. 'It's all rusty. I've got a spare one at home – a pink one that came off the bike I had when I was little. I'll find that and give it to her. David will fit it on her bike.'

'I'll put this in the bin, then,' Lynne said.

'Let's stick it in the time capsule.'

'Why?'

I shrugged. 'Why not? Got to fill it with something.'

'All right. See you tomorrow,' Lynne said, as I pocketed the bell and headed out to the street.

'Yeah, bye.'

I walked home feeling happy – we'd had a good afternoon and

there was a day at the farm and then the camping trip to look forward to. It wasn't a bad life, I thought, being twelve years old and enjoying a long hot summer with friends and family.

Chapter 9

Jo, 2024

I'd told Dad I was thinking about buying a bike but had done nothing about finding one yet. One day during the week after Ryan's visit, when I was walking back from the High Street, I spotted a bicycle, locked to someone's garage door with a piece of paper attached: *Lady's bike, in working order, £20. Just knock on the door.*

So I knocked and an elderly man came out with a key to the bike lock. I tried it out, pedalling up and down outside his house. It felt as though it needed a bit of oil on its chain and air in its tyres, but otherwise it was fine.

'Used to be the wife's,' the man said, and the sadness in his eyes told me she was no longer with us. 'She'd like to think someone was getting use out of it.'

'I'd love to take it,' I said. 'I've recently moved here and it'll be lovely to be able to pop out to the shops by bike instead of always using the car.'

His eyes lit up. 'That's exactly what my Shirley used to say. Well, then, you can have it for nothing, my dear.'

'Oh, no, I'll pay the twenty pounds,' I insisted, but he waved me away.

'I only put a price on it to stop kids who'd just dump it somewhere. You know what they're like these days.'

I grunted in reply, not really agreeing but not wanting to argue with him. Kids were the same now as they'd always been. No better, no worse. 'Well, I promise I won't dump it, if you're sure?'

'Totally sure. You enjoy yourself on it, but be careful not to fall off.'

'Thank you, I will.'

And, as simple as that, I rode my new bike home. The next day I spent an afternoon cleaning and oiling the chain, pumping the tyres to the right pressure and adjusting the brakes. Dad had taught David and me basic bike maintenance when we were kids. He always said that if we were going to go out alone on our bikes we had to know how to look after them. This bike seemed no different to the ones we'd had all those years ago.

That weekend was the first chance I could take the bike out for a proper ride. I'd spent some time peering at Google maps on my phone, planning a route along the half-remembered lanes around the village and into the New Forest. Back in the seventies, David and Rick were the ones who'd decide where we were going and who'd lead the way, with Lynne and me following behind. But those roads had barely changed in all these years, not once you went beyond the new estates.

I headed through the village, up the High Street, along Heather Avenue and out into Hawthorn Lane, passing Four Oaks Farm. The hill up towards it wasn't as hard as I remembered – my new bike's gears were much better than I'd had as a child. And the coolness of the March day made for easier cycling than those hot summer days in 1976. As I rounded the corner at the top I remembered what Lynne had said about Natasha Woods's farm shop, and decided to pay a visit. The shop was housed in an extension built onto the side of the original farmhouse. As I entered, a bell jangled loudly. A woman who looked to be about my age entered from a back room. She had a friendly, welcoming smile, and she positioned herself behind the counter. 'Anything I can help you with, just holler, all right?'

'Will do.' I returned the smile. The shop was beautiful. It sold fresh fruit and vegetables, eggs that were in a wicker basket so you could pick out your own to fill a box, a variety of handmade arts and crafts including some beautiful turned wood bowls. I picked one up, admiring the glossy smoothness. Underneath was a price sticker – £12. Not much for such a lovely item.

'Made by a local chap named John,' the woman behind the counter said. 'He's retired, spends all his time in his garage turning wood now.'

'It's gorgeous,' I said. 'He's very talented.' I put it on the counter while I perused the rest of the shop. There were jars of locally made jam and chutney that appealed so I chose a couple of those too. In the veg section there was locally grown seasonal produce – kale, leeks, parsnips, spinach. I wanted to grab bagfuls of each, and then remembered I was on my bike. Anything I bought had to fit in the small rucksack on my back. I reluctantly put the bag of spinach I was holding back.

'Grown in one of our fields,' the woman said.

'It looks amazing. But I've just remembered I'm on my bike. I'll have to drive back and stock up on all this.'

'We can deliver, if you like. We do weekly fruit and veg boxes of seasonal produce.'

'That sounds right up my street,' I replied. 'Yes, please.'

'Perfect. Sign up here – name, address, contact details, and preferred delivery day. I'm Natasha, by the way. I don't think I've seen you in here before?'

'You haven't, no.' I remembered Lynne talking about Natasha, Horace Thompson's sister. 'I've recently moved here. Although I used to live in Hareton Wick as a child.'

'Oh! We might have been at school together! Did you go to Brookhill?'

I grinned. 'Yes, but only for one year, then we moved away when I was twelve, in 1976.'

'Ah, I started at Brookhill in 1977.' As Natasha spoke, Horace emerged from a back room.

'Tash, I've done the spuds,' he said.

'Thanks, Horace. That's good you've got that job done,' she said, and his face lit up at the praise.

Apart from ageing, he hadn't changed a bit. He was staring at me, as though perhaps he recognised me from when I was in my car at Four Oaks Farm. I stepped forward, hand out to shake his. 'Hello. I'm Jo Atkinson.'

He shook hands, though his grip was weak. 'Hello, Jo. I'm Horace.'

'Jo's just moved to the area,' Natasha told him, and he nodded.

'Moved *back* to the area.' Horace grinned and went back out the way he'd come in.

'He must have heard us talking,' Natasha said. 'He's . . . um, he's my brother. He helps me out in the shop, a bit.'

Or perhaps he really did remember me, I thought. I decided not to say anything. That period must be so painful for Natasha and Horace. Natasha would have been only ten or eleven, but she'd remember it, I was sure. She'd remember, at least, her brother being sent away after it all happened. Lynne had said he'd been in Broadmoor for years.

I felt a pang of guilt that we hadn't made more time for Horace. Had we failed both him and Pippa, I wondered? Should we have spent more time looking after Pippa, so she wasn't on her own all day? Should we have sought out Horace and befriended him? Should we have spoken up more, at the end, when it had all gone wrong and Pippa had disappeared?

We were only twelve. I could hear Lynne's voice in my head, reminding me that what had happened wasn't our fault. Just as Ryan kept telling me what had happened to Stephanie wasn't my fault either.

'Right, well I've got all your details,' Natasha's voice cut into my reverie. 'It's nineteen pounds for the dish and the two jars. Thanks, Jo. So nice to meet someone new! We'll deliver to you on . . .' Natasha consulted my sign-up sheet, '. . . Tuesday evening. That won't be a problem. Most people want Thursday, Friday or the weekend.'

'Who does the deliveries?' I wondered if perhaps it was Horace, though I couldn't imagine him driving.

'That fellow John I mentioned. Same one who does the wood-turning. He says it's good to get out of the house, so he does a couple of hours most days for me, delivering.' She smiled, then turned to greet a couple of new customers who'd just set the bell jangling. 'Well, I hope to see you in here again, Jo. Nice to meet you.'

I packed my purchases into my rucksack and said goodbye. As I exited the shop, I remembered my promise to myself, that I'd talk to Horace. Apologise to him. He'd been locked away for all those years, and I was at least partly to blame. As I was mounting my bike he appeared from behind the shop and ambled over to me. This was my moment.

'You remember me, Horace?'

He nodded. 'Used to play with you. At Four Oaks. I liked playing with you.'

'We liked playing with you too.'

'Then I had to go away. They said I wasn't safe.'

'I'm sorry.'

'S'all right. They taught me lots. Then I came back to live here and work in the shop.'

I stood looking at him for a moment, wondering how to begin the conversation with him that I knew I needed to have. But would it help *him* at all? Knowing that the kids he remembered, whom he'd enjoyed playing with, had been the reason he'd been sent away from home, locked up for so many years?

Horace seemed to be waiting for me to say something more, and when I didn't he merely shrugged and pointed at the shop.

'I've got to get on, now. There's no one else who can do the jobs I do, Tash says.'

'You do a great job.'

He grinned proudly, and turned to leave, waving at me over his shoulder.

I climbed on my bike and watched him go, realising I was no further forward.

Chapter 10

Jo, 31 July 1976
Seven days before.

Before we were allowed out on our bikes on Saturday, we had to help get the stuff ready for the camping trip. David helped Dad load up the car. It was always a bit of a jigsaw fitting everything in the boot. We only had a Ford Cortina, not a big estate car, and there were four of us to fit in as well. In the past, when Mum used to help Dad load the car it often led to them fighting, so I was glad Dad had asked David to help him instead. And Mum dragged me off to the supermarket, to buy provisions for the week ahead.

Mum and I got back by lunch time, and my arms were nearly falling off with the weight of the bags she'd made me carry. Of course, because we were camping, with no fridge and cooking on a little stove, it was all heavy tinned foods. Tins of sausages, new potatoes, beans, spaghetti hoops, soup, mince. Not my favourite kind of food but as Mum said it was quick and easy to heat up. We'd also bought cereal, bread, crisps and a selection of non-chocolate biscuits. I was hoping there'd be a campsite shop, where we'd be able to buy ice creams each day. Otherwise I'd be in danger of melting in the relentless heat.

We packed the food into a box, then carried it out to the driveway, where Dad was triumphantly closing the boot of the car. 'There's this to go in as well,' she said, and Dad glared at her. He'd obviously forgotten about the food.

'That'll have to go on the back seat, between the kids.'

'Thought we were going to put the beach bag there?' Mum said. 'You'll need to make space in the boot for more.' Her tone was confrontational.

I'd wanted to put my bag of books and teddies in that spot, but decided to keep quiet. This was one of those moments that could escalate into a full-on parental row at any moment.

Dad looked at Mum, she stared back at him, hands on hips. Then Dad backed down. He sighed, reopened the boot, and began shoving things together to make a bit more space. 'I guess we can squash the beach bag in here.'

'I'll fetch it.' Mum turned to go back into the house. I sighed with relief. It was a small thing, but so often their rows began with small things. As though they looked for any excuse. But since their decision to take us camping, they seemed to be trying hard not to let any disagreement escalate. Long may it continue, I thought.

At last, it was all done, and David and I were allowed to go off on our bikes. This time our picnic was provided by Mum. 'Can't have Margaret Richards showing us up, can I?' she'd said.

After picking up Rick and Lynne we cycled the familiar route to the farm. The other two had been just as excited as David and me about the idea of burying a time capsule and had brought things to put in it. A recent edition of *Top Hits* magazine, a couple of rubber monster pencil toppers from David, and a Womble one – Orinoco – from me, a three-day-old local newspaper, some Black Jack chews and a handful of football trading cards. And I had the rusty bicycle bell from Pippa's bike. An odd collection, but as David said, it didn't really matter what we put in it. Anything we unearthed years later would spark memories of this long hot summer.

'Wonder if Horace will be here today?' Lynne said, as we parked our bikes and crawled through the gap in the hedge.

'I kind of hope not,' I confessed. 'He's all right, but my parents have said we shouldn't mix with him.'

'Really? Why?'

'They think he might be dangerous somehow. I think he's just like a little kid. Anyway, it'll be hard to explain what we're doing with the time capsule to him.'

Lynne nodded. 'I agree. So what'll we do if he shows up?'

I shrugged. 'I suppose we'll need to be nice to him, and try to include him, like last time. I'm not going to be the one to send him away. I just won't tell Mum and Dad. What they don't know they can't worry about.'

'Good plan. I'm not telling my mum we were here anyway. She says we shouldn't play here because it's private property even though it's empty.'

'We haven't mentioned we're coming here either.'

'Come on, girls!' Rick shouted to us. 'Stop standing there gossiping. We've got work to do! We need to bury the time capsule, eat the lunch, then after that we're going to build an assault course with these hay bales. Come and help!'

Lynne and I ran over to where David and Rick had begun putting the various items into a Marks and Spencer's green plastic bag, and then into the old ice-cream tub. David had brought some Sellotape and he used that to seal around the edge of the box. 'There. Reckon that'll be watertight now.'

'Where shall we bury it?' I looked around for a likely spot.

'Over there?' Rick pointed to a spot by the wall of the house. It had once been a flower bed but was now overgrown with weeds. 'It'll be easier to dig in a flower bed where the soil's been dug before.'

'Or there?' David pointed towards the hedge that separated the farmyard from the lane. 'In the ditch? Because if the farm is ever sold to someone else, they're likely to dig up the flower beds and replant them, and then they'd find our capsule.'

I nodded. 'Ditch is a better idea.' Rick realised he was beaten, and we all trooped over. 'How will we mark the spot so we can find it again?'

David pointed to a spot beneath a twisted beech tree that formed part of the hedge. 'Let's dig here. We can carve a mark on the trunk of this bush and we'll find it again. Even if the mark grows out it's quite distinctive. See the way the branches fork there?'

I looked at it, but all the other beeches in the hedge forked too. I counted from the gate. 'Or we could simply remember that it's the fifth beech from the gate.'

'That's easier,' Lynne said, with a smile.

David scowled, but I could see he knew Lynne was right. We retrieved the gardening trowels we'd brought in a rucksack and began digging. It was not easy. Weeks with no rain had left the ground rock hard. Only the fact it was a ditch, partly filled with the previous year's dead leaves, allowed us to make any progress at all. But we needed to get below the level of mulch and into the actual soil. After about half an hour, taking it in turns to use the two trowels, we'd dug a hole just a little deeper than the ice-cream tub.

'That'll have to do. I'm getting blisters,' Rick said, straightening up. 'If we put enough dead leaves back on top, they'll eventually turn to soil and bury it deeper. Anyway, no one's going to look here or stumble across it.'

We all nodded. No one wanted to spend more time digging. The tub was duly buried, soil packed down on top of it and last year's leaves pushed back. By the time we'd finished you couldn't tell that the area had been disturbed. At most it looked like an animal might have scrabbled around there for a bit.

'Right. That's that done, then. When will we come and dig it up?' Rick looked at each of us.

'Next year?' David said.

'Too soon. Five years?'

We'd be seventeen and eighteen by then. It was hard to imagine being that old. 'Yes, perfect!' I said. 'Let's do it then.' I loved the idea of revisiting our past selves by digging up the time capsule. I wondered if we'd feel like the same people we were now? One thing I was certain of is that we'd all still be close friends. That would never change.

'Yeah, that'll work. If we wait any later, we'll have left home or gone to university or something,' Rick said.

We shook on it and then headed into the barn to get out of the sun and eat the picnic Mum had made. Then the boys began making an assault course using the hay bales that were stacked in the barn, and Lynne and I pitched in to help build it. In a corner of the barn were some narrow planks of wood and a couple of empty metal barrels. Using those and the bales we soon had an obstacle course set up, where you had to climb over the barrels, balance along planks resting on bales, weave in and out of more bales and cross a finishing line made with a piece of frayed rope within as short a time as possible.

We were soon exhausted by both building the course and completing it. David had the fastest time. Mine, sadly, was the slowest. I'd never been very good at balancing and had fallen off the plank every time I'd tried it.

'Do you think Horace would enjoy having a go at this?' Rick asked, as we lay back on the bales, panting.

Lynne shook her head. 'I think he'd struggle. We should take it down before we leave today in case he comes and tries it and hurts himself.'

I smiled at Lynne. It was just like her to be concerned with Horace's wellbeing, unlike my mother, who'd thought Horace was more likely to hurt us.

We were just packing up the lunch debris when I heard a car in the lane. Instead of going straight past, as cars usually did, it slowed and stopped. Rick stepped outside the barn to see who it was, then darted back inside.

'Uh-oh. Think we're in trouble.' We all finished shoving our belongings into bags as fast as possible. David kicked over parts of the obstacle course.

'Oy! You kids, get out here now!' an angry male voice shouted. Not Horace. We glanced at each other, picked up our things and sidled out.

'It's Mr Willis,' I whispered to Lynne, as we stood in a line, waiting for him to approach. He had his hands on his hips. Behind him the gate to the farmyard was unlocked and stood open. His car, a bright-blue Ford Capri, was parked beside our bikes just outside the gate. My stomach plummeted. We really were in trouble. I darted a glance over to where we'd buried the time capsule. It was all right – it was well hidden, and I didn't think he'd notice.

'What the hell do you think you're doing? This is private property, not your playground! If you've done any damage you'll pay, or your parents will.' He pointed at David and me. 'I know you two. Alan Salway's kids. Do your parents know you're here?'

'Er, no, sir,' David replied.

'And who are you?' Mr Willis pointed at Lynne and Rick.

'Lynne Richards.'

'Rick Channon.' I turned to stare at Rick. His actual surname was Watts.

Oh, God. If Mr Willis complained about us to our parents we'd be grounded for the whole summer. I stared at the ground in front of me, trying not to let tears come.

'Well, look, if I see you or your mates here again, I will be calling round to complain to your parents, and I'll also have you up before the magistrates for trespassing. Is that completely clear?'

'Yes, sir,' David said. 'We haven't damaged anything, I promise.

We've only played hide-and-seek.' His tone and behaviour were as though he were being told off at school. I admired his cool.

'You'd better be right about that.' Mr Willis's tone softened a little. 'Now, go. The lot of you. Find somewhere else to play!'

We didn't wait to be told again. We grabbed our bags, walked quickly out through the gate, jumped on our bikes and cycled off. Rick was ahead and led us not back to the village but in the other direction, further along the lane.

We sprinted further up the hill then turned left, along an unsurfaced track that led between two fields, only slowing down once we'd rounded a bend and were out of sight of the lane.

'Channon,' David said, with a grin, turning to Rick. '*Mick* Channon's son, are you?' He named the Southampton footballer who'd been in the squad that had won the FA Cup back in May that year.

'First name that popped into my head.' Rick shrugged. 'I don't want him calling round to my parents to complain.'

'He already knows *our* parents,' I said with a grimace.

'I don't think he'll complain, Smudge,' David said, patting my shoulder. 'He's shouted at us and he'll think that's enough.'

'He's usually really nice to me,' I said, remembering times when he'd called round to our house and given me sweets.

'There's Horace,' Lynne said, pointing up the track. He was walking determinedly towards us.

'Ah, yes, this track leads to the farm where he lives,' Rick said.

'Are we trespassing again?' I had visions of Horace's dad being right behind him, shouting at us to get off his driveway.

'No, this is public land. It goes on to a few other cottages further along, and then to a car park by some woods. I've cycled it before,' Rick reassured us.

'Hello!' Horace had reached us. His eyes were shining, he looked excited to see us. 'Are we going to play 99999-In again?'

I sniggered at the extra nines.

'Not today,' Rick said kindly.

Horace looked disappointed. 'Can we play another game? I had fun playing with you. Can we go to the old farm and play?'

Rick shook his head. 'No, we can't go back there. A man came and told us off for playing there.'

'Oh. I go there a lot. I like it there. Can't I go there now?'

'I wouldn't if I were you, Horace. You don't want to get in trouble.'

'Was it Mr Willis? I call him the shouty man. He owns the farm but Mum said he doesn't want to be a farmer, so he doesn't live there, and one day he'll sell it.' Horace was out of breath at the end of saying all this and looked vaguely embarrassed, as if he didn't like being the one who knew more than others.

'Yes, it was Mr Willis,' Rick said. 'He was quite angry with us. Stay away, Horace.'

'But I like going there. It's my fun place.'

'It won't be fun if you get caught there by Mr Willis.'

'Are you going to stay away?'

We looked at each other. I could tell what the others were thinking – that we'd give it a few days and then go back, but we'd make sure our bikes were hidden next time. It was surely only the bikes that had caused Mr Willis to stop as he passed by. He'd have just driven past with barely a glance otherwise.

'Yes, I think we will,' Rick replied. But he turned to us and, out of Horace's line of sight, he winked. I knew that we would indeed still go back to play.

'I'll prob'ly stay away, then. Unless I see you lot there.' Horace grinned happily, obviously pleased with this decision.

'Well . . . OK. We have to go now,' Rick said. He turned his bike to head back down the track and we all followed.

'At least we warned him,' I said. 'It's up to him if he decides to ignore the warning.'

'We'll just have to be more careful not to be caught,' David said. 'We still haven't looked inside the house. I bet there's a cellar.'

'A haunted one. The girls'll be terrified!' Rick teased.

Lynne and I squealed. 'We'll be the ones protecting you if there's ghosts!' she retorted.

David laughed. 'Huh. I'd like to see that!'

That night at home Mum, Dad, David and I sat down to watch TV together, after tea. *The Generation Game* was on, and we had a real laugh yelling at the TV as the contestant tried to recall the prizes he'd seen pass by on a conveyor belt moments before.

'Food mixer!' Mum shouted.

'Pair of garden shears!' This from Dad.

'Cassette recorder!' yelled David.

'Cuddly toy!' I added, to everyone's laughter.

'There's always a cuddly toy, and I think he said that first,' David said.

Turned out though, he hadn't, and so he didn't win the toy. If ever I was on *The Generation Game* I'd call out 'cuddly toy' first.

It was a fun evening. It felt like we were a proper family again, watching telly together and looking forward to a holiday that started the next day. I had to hand it to Mum and Dad – they really were making an effort to put everything right at last. I decided we must have turned a corner, and now there was no danger of them splitting up.

Chapter 11

Jo, 2024

The next Sunday I found myself with a free afternoon. It was a warm, early April day and I decided to head out on my bike. The exercise would do me good.

I reflected on Ryan's visit the previous weekend. It had been a good one, and I felt proud to be Ryan's mum. I was divorced, I wouldn't have Dad very much longer, my brother lived in Australia and barely talked to me – I was grateful I had one family member who was a loving constant in my life.

Ryan had been on his own since his last girlfriend ended things a year earlier. I dearly hoped he'd find someone new soon – he was a lovely lad and would make someone a fabulous life partner. He'd be a good dad too, and I'd always hoped that one day I'd be a grandmother. But all this was out of my hands. All I could do was be a good mother to Ryan, support him when necessary, be there as his safety net or backstop when things got tough. As he had been for me, when I'd been at my lowest.

These thoughts were racing around my head as I cycled the familiar route through the village and out onto Hawthorn Lane.

At Four Oaks Farm I stopped. The farm buildings were exactly as they'd been the last time I came past, but as my neighbour Mr Simpson had said, a large board had been attached to the gate. *Four Oaks Close*, it read. *Coming Soon: A development of 12 luxury three and four-bedroom homes.* An artist's impression showed red-brick houses with block-paved driveways arranged in a circle around a green on which children were playing. It looked as though it'd be a nice place to live.

'Except it's a bit of a walk into the village to shop, and there's no pavements along Hawthorn Lane,' I muttered, imagining what it would be like for those future house owners. They'd have no option but to drive everywhere. From the upstairs windows there'd be pleasant views across farmland, and if you liked being away from built-up areas it'd be great. It'd be interesting keeping an eye on progress when the work began. In a way I was sad that the place hadn't been bought and restored as a farm. Everything changes, in the end.

I wondered what Charlie would think of the development. It had been his grandparents' farm, and I assumed he would have fond memories of visiting it as a child.

Thinking of Charlie gave me an idea. I pulled out my phone and sent him a quick message. *Hi! Just had a thought – if you're free today, do you fancy meeting for lunch at Julio's? I've been meaning to try it out since I moved back here!*

The blue tick indicating he'd seen the message appeared almost instantly, and within seconds he replied. *Great idea! See you there in about an hour?* I grinned and replied with a thumb's up.

As I turned to leave Four Oaks Farm, I glanced back at the hedge to the side of the new board. A distant memory surfaced – hadn't we buried something there? I had a vague memory of digging with garden trowels in rock-solid dry earth in a ditch under the hedge.

'The time capsule!' I blurted out. 'Of course!' I made a mental note to talk to Lynne about it, see if she could remember burying it too. What had we put in it? Lots of bits of 1970s teenage rubbish,

I supposed. It would probably have rotted away long ago.

Inside, I'm still that kid. That twelve-year old who'd played in the farm with her mates, who'd buried a time capsule, who'd sobbed at night in her bedroom when her parents were arguing. That child was still there underneath. The years since had added layers, but the core was the same. I suppose it's the same for everyone. You never really shed those past selves. You just add another skin around the outside of it all. Some of those layers were tougher than others. Some were so fragile that they ripped and tore very easily. Those needed to be protected by adding tougher layers on top. That's what I was doing, still. Building protective layers.

I cycled home, freshened up, put on a pair of cotton trousers and a pretty top under my leather jacket and set out to walk to Julio's. I was ten minutes early so I picked a small table and ordered a glass of sparkling water while I waited for Charlie to arrive.

One problem with being in a pub or café by yourself is knowing where to look. If you watch other people in the bar it looks as though you're being nosy, and you can get into trouble if caught staring. If you don't watch people there's nothing to entertain you. So you end up pulling out your phone and scrolling through social media. Before phones I suppose everyone took a book or newspaper to read. But I decided not to get my phone out. There were enough people in the bar that I thought I'd be able to get away with a bit of people watching while I waited. I was half wondering if I might recognise someone from my school days.

There was a couple at the next table who'd ordered food but were barely exchanging a single word. A group of five youngish men discussing the football stood by the bar, drinking pints and getting louder and louder. A couple of old men, probably in their eighties, sat by a window at a table that I guessed was their regular spot. One was drinking Guinness, the other had a pint of real ale.

Even though I'd suggested meeting for lunch I felt strangely nervous as I sat there watching the door. Was this a date? Would Charlie think it was? We'd met just a handful of times as children and twice since I'd moved back to Hareton Wick. But undeniably I'd felt a spark of attraction between us each time I'd seen him. Did he feel the same?

It wasn't long before he walked in, wearing a loose linen shirt and jeans, a jumper slung casually over one shoulder. He greeted me with a kiss on the cheek. 'Jo! Good to see you again! I was so glad you messaged me. I was just wondering what to do with my day – although I do need to visit Dad this afternoon. Lovely idea to come here.'

'Well, I thought we could have a proper catch-up. We couldn't really do that at my house-warming, could we?'

'No, you needed to mingle with your new neighbours. They all seemed like a nice bunch. And your son Ryan's a good lad. What're you drinking? I'll go to the bar.'

'I'm all right with this water, thanks.' I picked up my glass.

'OK. Mind if I have a pint?'

'Not at all – please go ahead.'

As he went to the bar, I considered how thoughtful it had been of him to ask if I minded him drinking. He didn't know about my drink problem but wanted to make sure I was happy if he had alcohol in front of me anyway. That was sweet.

He was back in a minute with a pint of real ale and two menus. 'I've eaten here a few times before and can recommend the wild boar sausages with mash.'

'Mmm, sounds good!'

We ordered our food – both of us chose the sausages – and relaxed into chatting about our lives.

'So, Jo. When did you move away from the area?'

'Oh, when I was about twelve. My parents split up and sold the house. My brother and I went with Mum. Dad moved to Southampton to be nearer his work, and we went to Northampton near my grandparents.'

'That must have been tough. I always worried my parents would divorce, but somehow they stayed together. Mum died when I was in my thirties.'

'Sorry to hear that. I lost my mum at a young age too. But we still have our dads.'

'Yes, although my dad's dementia is so bad that some days he barely recognises me.'

'That must be horrible.'

'It is. But let's not dwell on the sad subjects, eh?' He smiled. 'You know, it occurred to me that if I'd been at Brookhill with the rest of the local kids I would probably have known you and your brother much better, back then. We might have hung out together at the rec.'

'You called it the rec too? So did we!'

'I used to climb the big tree there whenever I was home. I'd sit in it and watch the world go by from up there.'

'So did my friend, Lynne, and I! It was our favourite place to sit and gossip.'

'Oh, *you* were the girls who hogged the tree when I wanted to climb it!' he said with a wink. 'Where else did you used to play?'

I thought back to that last summer. 'We used to ride our bikes in the New Forest, take buses into Southampton to go swimming. All sorts of places.'

'See, I missed out on all that, being away at boarding school and having few local friends.'

'Aw, poor you. Can I tell you a secret?'

'Go on.' He leaned forward, his eyes twinkling.

'We used to play at Four Oaks Farm. We'd squeeze in through a gap in the hedge and play in the barn, climbing on the hay bales. We were shouted at by your dad for trespassing once.'

'Ah! So it was you! I remember Dad got the place boarded up to stop kids getting in.'

I blushed. 'I'm sorry. We shouldn't have gone in . . . but it was that long hot summer, 1976, and the barn was such a great place to play.'

'I remember that summer. Didn't a kid go missing?'

'Yes. We knew her. Pippa Jenkins. She sometimes hung out at Lynne's with us.'

'Was she a friend of yours?'

I shook my head. 'Not really. She was quite a bit younger than us. We only tolerated her being around because she was so often left alone.' The familiar pangs of guilt rose up in me as I remembered how sometimes we'd actively try to avoid Pippa. If we hadn't, if we'd searched her out to play with us more, she might not have disappeared.

Charlie reached across the table and touched my hand. 'Still. Must be awful for something like that to happen to someone you knew. What did actually happen? I was away for a lot of that summer, staying with a friend.'

'No one really knows what happened to her. She just disappeared. The police questioned everyone, including me, my brother and friends. The men of the village, including my dad, formed search parties and looked everywhere but found no trace.'

'I think my dad helped with the search too. It must have been terrible for her family.'

'Her parents were divorced. Her mum moved away the following year, so Lynne told me.'

'But no closure for her.'

'No.'

We sat in silence for a moment, contemplating how awful it must have been for poor Mrs Jenkins. I was struck by how kind and caring Charlie seemed to be. I liked him.

Our food arrived, then our conversation moved on to the tastiness of the boar sausages and the creaminess of the mash. It was a very pleasant lunch in very pleasant company, and I didn't want it to end.

When Charlie said he needed to go to visit his dad, I couldn't help but look disappointed that our lunch date was coming to an end.

'Unless,' Charlie said, his head tilted to one side, 'you'd like to come with me to Dad's? I never stay long because he gets tired quickly. Then afterwards we could get a coffee or go for a walk or something?'

'I used to like your dad,' I said, 'so, yes. I'm very happy to come along.'

'Excellent! I'll pay this bill and then we can go.'

I protested but Charlie insisted on paying the whole bill, saying it could be my treat next time. I was pleased he was expecting a 'next time' because that was precisely what I wanted too.

Crispin Willis's care home was on the edge of the village, on the road that led towards Southampton. It was about a twenty-minute walk from the pub. The day was sunny and warmer than usual for the season, so it was a pleasant walk. It looked like a nice place, probably expensive, with well-kept grounds and neatly uniformed staff, who greeted Charlie by name as we signed in at reception.

'He's in his room,' a nurse said. 'He's on good form today.'

'Oh, good. We'll go in to see him now.' Charlie led the way along cream-painted corridors to a room at the end that overlooked the garden. The room was large, with a hospital bed on one side, a door to a bathroom, and a cluster of easy chairs by a bay window. Sitting on one of these with a blue blanket over his knees was an old man whom I barely recognised. Whatever I remembered of Crispin's looks from fifty years ago was either inaccurate or he'd changed with age. Probably a mixture of both.

'Hey, Dad,' Charlie said, as he pulled up a couple of chairs beside his father. 'How are you today? I've brought a friend for you to meet. This is Jo.'

'Hello, Mr Willis,' I said. The old man looked up at me with rheumy eyes and offered a limp, blue-veined hand for me to shake.

'Who are you?' he said.

'This is Jo,' Charlie said, patiently. 'My friend.'

'She's not your friend,' Crispin said, and his mouth broadened into a wide smile. 'Silly boy. She's your mother. My Barbara. My lovely Barbara.'

'Dad, she's not . . .' Charlie began, but I put a hand up to stop him.

'Crispin, it's been a long time since I last saw you,' I said, not untruthfully, smiling as I sat down beside him.

'Why don't you come, Barbara? No one ever comes.'

'I come every two days, Dad!'

Crispin waved a dismissive hand in Charlie's direction. 'Oh, I know *you* come. But no one else. My lovely Barbara. You're here now. Will I make you a cup of tea?'

'I'll do it,' Charlie said, jumping to his feet. There was a little kitchen area we'd passed on our way to Crispin's room. He headed out to make the tea after I nodded to say I was happy being left alone with Crispin.

'I remember you in your blue dress most,' Crispin said while Charlie was out of the room. 'At Muriel's birthday party. You remember?'

'I liked that dress,' I said, playing along.

'It suited you. And you told me I was your handsome prince.' Crispin chuckled. 'Your handsome prince. They don't tell me that now. They leave me in this room. But they do let me watch the TV. We used to watch the TV, Barbara. We were the first to have a colour telly, weren't we?'

'We were indeed. Not many had them back then.' My own family had stuck with a black-and-white one until the mid-seventies, I remembered.

'You needed a colour one if you were watching the snooker. Or you couldn't tell what colour ball they'd potted!' Crispin chuckled.

I laughed too.

Charlie came back in carrying a tray with mugs of tea, milk and sugar. 'Wasn't sure how you like your tea?' he said to me.

'She likes it white with one sugar,' Crispin said. 'I remember that. Don't know how you don't, Charles.'

I much preferred it with no sugar but I put a spoonful in anyway.

Charlie grinned. 'It was good to hear you laughing, Dad, when I was out making the tea.'

'Doing me a power of good, seeing my lovely Barbara, son. Power of good, it's done me.' Crispin smiled at me fondly.

'It's lovely to see you too, Crispin.'

We chatted for a quarter of an hour, with Crispin coming up with disjointed memories. Charlie and I followed along as best we could. Charlie shot me grateful glances now and again.

We left when Crispin had finished his tea and was looking tired. Charlie cleared away the cups. 'You have a nice nap this afternoon, Dad, and I'll come to see you again on Tuesday, all right?'

'Isn't it Tuesday today?'

'No, Sunday.'

'Barbara, you'll come again?'

I smiled. 'Yes, I will when I can.'

Crispin smiled back and reached for my hand, which he held to his cheek. 'My lovely Barbara.'

As we left the care home Charlie turned to me. His eyes glistened with unshed tears. 'I haven't seen him look so happy, or heard him laugh like that, for so long. Thank you.'

'No problem. I remember reading somewhere that it's better to play along than to try to explain. I'm glad he seemed to have a nice time. And I'm happy to go back again, another time.'

'Thank you.' And now it was Charlie's turn to catch my hand, raise it to his lips and kiss it.

Chapter 12

Pippa, 31 July 1976
Seven days before.

Since Mum and Dad split up, Pippa had lived with Mum, but every two weeks Dad came to take her out for a day at the weekend. Those days had been brilliant to start with. Dad would treat her to ice cream and chocolate, and would take her somewhere exciting – the beach at Bournemouth, the cinema in Southampton, shopping for toys. She'd had some lovely times with him and had always looked forward to those days. He'd bought her a ballerina watch that she wore every day, even though Mum said it was a silly one that wouldn't last.

Once or twice, she'd come home from days out with Dad feeling a bit sick from too much ice cream, and there'd been that time at the beach when they'd gone in the sea and he'd tried to teach her to swim, and she had ended up out of her depth. She'd been floundering but Dad had just laughed, thinking she was playing around. When eventually he'd come to her rescue and carried her back to the beach he'd still been laughing. She'd had to pretend it was all a joke, even though actually she'd been terrified she was going to drown. That sort of thing never happened with Mum, who kept a much closer eye on her. At least she did if she didn't have to go to work.

Today was a weekend and it was a Dad day. He'd collected her late, and Mum had grumbled about it but eventually he'd turned up in his purple Ford Cortina. 'Daddy's taking you to the zoo tomorrow, zoo tomorrow, zoo tomorrow,' he sang, then stopped. 'Zoo *today*, actually, kiddo! Come on, are you ready?'

'Yes! The zoo!' Pippa jumped up and down with excitement but Mum was frowning.

'Southampton zoo? That place is awful. The poor animals are in such cramped pens and they're not well looked after. Paul, I don't like you taking her here.'

'Not Southampton zoo. We're off to the new one, Marwell zoological park, where the animals have lots of space to roam around. Don't you worry, Joyce. Pippa will love it.'

'Well, all right then. Bring her back by five o'clock for her tea, won't you?'

'Of course.' And with that the goodbyes were said and Pippa climbed into the back of Dad's car. She knew that as soon as they were round the corner, out of sight of Mum, she could climb over into the front seat and sit next to Dad. Mum didn't like her riding in the front, telling Pippa it wasn't as safe as in the back in case Dad crashed the car.

But Pippa liked it, and she knew Dad was a good driver. He wouldn't crash. He said he liked her sitting beside him, so once they were out of Beechmount Road she climbed through the gap between the front seats and slid into the passenger seat next to him.

'That's my girl,' Dad said, grinning at her.

'Shall I put the seatbelt on?' she asked.

'Only if you want to. You're probably too small for it.'

Pippa decided to leave it. Dad wasn't wearing his, in any case.

It was about a half-hour journey to Marwell, and the journey passed quickly, with Dad asking her about what she'd been up to lately. Mum had told her not to tell him that she was often left alone, so she spent most of the time talking about the day she'd spent in Lynne's garden and pool. 'And Lynne gave me her old Barbie doll to take home. I've called her Bambi because I already had a Barbie.'

'You still playing with dolls, Pippa? Thought you'd have grown out of them by now.' Dad reached across and ruffled her hair.

'Barbie is like a grown-up's doll. Not like Tiny Tears.' Pippa pouted. She didn't like it when Dad made fun of her.

'Still a doll,' Dad said. 'Anyway, nice that you could play in Lynne's pool. Are you better at swimming now?'

'A bit.'

'Good. Look, we're nearly there.' Dad turned off the road and into a car park. He drove up and down the aisles muttering, before going into an overflow car park. 'They ought to tarmac over this field too, if they're getting this number of visitors,' he said, as they walked over to the ticket booth.

Pippa was skipping alongside Dad, wishing he'd hold her hand. Even though she was eight it was still nice to hold hands with an adult now and again, but he didn't seem to like it.

The zoo wasn't like she'd expected. The animals had large enclosures and because it was hot, most of them were sheltering under trees or had gone inside their barns so they were hard to spot. There were no lions, and the Siberian tigers were nowhere to be seen. There were several different types of antelope, and a pond with lots of pink flamingos, which she liked. You had to walk on long paths to get to each part of the zoo, and soon Pippa sensed that Dad was getting bored.

Sure enough, when she was peering through a fence trying to spot the wild boar that were supposed to be in that enclosure, he sighed. 'I've had enough. There's a café here somewhere. I'm going to get a drink of something. Want to meet me there when you've seen everything?'

'I don't know the way, Dad!' Pippa said.

'Back near the entrance. You'll find it. No hurry though – you enjoy yourself.' And with that he strode off.

Another day, another parent, but still she was on her own. She watched him walk away, noting the direction. Might as well carry on going round the zoo, she thought. Somewhere there were supposed to be giraffes, and she wanted to see those. She carried on along the path they'd been following, past pens containing okapi, oryx, and Przewalski's horses, according to the information boards. What funny names some animals had, she thought. The okapi was the only one she spotted – its stripy backside like a zebra's stood out against the brown vegetation. She watched it for a while and then moved on.

It was hot, and growing hotter, and after a while she wished she'd gone with Dad to the café. He'd have bought her an ice cream, and maybe a Fanta with ice. Anything to help her cool down.

There was no sign of the giraffe enclosure. Maybe it was near the entrance. She turned to head back, but became unsure at a junction – was it left or right here? She looked for someone to ask – a member of staff in their green T-shirts or perhaps a mother with children of her own who might know, but she felt too shy to approach anyone. Mum was always telling her never to speak to strangers.

She turned left on a path that led up a slight hill. In the distance at the top was a signpost. That would help.

But the sign said the café was back in the direction she'd just come, so she went back down and took the other turn. She was hotter than ever now, after walking up that hill, and felt annoyed with Dad. He shouldn't have left her alone. It was supposed to be their day together. He was worse than Mum. At least when Mum left Pippa alone it was because she had to go to work, and Pippa was at home with food and drink left in the fridge for her.

'Better than stomping round a boring old zoo,' Pippa muttered. 'There's not even any monkeys or chimpanzees here. Or elephants. Or lions and tigers, and I can't find the giraffes!'

'Giraffes are over that way,' a man said as he passed her, pointing back in the direction she'd just come from. Pippa just glared at him and carried on walking. Sooner or later she'd find the café, and if she didn't, she'd go to the exit and then to the car and just wait there for Dad. There were some trees at the edge of the overflow car park so at least she could sit in the shade.

She saw buildings ahead. One of them must be the café. And thankfully, it was. But there was no sign of Dad.

Pippa went in anyway and took a seat at a table near the door. Perhaps Dad had gone to the loo. She felt tears pricking at the corners of her eyes. The last thing she wanted to do was cry – it was supposed to be a good day out with Dad, who she only saw once every two weeks. Why did her parents have to be divorced? Everyone else at the zoo was a family – mums and dads together with two or three children and babies in pushchairs. All happy and having fun. Kids with sunhats on to keep them cool, and dads carrying rucksacks that she would bet contained drinks bottles.

And then she spotted Dad. He was by the café's self-service counter, talking to the woman at the till, laughing and joking with her. He had no tray, and it didn't look as though he was buying anything. As Pippa watched, they broke off their conversation so the woman could serve someone in the queue, but Dad stayed at her side to continue chatting. It was clear he was not going to leave to take a seat, so Pippa went over.

'Dad?' she said, as she came alongside him.

'Ah, here you are. Did you like the zoo?'

'Not much,' she said. She'd meant to tell him she'd loved it, but now she felt so cross about being abandoned and having to spend so long finding him again that she decided to be truthful. 'There aren't any interesting animals here.'

'Oh, you've a right little madam there, haven't you, Paul?' said the woman at the till with a chuckle. She had the biggest, blackest eyelashes Pippa had ever seen, and her hair was what Mum called 'bottle blonde.'

Dad laughed and rolled his eyes. 'I certainly have. Better get her into the gift shop, I suppose. She'll want a teddy bear or something. She still plays with dolls, you know.'

'I don't want a teddy!' Pippa almost screamed the words at him and stamped her foot. 'But I do want a drink.'

'Well, ask nicely then!'

'Can I have a drink, *please*,' Pippa said, glaring at Dad.

He laughed and again rolled his eyes at the till-woman, then picked up a can of lemon Fanta. 'Better get the little madam what she wants, eh?'

'That's fifteen pence, please, Paul,' till-woman said, and Dad rummaged in his pocket to find the coins.

Pippa hated lemon Fanta. She much preferred orange, but Dad and the till-woman would only make some remark about her being fussy or something, so she decided to keep quiet. At least the can had come out of a fridge and would be cold. She took it to a table and dug her fingertips under the ring-pull. Usually she'd ask Dad to open it for her, but this time, she decided she'd do it herself, even if it hurt her fingers.

It did hurt her, and she broke a nail, but she managed it, and the drink, although disgusting, did make her feel a bit better. Dad stayed at the till talking and laughing with the woman. Some day out this had proved to be. Maybe it was better being left at home by herself after all, especially if she could go round to Lynne's.

On Dad's next visit he'd said she was going to stay with him overnight. 'For a proper holiday,' he'd said, and Pippa had felt excited at the prospect. Now she wasn't. Not if today was anything to go by.

Chapter 13

Jo, 2024

I was settling into a relaxed but busy life of working on my latest IT training project most days until about three o'clock, then going out for a walk or a bike ride, or perhaps meeting up with Lynne for tea and cake, or doing Dad's shopping. My plan was to spend weekends visiting Dad and doing chores around the bungalow. My work was easy and I liked the way it filled part of my week. In a few more years, I'd retire. But for now, I was happy to earn a bit extra, add to my pension pot, and feel productive.

Ryan generally called me on Wednesday evenings. I wasn't sure if he'd call that week as he'd only just visited, but he did. And he sounded distracted.

'Is something wrong?' I asked him, picking up on the worried tone in his voice.

'Not with me,' he answered, 'but . . .'

'But?'

He took a deep breath. 'There's a kid from school. In my class. He's gone missing.'

'Missing?' A cold hand of dread clutched at me.

'Last seen on Monday after school.'

'Oh, no. What do they think happened?'

'I don't know. There's been search parties, obviously all his friends have been spoken to . . . police have checked all the places the kids hang out . . .'

'History repeating itself,' I muttered. Visions of Stephanie and memories of little Pippa inevitably sprung to the forefront of my mind.

'What?'

'I've told you before, I think? About the little girl who went missing here in Hareton Wick that last summer I lived here.'

'I vaguely remember. What happened to her?'

'She was never found.'

'Oh. That's not very comforting,' he said. 'Thanks for cheering me up, Mum.'

'Oh, I didn't mean . . .'

'It's all right. It's just a bit stressy. Ben being in my class and everything.'

'Of course. God, I hope they find the poor little boy.'

'Well, yes. So do we all. I suspect it's going to be on the news tonight. The poor lad's only eleven so they're making a big thing about it all.'

'I'll catch the six o'clock news, then.'

'Yeah, you do that. So, everything OK? I phoned Granddad yesterday. He sounded in fine form.'

'Oh, good. I'll be seeing him tomorrow. I usually get his shopping on a Thursday afternoon.'

'He said you'd been doing an excellent job looking after him since you moved closer. Said he was lucky to have you as a daughter.'

I felt tears well up at the praise. Dad was rarely forthcoming in saying things like that to your face, but it was good to hear. 'I do my best.'

'I think he's missing Uncle David.'

'Yes, he is. I wish David would come over.'

'Me too. Haven't seen him since I visited Australia after graduating.' Ryan had stayed with David for a month in Sydney and they'd got on really well. It was a shame they hadn't been able to continue that relationship. David was long overdue visiting the UK. 'Does he know how frail Granddad is?'

'I think so . . . I'll email him again,' I said.

'I think you should. Anyway, I'll let you go now. This conversation's been all doom and gloom. After what's going on at school I need a bit of cheering up. Think I'll go down the pub with Liam if he's around.'

'OK, have fun. I really hope that child is found safe and well soon.'

'Yes. Thanks, Mum. Talk next week, eh?'

'Or before, if there's any news. Keep me informed. It's a horrible thing to have to go through, I know.'

We said goodbye and hung up. I sat quietly for a while, hating what my poor boy was having to deal with. I realised I hadn't asked if he'd been questioned by the police. I assumed he would have been, as Ben's teacher. Or maybe not, as the boy had gone missing after school hours.

That evening, I watched several news bulletins and followed updates on news websites. The boy's friends hadn't seen him since school finished. He'd been reported missing after his mother came home from work. Normally he'd be at home by then, doing his homework. Or at a friend's house, playing video games. But none of his friends had seen him since classes ended. His parents were divorced and his father lived abroad. He was generally thought of as a well-behaved child, who'd never run off before, and the suspicion was that someone had taken him.

It was so similar to what had happened with Pippa. That of course had been in the school holidays, but again the child was expected to fend for themselves until their only parent came home from work. Ben was eleven – to my mind that was still too young to leave a child alone. Back in the seventies it was normal to have a child let themselves into their home after school. But now? Now, when there seemed to be predators around every corner? Was it really a sensible thing to do?

The TV news bulletin showed an interview with Ben's tearful mother. My heart went out to her as she dabbed at her eyes and pleaded with whoever was holding Ben to let him return home safe.

'Please let him be all right,' I whispered.

That night I couldn't sleep. It was just like it had been after finding Stephanie. I tossed and turned all night; images of her discarded body jumbled up in my mind with memories of Pippa and the details I'd heard on the news about Ben. Somehow in the cold, dark hours of the night I began feeling guilty for all of them. I could have done more for Pippa. I should have left home earlier and prevented Stephanie's murder. There was nothing I could have done for Ben, but even so I found myself wishing that Ryan had been a better friend to him. Maybe Ryan could have run an after-school club for children like Ben. If I'd been a better mother, would Ryan have become a more caring teacher?

My mind whirred for hours, round and round, blaming myself, even though rationally I knew none of the events had been my fault. I finally got out of bed at five-thirty and made myself a cup of chamomile tea. Had there still been wine in the house left from Ryan's visit, I might well have poured a glass. Anything to take the edge off, to help me sleep.

I must have gone back to sleep in the end. I woke just before seven, groggy from the bad night, but feeling more together than I had been earlier. Of course Ben's disappearance was nothing to do with me. Of course there was nothing I could have done for him. *You silly woman*, I told myself. *It's sad, it's traumatic for all involved, but you're not involved, Jo Atkinson. All you need to do is support Ryan if he needs it. He's the one close to it.*

I wondered how Ryan was feeling. I knew he didn't leave for

school until about eight o'clock so I had time to call him over breakfast.

He answered straight away and sounded stressed.

'How are you, Ryan?' I asked. 'Handling it all OK?'

'Hmm. It's tough. I was at the police station for hours yesterday after we spoke.'

'At the station?' I gasped.

'Being questioned. Turns out I was the last person to see Ben. He stayed behind after school for a little while, helping me tidy the classroom and put some displays up. He often did. I had the impression he didn't much like being at home on his own before his mum got back, so I always let him stay behind if he wanted to. Anyway, he was helping me for about half an hour after school, maybe a little more. Then, as it was raining, I offered him a lift home. I dropped him off on the corner of his road and no one's seen him since.'

'Oh, Ryan!'

'I was questioned under caution, Mum.' He took a long shuddering breath. 'They think I've done something to him.'

'No! Surely not. Just that you're the last person . . . of course they want to retrace all Ben's steps.'

'Yes, but it was the way they questioned me. Two of them. Good cop, bad cop, it felt like. It was horrible. Made me feel as though I was supposed to be guilty, if that makes any sense. I began doubting myself.'

'I know that situation well, both from Pippa all those years ago and also . . . more recently.' I sighed.

'I think they believe I've hurt him.' Ryan spoke in a whisper, as if saying it out loud might make it true.

'Oh, my God.'

'They kept me there for hours, Mum. Honestly, I thought they were going to keep me all night and stick me in a cell. But they sent me home around midnight.' He sounded close to tears. 'They told me not to leave the country. And today, I have to teach, but the head's going to sit in on all my classes. They don't want me left alone with the kids . . . in case it turns out it was me. Mum, it's horrible.'

My heart went out to him. I wanted to soothe him, to hold him close, the way I had when he was little, and make all the horridness go away. But my words came out wrong. 'Now you know how it feels to feel guilty and wonder if it's somehow partly your fault. If there was something you should have done . . .'

'It's not my fault, Mum. It's nothing to do with me.'

'I know, Ryan . . . I don't doubt that for a second.'

'Really? Because it sounds like you do. Like you think I might have hurt that boy. Jeez, Mum, I couldn't hurt a child. Surely you know that?'

'Of course, I just—'

'Just said the wrong thing, you're going to say. You sound like you think I'm involved, somehow. Even if you don't believe I could hurt him you think I could have done something to help him. Don't you think I've gone over every minute of that afternoon? Both with the police and by myself? I was awake half the night wishing I'd dropped him right by his door, made sure I'd seen him go in, rather than leaving him at the corner. Or wishing I'd not offered him a lift home. We're not supposed to. But he'd been so helpful and it was raining . . .'

'I'm sure you—' But Ryan still wasn't ready to hear anything from me.

'Maybe I shouldn't have let him stay and help. But he wanted to and he's a good kid. The police made a lot of that, you know. I let slip that Ben had often stayed behind and done a few small jobs in the classroom. Once he sat there playing on his phone while I got on with some marking.'

'His phone . . .' I managed to say.

'That day he went missing it was out of charge. He was cursing it. He'd have played on it rather than help me, I think, if it had any charge.'

'So the police can't contact him.'

I could almost hear Ryan's eyes rolling. 'No, Mum. Obviously calling him was the first thing his mum tried.'

'Well, I just meant—'

'You're not helping. Useless suggestions as to how the police might do their job, and insinuating I might be guilty somehow. Fuck's sake. I can't . . . I just can't . . .'

And then he hung up.

Ryan had never hung up on me before. Never. We'd always had a good, close relationship. There'd been a few clashes, of course, especially in his teenage years. But Ryan as an adult had felt more like my friend than my son.

An awful thought flitted through my mind. Ryan was the last person to see Ben. Ben had often stayed behind in class, just him and Ryan. Surely Ryan couldn't— No. I wouldn't believe it of him for a second. Even though he thought I did.

And that was the thought that broke me. That Ryan believed I could think so badly of him. I began to shake, to cry, and I knew there was only one thing that would fix this. Without giving it a moment's more thought I grabbed my keys and purse, got in my car and went straight to the supermarket. I hurried past the fruit and veg, the bakery and deli bar, and into the corner where the alcohol was. I grabbed a bottle of merlot in each hand and strode towards the checkout. I'd be home in five minutes, the first rush of alcohol into my system would soon be mine. Just five minutes until I could start the process of hurling myself into drunken oblivion where all my worries and hideous thoughts were buried under a bottle or two of wine.

A woman with a fully laden shopping trolley and a toddler in the child-seat was approaching the checkout – the only one that was open – at the same time as me. I hurried to get there first – after all I was only buying two items, but she was ahead of me. I tried to catch her eye to indicate perhaps she'd like to let me go first, but to no avail. I had to wait in line.

As I waited the child looked up at me and smiled cheekily, then he hid his face in his hands to play peekaboo. He was just like Ryan had been at that age – all white-blond hair and dimples. I watched him for a bit while his mother took forever to unpack her trolley. And gradually I found myself smiling, chuckling a little at the child's evident joy in having a captive audience. I wanted to play peekaboo back at him, but my hands were occupied holding the two bottles of wine. I looked at what I was holding. Merlot. I didn't even particularly like merlot.

I put the bottles onto the magazine rack that divided the checkout from the next one, and joined in the game, sending the toddler into paroxysms of laughter. His mother turned and smiled at me. 'Thanks for keeping him amused. You're a lifesaver,' she said, as the cashier started to scan her purchases.

But she was wrong. It was her little boy who was the lifesaver. I stayed in that line playing peekaboo with him until she'd finished bagging and paying for her shopping. And then I grabbed a magazine to buy off the rack, leaving the bottles there.

Back home, with only a copy of *Woman's Weekly* to show for my excursion, I put the kettle on and made some tea. That had been a close call.

Jo, you'll be of no use to Ryan, who needs you, if you're back at the bottom of a bottle, I told myself. It wasn't him who'd hurt Ben. It couldn't be. I knew him too well, I knew he wasn't capable of such a thing or anything approaching it. It had just been the way it had brought Pippa's disappearance to the forefront of my mind – another child missing, my family involved. That's what had so very nearly tipped me over the edge. Thank God for that small child.

I needed to stay strong, to stay sober. Although Ryan had taken what I said the wrong way and hung up on me, it was only the stress of what he was going through. And, surely, I of all people understood that?

It was well past the time that I should have started work for the day. Maybe it would take my mind off things. I switched on my laptop and tried to get stuck in.

As it turned out, I spent half the day refreshing news websites to see if there was any more news on the missing boy. But there was nothing. My heart gave a lurch at one point, when I read that a local man was 'assisting police with enquiries' – was that my Ryan they were talking about?

I messaged him. *Sorry if what I said came out wrong this morning. You know, you MUST know, that I'm always here for you if you need me. Xxx*

Chapter 14

Jo, 1 August 1976
Six days before.

It all kicked off in the car, on the way to Devon. We were nearer to the campsite than home so we couldn't simply turn back.

It was hot, very hot, in the car. Dad wound down his window to let some air in.

'Wind that back up, will you. It's ruining my hair. I've only just had it done,' Mum said.

'It's too hot,' Dad replied, and I had to agree. Sitting in the back seat behind Dad I'd felt thankful for the blast of air.

'But my hair!'

'Why on earth did you get your hair done just before a camping trip?'

'Because it needed it, and I wanted to look nice for my holiday!'

'You'll be on the beach and in the sea. It won't last five minutes so it doesn't matter if it gets a bit windblown now. Anyway, I'm driving and I need the window down so that's all there is to it.' Dad's tone brooked no argument, but Mum went on anyway, asking whether he cared what she looked like anymore, whether he was going to give her money to get her hair done again in Devon, whether there was any point her making any effort when he was just going to sabotage it all. He retaliated, of course he did, telling her she was a vain woman, and of course he didn't mind what she looked like, no more than she minded what he looked like. And the whole thing spiralled out of control.

In the back seat, David kept his eyes fixed on a book he was reading, though I noticed he hadn't turned a page for some time. I stared out of the window at the passing scenery and did my best to block out what they were saying.

At last, we arrived at the campsite. The final section of the journey had passed in an uncomfortable silence. Mum had sat with her arms folded, staring out of the window. Dad had reluctantly wound the window up but had turned the fan on full. I could see damp patches under his arms where he was sweating.

We parked up and began pulling things out of the car. The next argument, thankfully a short one, was to do with how to pitch the tent. Mum wanted it under a tree for shade, Dad thought the tree would drop branches or sap onto the tent and ruin it. Mum got her way this time, mainly because David chimed in, pointing out that it would be very hot in the tent in the mornings if we had no shade.

I was trying to ignore it all, as usual. I couldn't wait for us to have everything sorted out so we could walk down to the beach and get in the sea. Our campsite was just a few minutes' walk from a village and a beach. It was one of those wonderful flat beaches where the tide went far out exposing huge expanses of sand. The sea was the Atlantic which meant there were lovely breaking waves. I'd already spotted that you could buy surfboards made of plywood from the campsite shop, and I wanted to get one and go down the beach to try it out.

But after the tent was up, we were hungry and it was well past lunch time. So we needed to make some sandwiches, eat and clear up before we were allowed to leave the campsite. It was three o'clock before we got away from our pitch. David and I bought a surfboard each, but Mum said we'd wait until tomorrow before we went to the beach. We had to take them back to the tent, then run to catch up with Mum and Dad, who were walking hand in hand (a good sign!) towards the village.

I guessed Dad had agreed to wait before going to the beach so Mum could have one more day before her hair was messed up any more. If that stopped another row, I was happy with that plan.

We finally went to the beach the next morning. We'd got up pretty early because, despite the shade of the tree, the tent became stifling hot as soon as the sun came up. Actually it had been too hot all night. I'd slept on top of my sleeping bag, in the tiny partition of the tent that was my 'bedroom'. Mum and Dad were in the main partition and David was in the section next to mine, separated from me only by a thin sheet of fabric that hung down. We'd set up the camping stove outside, along with a tiny camping table and deckchairs for Mum and Dad. David and I had to sit on mats on the ground for breakfast.

Straight after breakfast we headed to the beach, hoping to beat the crowds, but there were already loads of people there. It was a massive beach and the tide was way out so there was loads of space for us to set up. But then Mum looked around and realised every other family had a huge beach umbrella providing some shade, and we didn't.

'We should have one of those,' she grumbled.

'If you want shade, stay under the tree at the campsite. We're here for sunshine,' Dad replied, but he already looked hot and sweaty from carrying bags of beach stuff across the sand.

'Still, I'm going to buy us one.' Mum dropped the bag of towels and deckchair she was carrying and marched back up the beach towards a row of beach supply shops.

'I guess that means we're setting up here,' Dad said moodily.

He unfolded a deckchair and sat down, while David and I spread out the picnic rug.

'Can we go into the sea?' I asked.

'If you must, but look the tide's a long way out.'

'Doesn't matter.' I couldn't wait to try out my surfboard.

'Go on, then. Don't forget where we're sitting on the beach, eh?'

I looked around, noting landmarks nearby. 'Between those two blue-striped beach umbrellas and a little bit up from the orange windshield people.'

Dad nodded. 'Have fun. Be careful.'

And then David and I grabbed our boards and legged it down the beach towards the endless series of waves that broke onto the sand. Dad was right – the tide was a very long way out and it took us a good five minutes to reach the sea and wade out far enough to start catching waves. The boards were brilliant – we soon got the knack of diving onto our bellies on them just as the wave broke and letting it bring us all the way on to the beach. If you got it just right, you ended up skimming over the wet sand in just an inch or two of water as the wave finally petered out. If you got it wrong, you kind of fell off the back of the wave and had to get off the board and wait for another. Further along the beach were people with proper, stand-up surfboards but we loved our pieces of plywood with their curved-up ends, and boy, did we have fun.

I don't know how long we stayed in the water but eventually we became tired and hungry and headed back up the beach to our parents. The tide had come in some way so it wasn't nearly as far to walk back. We easily found the spot where we'd left them. But there was only Dad, sitting with a stupid-looking sunhat on his head, reading a newspaper.

'Where's Mum?' I asked, expecting him to say she'd gone into the sea.

'She couldn't find anywhere that sold beach umbrellas, so she decided to return to the campsite.'

'Oh.' I grabbed a towel, though actually I'd dried as I walked up the beach.

'You two look sunburnt. Better put some clothes on.'

I inspected my arms which looked OK to me, then noticed David's shoulders which looked rather pink. I did what Dad said and slipped my T-shirt on, which felt scratchy on my skin. It was too hot, out of the water, with no shade. 'Are we staying long?'

'Not if you don't want to,' Dad said. 'I'd like a quick dip, then we can pack up and go. It is a bit hot for me.'

He'd never liked the sun much, despite what he'd said to Mum about not wanting a beach umbrella. I watched as he jogged down the beach to the sea, still wearing his T-shirt, shorts and sunhat. David and I stuffed things into bags and folded deckchairs, ready for his return.

Back at the tent Mum had left a note saying she'd gone shopping. David and I spread the picnic rug on the ground under the tree, ate our lunch and spent the afternoon reading books while Dad went for a walk somewhere.

We had dinner out at a pub that night, sitting in the pub garden. Children were only allowed there up until eight o'clock, so we had to leave then. Shame, as it was only just becoming cool enough to be enjoyable.

The next few days were similar. Beach in the morning for a couple of hours until we all felt too hot. Then it was a scramble to find shade. Museums were good, we decided, as they were pleasantly cool inside, so we went to every local one we could find. Visits to tourist attractions were chosen if there was likely to be shade and shunned otherwise. Often, we went with just one parent. It was as though they'd decided to spend as little time in each other's company as possible to reduce the possibility of getting into fights. As a result, it wasn't like family holidays used to be. There were too many occasions when the parent who was with us seemed bored, or the parent who had done their own thing that day seemed tetchy afterwards, as though they'd missed out. David and I were at a loss. There was nothing we could do to make things better and the entire holiday became something to be endured before we could go home and see our friends again.

Only the fun of surfing each morning kept David and me enjoying ourselves.

'Not going well, is it?' David said to me, about halfway through the week, when we were on our own at the campsite.

I looked up from my book, a Nancy Drew mystery I'd borrowed from the library, and glanced at him. 'I like the beach, and the campsite's OK.'

'Not what I'm talking about.' There was something infinitely sad in his tone. Of course I knew what he meant. Our parents' relationship. If this holiday was supposed to be them trying hard to get on, it wasn't working. The first row had begun less than fifty miles from home.

'What can we do?' I asked.

He shrugged. 'It's for them to sort out, isn't it? Wish they would. We're stuck in the middle.'

'I thought it'd be better, away from home.'

'So did I. They've just brought their arguments with them, though.' David sighed. 'I suppose we just have to make the best of things and try to enjoy ourselves anyway.'

'Yeah.'

'Glad you're here, Smudge. It'd be worse if we didn't have each other.'

'Yeah.' I didn't dare say anymore. I felt too much like crying.

Chapter 15

Jo, 2024

There was no further news during the rest of the week about Ben's whereabouts. But I did get a text from Ryan in which he reassured me the police had eliminated him as a suspect. Thankfully, a neighbour had seen Ryan dropping off Ben at the end of the road and had watched him drive away. Ryan had called in at a supermarket after that, and there was CCTV of him entering and leaving, so the police were satisfied that his story panned out.

The neighbour had also seen Ben enter his house. So the time frame for his disappearance had narrowed to between then and when his mother arrived home, just forty minutes later. It was a mystery.

I was concerned for the child still, of course, and so was Ryan, but I was supremely thankful my boy was off the hook. Of course it hadn't been anything to do with him. How could it? I hadn't ever really thought it could have been. But I couldn't deny the idea had flitted across my mind. I was so ashamed of myself; both for the thought and for almost turning back to drinking.

I tried calling Ryan, but he didn't answer, and didn't return my calls. *Give him time*, I told myself. He knew I was there for him, if he needed me or wanted to talk.

And then on Thursday night I had a different call – from Charlie Willis. 'Fancy a lunch out on Saturday? There's a lovely New Forest pub that's been done up that I'm dying to try. It's just reopened and has a great-looking menu.'

'I'd love to,' I replied. It would be a great way to put the week's worries out of my mind.

'I'll pick you up at twelve, then?'

'Perfect! I could drive if you prefer, if you wanted to have a drink?'

'What about you having a drink?'

'Ah . . . I don't. Drink, that is. So it makes no difference for me.'

'I don't generally drink at lunchtimes either. So it's OK. I'll pick you up.' I had the impression he'd said that only to be in solidarity with me. Perhaps he'd guessed I'd had a problem with drink and didn't want to put me in a difficult situation. It was very gentlemanly of him, I thought.

I found myself very much looking forward to the date, if that's what it was, as the week progressed. Between having something to look forward to and the relief that Ryan was off the hook, I felt a lot better.

On Saturday morning I spent an agonising half hour deciding what to wear to meet Charlie. It was a cool spring day, with a strong breeze and intermittent sunshine. Might we go for a walk after? Or would we only go to the pub? I decided on some smart jeans, a nice top with my leather jacket, and a pair of flat shoes. I chucked a pair of trainers and a fleece in a bag just in case a walk in the New Forest was suggested for the afternoon.

Charlie was right on time, ringing my doorbell at midday exactly. 'You look lovely,' he said, kissing my cheek in greeting.

'So do you!' I said. He was dressed in jeans, a white shirt and a brown leather jacket. 'You obviously got the dress code memo.'

He laughed. 'I did, yeah. Well, if you're ready, we can go straight there.'

'I'm ready,' I replied, and went out to his car. He drove a mid-range Audi – a decent car, but not too showy. It fitted with what I knew of him so far.

It was a pleasant drive into the New Forest, through some forested areas and then across open heathland, skirting groups of ponies that congregated at the roadside. We ended up at a pub on the edge of a small village. It had a newly thatched roof, exposed beams inside and was thoroughly charming.

'Recently renovated, as I said on the phone, but looks like they've been sympathetic to its age and kept the original features,' Charlie said, as he admired the huge inglenook fireplace on one side of the main dining area, its walls adorned with hundreds of horse brasses.

'I love it,' I said, as I gazed around. It was perfect. Just the sort of place I like. 'Was there no chance of restoring Four Oaks farmhouse?'

'No. It's far too derelict. Been left too long. Shame, really.' Charlie looked wistful and I had to agree. It was a shame the farm had been left to rot all these years.

Our table was in a corner, with a good view across the room and a window nearby that looked out onto an attractive beer garden that I imagined would be lovely in warmer weather. The menu was interesting – a definite step up from regular 'pub grub'. I chose a goat's cheese tartlet as a starter and a chicken risotto main course, with a glass of sparkling elderflower to drink.

'This all right for you?' Charlie said as we sipped our drinks and waited for the food to arrive.

'It's perfect,' I replied.

'I used to come here years ago. Way back when I was a young fellow, haring around the countryside in a Triumph Spitfire with my latest squeeze at my side. It was a bit more rough and ready then, but the girls seemed to like it, so I brought them here.' He laughed and put a hand to his mouth. 'Oh, God, sounds like I haven't moved on at all, doesn't it? Like I'm still driving through the New Forest bringing dates to the same pub! Believe me, the pub has changed a lot.'

I laughed too. 'So we're revisiting your youth, are we? Well, I can't complain about you doing that, can I? Given that I've just moved back to the place where I grew up.'

'And I never really moved away.' Charlie looked thoughtful. 'I think I was away so much as a kid, at boarding school then university, that when all that was over I just wanted to settle in one place. Dad needed help with his various businesses so it made sense to stay with him. Mum and Dad lived in a massive house so although I lived with them, I had my own wing, practically.'

'Are you still there now?'

'Oh, God, no, though Dad still owns it. I married, and we bought a new house, outside the village. You know Southampton Road? It's along there – a private lane off to the left, just after you go up the hill. My house is at the end.'

'Ah, yes.' I vaguely knew where he meant. His mention of being married had thrown me, though. I'd thought this was a date.

My confusion must have been written all over my face. 'I'm widowed now. Clara died seven years ago. It was cancer.'

'Oh, I'm sorry. That's so tragic.'

He nodded. 'We had four children. Had to, really, as we lived in such a large house – it seemed only right to fill it. Now the kids are spread all over the place. One in France, one in Australia, and two in London. I'm not sure why I keep the house just for me, but it is nice when they come to visit and bring their partners and my grandchildren, so I suppose I'll stay put. Seems to be a Willis habit – owning unnecessarily huge houses. You can see why I sold the old farm as soon as I could.'

'Why did your father own that farm if he never lived in it?'

'He inherited it from his parents. When they died, he sold off the land. I think he had meant to do something with the farmhouse itself but then never got round to it.'

'I remember the farmhouse being boarded up in 1976.'

'Yes.' Charlie's eyes twinkled. 'Dad didn't want kids breaking in and playing there.'

I blushed. 'Hmm. You remember what I told you last time we met, obviously.'

'I remember every moment of it,' he said, his voice soft. I blushed harder. Time to change the subject, I thought.

'So, anyway, you've sold it now.'

'Yes, it's paying for Dad's care home nicely.' He took a sip of his drink. 'You know, when he, um, goes, I'll sell his house. And probably mine. Might sell Dad's businesses too. I could buy a nice little bungalow up the road from you, live there in the summer, and live on cruise ships travelling the world in the winter.'

I smiled. 'That sounds like an amazing lifestyle. I'd join you, if I could afford it.'

'I could pay for you too!' He laughed, to show he didn't really mean it. 'It'd be great fun. Imagine waking up and thinking: "Where are we this morning? Well, if it's Monday it must be Barcelona . . .". Have you ever been on a cruise?'

'Only one short one to the Norwegian fjords, many years ago.' It had been with Colin, after Ryan had started university, and not long before we split up. Before he sheepishly announced to me one weekend that he'd fallen in love with his secretary and wanted to end our marriage so he could be with her. He hadn't been unfaithful, he insisted. Not yet, anyway. But it was clear Marion had won his heart. What could I do other than let him go gracefully? I was glad I did. Colin and I have maintained a good, friendly relationship, and Marion became a friend too, of sorts.

'You look pensive. Good or bad memories of that cruise?'

I liked that he seemed so sensitive. 'Mixed, I suppose. Like so many things in life. I split up with my husband not too long after.'

'I'm sorry.'

'It's fine. We actually have a good relationship. Our marriage had run its course, he'd fallen for someone else. Our son was grown-up and had left home, so us splitting up didn't hurt him.'

'That sounds like the perfect divorce.'

'I think it was.'

'You have just one son?'

'Yes. Ryan. He's a schoolteacher.'

'Great job to be in. You get on well with him too?'

'Well . . . generally, yes. Had a bit of a hiccup this week.'

He pulled a face. 'Happens too easily, doesn't it? I'm not entirely sure if my youngest is talking to me right now. I upset her by accident the other day, when I made a joke she took personally.'

'I said something that Ryan took the wrong way, too.' Suddenly I felt I wanted to talk about it. I'd said nothing to anyone about Ryan's closeness to the missing boy. But now, here was a charming, warm, sympathetic man whom I liked a lot, sitting right opposite me. And we were still waiting for our starters. 'You might have seen on the news, something about a boy called Ben, who's gone missing after school?'

'Oh, yes. I saw that.'

'He's in Ryan's class. Ryan was the last person to speak to him that day. He was questioned closely by police. It was all quite traumatic for him.'

'I bet it was.' Charlie nodded.

'I said something, and he took it to mean that I thought he *was* guilty.' As I said it, I realised it didn't make sense unless I also told Charlie my deep-seated guilt about Pippa Jenkins, and how that had fed into my breakdown after the trauma of finding Stephanie.

But Charlie didn't look confused, didn't ask, just gave me a caring look and reached across to touch my hand. 'I imagine he was reacting out of stress—'

He was about to say something more but at that moment our starters arrived, and we broke off the conversation as the waitress put our plates in front of us. By the time she'd left the moment had passed. 'This looks delicious,' I said, gazing at my beautifully presented goat's cheese tartlet.

'So does mine. Let's get stuck in, shall we?'

We ate our starters more or less in silence, making comments only about the food. When we were finished and the plates pushed aside, Charlie looked at me meaningfully. 'I was going to say, that Ryan perhaps took what you said the wrong way merely because of the stress he was under. Being questioned by police is never fun. Not that I've ever experienced it, myself.'

'I have. That's kind of why I said it, I suppose. Thankfully after he was questioned the boy's neighbour came forward, and they realised Ryan can't have had anything to do with it.' To my horror I felt tears welling up. 'God, I was so relieved to hear that. But since then, I haven't spoken to Ryan. He's not accepting my calls.'

'That's tough. Give him time. He'll know you didn't mean it, and that you support him.'

'I hope so. I miss him, in a way. I only saw him last weekend but I so want to chat with him again, find out how he's feeling now.' I looked down at the table for a moment, and then surprised myself by opening up yet more. 'Thing is, when I went through a traumatic time a few years ago I didn't talk to anyone enough and ended up spiralling out of control. It's why I don't drink, now. I used it as a crutch to get through. And I don't want Ryan to go through anything similar.'

'Was your trauma anything to do with what you just said about having experienced police questioning?' Charlie asked carefully.

I nodded. 'Yes. I . . . found the body of a young woman who'd been murdered.'

'Oh, my God!'

'It was awful. The poor woman. It could have been me . . . if I'd set out on my dog walk a little earlier. But what tipped me over the edge was thinking if only I'd left sooner, I might have stopped it. I might have been able to do something to help her.'

He shook his head. 'Yet you know you couldn't really have prevented it, and it's not your fault.'

'I told myself that; so did everyone I knew; so did my therapist later on. But even so, at three in the morning that's what was keeping me awake and sending me to the solace of the wine bottle.'

'Oh, Jo.' Again, he reached across the table and briefly touched my arm. A small gesture, and one that was oddly comforting. I liked it.

Other than my family and therapist, no one else knew about Stephanie. I barely knew this man and yet here I was burdening him with my innermost secrets. But there was something about him that made me want to be honest and open with him, to hide nothing, to let him see me, warts and all.

'And weirdly,' I went on, 'I connected finding her with the mystery of what happened to Pippa Jenkins all those years ago. I was questioned by the police then, you know. We all were. Because she had quite often come round to Lynne's house when her mum was at work and hung out with me and Lynne. We'd found it a bit annoying, if I'm honest. She was a few years younger than us, and we felt she got in the way a bit. Although we felt sorry for her, being left alone like that all day.'

'That should never have happened. Her mum had a lot to answer for.'

'I don't think she felt she had a choice. She was a single mum, and in those days, there wasn't the childcare support available that there is now.'

'Still, she should have made proper arrangements for someone to look after her daughter.'

'Well, yes. But it was all more informal in those days, wasn't it? We'd be in and out of each other's houses, always using the back door, playing out in the street from a young age. I felt guilty, though.'

'Why?' Charlie's expression was one of concern.

'Because Lynne and I sometimes actively tried to avoid her. We didn't want her hanging around. If we'd been kinder, she might not have disappeared. That's why, my therapist said, I link it with finding Stephanie's body. In both cases I keep thinking, *if only*.'

'Neither tragedy was your fault, Jo. If you'd done something different, the tragedies might still have happened, just a bit differently.'

I nodded. 'I know. I *do* know all that, and I had a year of counselling to make myself understand it. But now and again . . .'

'. . . it comes back to haunt you. I do understand. And Jo, I'm glad you've felt able to tell me all this.' He gave me a small, reassuring smile.

'You're very easy to talk to.'

'Thank you. I like listening to people. If it helps, talking it all through, I'm always available for you.'

'Thank you.' Our main courses arrived then, and we ate in companionable silence. I was mulling over what had just happened. How I'd opened up. How he'd said he would always be available to listen. And I found myself reconsidering my plans for how my later years were supposed to pan out. Might there be space for someone else? A man, someone exactly like Charlie? I really liked him, and I had the impression he quite liked me too.

I smiled, and looked up to find him smiling at me as well. *Just wait and see, Jo. Take it slowly. Don't rush into anything. Let it develop in its own good time.*

Chapter 16

Jo, 5 August 1976
Two days before.

After five days of surfing for hours each morning our shoulders were so sunburnt Mum said we weren't allowed to do anything without T-shirts on. But she wouldn't let us go in the sea wearing T-shirts in case it ruined them. The sun cream we had was obviously useless. Dad's nose was burnt too. Only Mum had avoided getting burnt, but that was because she was staying off the beach and out of the sun.

'Not sure what the point of coming here was, if you're not going on the beach at all,' Dad grumbled. 'All this way and you're spending the days shopping or sitting in cafés. You can do that in Hareton Wick.'

'We came for the children,' Mum said, rolling her eyes at him. 'They're having fun.'

'They *were* having fun, until you ruled they can't wear T-shirts in the sea, and they're not allowed to take the T-shirts off.'

'The sea will ruin their clothes. If you had to do the family laundry, you'd know.'

And so, another argument began. David and I pulled the picnic rug away from the tent to an empty nearby pitch that had some shade. We could still hear them bickering but not as loudly.

'Will they ever stop?' David asked. He looked worried.

'I don't know. I thought things were going to be different. Before we came away it was like they were making an effort.'

'I thought so too. Didn't last long though, did it?'

'Nope. Hey, Dad's coming over.'

We stopped talking as Dad approached. He was forcing himself to smile. 'Hey, kids. We've had an idea, your mum and I. As it's so hot and we're all sunburnt, it feels like there's not much point staying here until the end of the week. We could head back home, and you'll be able to go out on your bikes and see your friends. Not much to do here other than the beach, and I think you're a bit fed up of that now. What do you say?'

'Go back early?' David asked.

'Yes, we'll cut it short by a couple of days. It's been fun, but it's pretty uncomfortable in the tent in this weather, isn't it?'

I just shrugged.

'Jo? Is it OK by you?'

'Suppose so.' I didn't quite know what to think. I'd been enjoying the surfing and the lazy afternoons, and I'd read loads of books – all that I'd brought, in fact. Now I was working my way through an Arthur C Clarke anthology of science fiction stories that David had brought and finished. As long as we kept out of the way of the parents when they argued, it was all right, as a holiday. But I rather liked the idea of going back to days cycling out to the barn, and I missed Lynne.

'Well then, we'll get up early tomorrow to take down the tent and pack the car before it's too hot. We'll be home by early afternoon.' Dad looked pleased with the plan, and went back into the tent to begin packing away things we wouldn't need to use before we left.

'Oh. Well, that's that, then,' David said. 'At least we had a few days away.'

'Yes.' For some reason I felt tears prickle at the corners of my eyes. It felt as though this was the end. Not just of a short holiday, but . . . of something more. Our family life, the way it had been. I couldn't imagine us going on another holiday, all together. Not after this. I didn't want to think about it too deeply. I'd only get upset.

'Jo, let's go up to the campsite shop and buy ourselves ice creams,' David suggested. I jumped up, happy to be pulled out of my morbid thoughts.

'You all right?' David said to me, once we were out of earshot of our parents.

'Yeah.'

'We probably have more fun at home anyway. Apart from the surfing.'

'Apart from the surfing,' I agreed.

'We'll go back to the farm. If we hide the bikes there'll be no chance of old man Willis seeing us if he drives past. I want to look inside the house.'

I stared at him. 'How can we? It's locked. We can't, like, break a window or something to get in. We'd really be in trouble for that!'

'I bet we can find a way. Maybe a window's a little bit open or something. Must be some way in if we really check. We wouldn't damage anything. Just want to, you know, have a nose around. See what's inside. See if it's haunted.'

I laughed. 'Ghosts! Huh. I don't believe in them.'

'You never know, though, Smudge,' David replied. 'Just because you've never seen one doesn't mean they don't exist. Woooo!'

We'd reached the campsite shop, where we bought ourselves an Orange Maid ice lolly each. I loved the way they turned your tongue bright orange.

The wind was picking up, so we decided to spend the rest of the day flying kites from the hill behind the campsite. The breeze kept us pleasantly cool, and for the first time on the holiday, other than when we'd been in the sea, I didn't feel too hot.

*

Our journey home the next day was uneventful and passed pretty much in silence. Even David and I dared not say much. We all just sat quietly, staring out of the window, for the four hours it took to drive home.

'I'll unpack the car,' Dad said. 'David, can you help me, please.' Mum had already gone inside with what was left of the camping food, muttering something about needing to work out what to cook for dinner.

'Shall I help?' I asked, but Dad shook his head. 'Just take your own stuff inside, that'll do. I need David to help me put things back in the loft.' His shoulders slumped as he gazed at the contents of the car. It hadn't been nearly as well packed coming home. David and I had sat with our feet on top of bags of clothes and wet towels, and with a crate of gear between us.

I did what Dad said – took the bag of my own clothes inside and unpacked it. Most of the things needed to go in the wash so it didn't take long. I ate one of the sandwiches Mum had hurriedly prepared for lunch, then went out to see if Lynne was home. There was an atmosphere in the house I didn't like. Any moment everything would kick off again, and I honestly thought I couldn't cope. It'd make me cry and I didn't want them to see how badly I was affected by their rows.

As I turned into Lynne's road I spotted little Pippa playing in the street with her skipping rope. She was on her own. She smiled shyly at me as I approached.

'Hello, Pippa. How's things?' I asked, smiling back at her.

She shrugged. 'Things are OK. Are you going to Lynne's?'

'Yes. We got back from our holiday today.' I didn't want to mention we'd cut it short.

'Lynne's not home. Think her mum has taken her out somewhere.'

'Oh.' I looked up and down the street, deciding what to do next. I didn't want to go home.

'My dad's taking me on a little holiday soon,' Pippa said, starting to skip again.

'That'll be fun!'

She stopped skipping and shrugged. 'Might be. Might not be. Last time he came he took me to Marwell zoo, but it wasn't any fun. He wasn't interested in the animals. He just wanted to talk to a lady in the café.'

'Parents, eh? Where does your dad live?' I was interested in how divorced families arranged their lives. Might be us, soon.

'45 Sea Road, Gosport,' she recited. 'Takes ages to get there.'

'Where are you going on your holiday with him?'

'His house. Dad said we'd go to see some big ship called HMS *Victory*.'

'You'll like that.'

Pippa made some noncommittal grunt and began skipping again, twirling her rope and counting. I had a sudden idea. 'Want to learn a new skipping game, Pippa?'

Her eyes lit up. 'Yes, please!'

'OK, then. You skip, and I'm going to jump in with you, all right? I'll say the words and you join in.' I began chanting, 'I like coffee, I like tea, I like Joanne IN with me.' I tried to jump into the loop of the rope on the word 'in'. The rope snagged round my shoulders. I was too tall to skip in with Pippa. Also, I hadn't tried this for years, though back when we were Pippa's age, Lynne and I had been world experts at double skipping.

'How about I twirl the rope and you jump in with me instead?' I suggested, so we tried that next. 'I like coffee, I like tea, I like Pippa IN with me.' This time it worked, and we were jumping the rope in tandem, with Pippa giggling.

'Ready for the "out" part?' I said, and Pippa nodded as she jumped. 'Right then – I don't like coffee, I don't like tea, I don't like Pippa IN with me.' She got the idea and ducked out from under the rope at the right point, while I carried on skipping.

'Well done!' I stopped twirling and handed her the rope back.

'Can we do it again?' she said, breathlessly, and so we did. Several times. I was hot and sweaty but somehow it was fun, and

I liked that she was enjoying herself. I remembered what Lynne had said about Pippa not having any friends her own age living nearby, and that we should feel sorry for her. Well, I had nothing else to do; Lynne wasn't around, and I didn't want to go home, so why not spend the time with Pippa?

When we were exhausted from skipping, we went to sit on someone's garden wall, under the shade of a tree. Pippa was humming, and I recognised the tune to 'All Things Bright and Beautiful', so I joined in.

'It's my favourite hymn,' Pippa told me solemnly, and then we sang all the verses we could remember, giggling when we forgot a line and had to hum instead.

Down the end of the road was a corner shop. I felt in my pocket and pulled out a couple of ten pence pieces. Just enough to buy us both a treat. 'Shall we go to the shop?' I said, and she nodded.

As we walked up the road, she began chattering to me about her favourite teddy bears and her idea to hold a teddy bear picnic, and would I like to come? And maybe Lynne too? And we could do it in her garden, and her mum would make us a chocolate cake for the teddies. 'Though actually,' she said conspiratorially, 'the toys don't eat anything, it's just pretend, so we'll get it all.'

I laughed but pretended to be surprised. 'It sounds wonderful. I'd love to come to the picnic and I bet Lynne would too. What do you want from the shop? Ice pop to cool you down, or a Freddo Frog?'

'Freddo Frog, please.' We went in, and I bought us each a chocolate frog, which of course we ate straight away, before they had the chance to melt. I felt strangely proud and grown-up using my own money to buy the little girl a treat, even if it was just six pence. I think it was almost the last of my pocket money, as I'd spent the rest on ice creams at the campsite shop.

We ate the chocolate standing outside the shop, in the band of shadow it cast across the road. 'What time is your mum working until today?' I asked her.

'She stops work at three o'clock. Then she comes home on the bus. I go home at four o'clock and she's back then.'

'Four o'clock. What time is it now?' Pippa was wearing a child's watch that was pink with a picture of a ballet dancer on its face. She looked at it for a while, working out what it was telling her.

'Twenty past three.' She smiled, pleased with herself. Or was she pleased that there wasn't too much longer until her mum got home? It must be hard, I thought, being left alone for much of the day when you were only eight.

'Do you have lots of friends at school?' I wondered why her mum didn't arrange for her to play at friends' houses when she had to work.

'Some.' Pippa shrugged. 'Not round here though.'

'What school do you go to?'

'Oakwood.' She named a school the other side of the village. Lynne and I had gone to one much closer, before we'd moved up to the secondary school.

'So all your friends live near that school?'

She nodded. 'We used to live near Oakwood school. Then Daddy moved out to Gosport, and Mummy and me moved here but she didn't want to change my school.'

I guessed her mum had thought it'd be too much disruption all at once for her to cope with – her parents divorcing and a house move. I was glad she'd been able to stay at the same school and keep her friends, but it was difficult during the holidays for her, with no one around.

'Does your mum drive a car?'

Pippa shook her head. 'Not now. She did. But then the car broke down and since then she gets the bus to work.'

So her mum couldn't drop Pippa off at a friend's house when she was working. That explained why she was often at Lynne's, the only other child anywhere near her age on her street. Not for the first time I felt sorry for her. But also . . . I supposed this was how it would be, if or when my parents split up. David and I would stay with Mum, the house would be sold and we'd end up living . . . who knew where? Hopefully still in Hareton Wick so that we'd keep going to the same school as our friends. I couldn't bear the idea of leaving Lynne.

'Where do your grandparents live, Pippa?' I felt sure there ought to be somewhere else she could go.

'Granny and Granddad live in London. And Nanna and Pops live in Scotland. They're Daddy's parents.'

Both a long way off, then.

'Mummy says we might move to London near Granny and Granddad, only it's expensive living there. I don't want to move again though.' Pippa sniffed, and I had the horrible feeling she was going to start crying. We'd finished our chocolate. There was still about half an hour before her mum was due home. I felt like I shouldn't leave her, even though I was fed up of being out and just wanted to go home and sit under a tree in the garden with a book.

Tree. That was it. I'd take her to the climbing tree. Even if she couldn't climb it, we could sit in the cool of its canopy until it was time for her to go home to her mum.

And that's what we did. With a bit of help she managed to get up to the first set of branches, just below where Lynne and I usually sat. I climbed up to the usual place, and Pippa sat on the lower branch with a leg dangling either side. It wasn't far off the ground so I thought even if she fell she wouldn't hurt herself.

'First time I've ever been in a tree!' Her face was flushed with excitement and effort, and I laughed.

'Lynne and I come here all the time.'

'You're lucky having Lynne as a friend. She's nice. So are you.'

'And so are you,' I said, kindly. 'What time is it now?'

'About . . .' She paused, scrutinising her watch while trying to hold on to the tree trunk. '. . . two minutes to four o'clock.'

'Time you went home to your mum then.' I slipped down from

the tree, then held up my arms to help her down. Thankfully she managed it all right, and I walked her home. As we turned the corner into her street a woman was walking from the bus stop. She spotted us and stopped walking, smiling and waving.

'That's my mum,' Pippa said, and broke into a run towards her, throwing herself into her mother's arms. 'Mummy, this is Jo. And she taught me a skipping game and bought me a Freddo Frog and then we climbed a tree!'

'Climbed a tree? You little monkey, eh?' Mrs Jenkins kissed the top of Pippa's head as she hugged her, then looked at me. 'Jo, you're Lynne Richards' friend, I think? I've seen you around.'

'Yes, that's right. Lynne's out for the day with her mum. I just got back from a camping trip and . . .' I'd been about to say I came across Pippa playing on her own in the street but decided not to, in case she wasn't supposed to do that. For all I knew Mrs Jenkins might tell her to stay at home if she couldn't be at Lynne's.

'Well, thank you, Jo. It's very kind of you to play with her.' Mrs Jenkins looked down at her daughter and ruffled her hair. I thought I spotted the beginnings of a tear in her eye. It must be hard for her too, being a mum on her own.

'That's all right,' I said. 'Maybe we'll see you tomorrow, Pippa?'

She nodded enthusiastically. I smiled at seeing her look so happy.

'Well, thanks again,' Mrs Jenkins said. 'Say bye now, Pippa. I'll cook us fish fingers for tea if you like?'

'Yes, please! Bye, Jo.' Pippa waved cheerfully as her mum took her hand and led her home.

Chapter 17

Jo, 2024

I went to visit Dad on Sunday, the day after my lunch date with Charlie. I had all day spare, and Dad had asked me to come for longer, to spend some time 'going through paperwork'. I suspected he'd fallen behind with filing away his bank statements. Or maybe he had a few outstanding bills he needed to pay. This was the point of moving closer to him, so I could be on hand for this sort of task. It made me feel a little uncomfortable – being privy to his financial details like that. Dad had always been so independent, so on top of everything. He's the one I'd always gone to for advice and help, and now, here we were with our roles reversed.

It had been different with Mum. That was all so long ago, and such a shock. I hadn't had time to get used to doing things for her before her end came.

When I arrived at Dad's he had piles of folders spread out across his dining table. His glasses were on the end of his nose and he was peering at papers, sorting them into stacks. I noticed a tremor in his hands as he moved the sheets around.

'Hi, Dad. What do you need me to do, or shall I make us some tea first?'

'Hello, Jo. I've just had a cup, but you make yourself one. I think you're going to need it.' He pulled a wry face and gestured to the piles of folders.

'What are you doing with all this?'

'Sorting it out. Making sure you know what's what, and where I keep everything. Because one day you'll need to know. If you have a good understanding of all my financial affairs now, it'll be easier . . . later on.'

He was talking about when he died, I realised. I didn't want to think about such things. He was frailer than he had been, but I hoped he still had years ahead of him. 'Well, if you really want to . . .'

'I do, Jo. I'll be easier in my mind if I know you are up to speed on all this. I don't want you to be thrown in at the deep end, when the time comes. So, go on, make your cup of tea, then come and join me here, and we'll make a start.'

'OK.' I went to the kitchen and put the kettle on, taking a moment to dab at my eyes. I hated thinking about Dad's decline. Obviously, I knew I'd lose him one day, sooner rather than later, but I wasn't ready for it to happen yet. Although getting on top of his affairs was a good thing for him to do, and he was right. The more I knew about it now, the more I understood it all, the better it'd be in the long run.

Once my tea was made, I went back to sit beside him. 'Right. I'm ready.'

And we spent the next hour going through the bank accounts he had, what stocks and shares he held and how he managed them, and which credit cards he held. 'I'm going to simplify things over the next few weeks,' he said. 'I'll close some accounts I don't need, consolidate things a little. I'll keep this up to date.' He patted a notebook in which he'd written details of everything including account numbers, log in details and the like. It was just like him, making it as easy as possible for me. Because it would be down to me. While David would, I hoped, come over for a funeral at least, he was unlikely to stay long enough to help.

Once we'd finished for the day, I helped Dad bundle up the papers and put them away in his filing cabinet. We'd cleared out some old stuff and I fed that into the shredder.

'There. A good job done,' Dad said, looking pleased. He looked tired too. I wondered if I should leave him to take a nap. But he waved towards the kitchen with a smile. 'I wouldn't mind that cup of tea you offered me earlier, now.'

So I made more tea and brought it back into the sitting room. Dad obviously had something else he wanted to talk to me about.

'So. This thing with Ryan.'

'Ye-es . . .' I said, hesitantly. I wasn't sure how much Dad knew about what had happened at Ryan's school. I'd never had a chance to discuss with Ryan whether or not Dad should be shielded from it.

'He called me on Friday. Told me about that poor boy going missing. I'd seen it on the news of course, but hadn't made the connection with it being Ryan's school.' Dad wasn't looking at me as he spoke.

'I wasn't sure whether to tell you. Didn't want to worry you.' It had almost sent me back to my drinking ways. I hated to think what that kind of worry could do to Dad.

'Yes, I understand that. Ryan says you thought for a while he might be guilty of something awful.'

'No, I didn't! It came out wrong. I didn't for a second mean to imply I thought he had anything to do with it.'

Dad looked up at me for the first time since beginning the conversation. 'He was under stress, he took it the wrong way. And you perhaps ought to have been more sensitive. You've been there, you should know how it feels.'

'I do! That's what I was trying to say!'

'Ryan needed your support more than ever. It might not be my place, but I don't like to think of my family members falling out. I've little enough time left . . . I think you ought to apologise to him. Even if you don't believe you said anything wrong, you're the parent, and you ought to take the blame.'

'Dad, I've been trying to call him for days. He's not taking my calls.'

'How about messaging him?'

'I've messaged him asking him to ring me when he can.'

'Message him to say you're sorry.'

I made a dismissive gesture with my hands. 'I already did, immediately after we had our row. Not sure why I should have to do it again.'

'Because you're the adult.'

'He's an adult too!' As I said it, I realised I sounded like a petulant child.

'You're the *parent*. He's the one who was under stress. You'll need him, one day. Like I need you.'

'You at least had two children. So when one of them buggered off to the other side of the world and refused to come back to visit, at least you still had one mug hanging around to help you.'

'Well, I'm sorry if I'm taking up too much of your time,' Dad said, folding his arms.

'I didn't mean—' I began, but Dad cut me off.

'I think you did. I appreciate all you do for me, Jo, I really do, and I hope you know that. But I don't want to feel that you're doing it begrudgingly. Maybe I shouldn't have asked you to come on a weekend. You need the days off to relax and see your friends.'

An image of Charlie ran through my mind. 'I saw a friend yesterday. Honestly, Dad, I don't mind coming here at least once a week. Twice if you need me. I just sometimes feel bitter towards David, for leaving us and never coming home to visit. He doesn't call you often either, does he?'

'Well, the time difference . . .' Dad said, but I could see in his eyes he was hurt too that he didn't speak to his son very often.

'Anyway. Let's put it behind us. I'll message Ryan again. As for David, we'll just have to accept that his life is in Australia.'

'I suppose you're right. Well, we're done here, with the paperwork. I'm actually quite tired. Think I'll have a little nap, now. Thanks again, Jo. And if you've something else on next weekend, it's all right with me if you can't make it. Just give me a call, instead.'

'I'll come, Dad.' I stood up and went over to him to kiss his cheek and received a vague pat on the back in return.

I felt a bit down that evening. I'd messaged Ryan again, with an apology as Dad had suggested, but received no reply. An image of a comfortingly full glass of Cabernet Sauvignon appeared in my mind and I wondered, just for an instant, if . . .

No, Jo. That's the way you used to deal with stress. Not the way you deal with it now, I told myself, sternly.

I turned on the TV, channel-hopped for a few minutes but couldn't settle to anything. I needed to talk to someone, I realised. But who? I could phone Colin, but it didn't seem fair. He'd made a good new life for himself and it didn't include me or my woes. In an emergency I knew he'd help me out, but this was just a vague feeling of depression. Same went for Marion.

I considered Lynne – but there was too much I still hadn't told her about.

My old friends from Northampton had mostly either been Colin's friends, or had drifted away when I had my breakdown.

'Sorry, Charlie,' I muttered. 'It'll have to be you, then.' My newest friendship, but the person I instinctively knew would be the best for me to talk this through with.

Without thinking any more about it, I picked up my phone and called him. The call went to voice mail. I left a brief message saying I'd hoped to speak with him and would try again later, and hung up feeling annoyed. Why wasn't he available to take my call at this time on a Sunday afternoon? Where was he, and who was he with?

And then I was annoyed at myself. I'd only met him a handful of times. I didn't own him. It possibly wasn't even fair that I was calling such a new acquaintance just so I could offload my problems. And yet, it's how I felt.

I went to make myself a cup of tea. Something to sip at, to take my mind off the desire to sip something stronger.

My phone rang while I waited for the kettle to boil. It was Charlie.

'Hey. You rang?'

'Yeah. Had a bit of a bad day and I . . . um . . . needed to talk about it.'

'Oh, no. Sorry to hear that. What happened?'

I shrugged, even though he couldn't see the gesture. 'Went to see Dad. He had a go at me for having upset Ryan. Then I said something that upset him too.'

'Oh, dear.' Charlie, normally so sympathetic, didn't sound very concerned.

'I suppose it's a little thing, but—'

'Jo, listen, sorry but I can't talk long. I was driving, saw it was you on the phone, and pulled over. But if it isn't anything urgent, I need to be on my way. I'm not parked in the best place.'

'Oh, well I—'

'Look, I'll call you back when I'm home, OK? Should be in about an hour and a half. You can tell me all about it then, and I promise I'll listen properly. Sorry, Jo. Got to go.'

And with that he hung up. Obviously, I didn't want to put him in danger, keeping him on the phone if he wasn't in a safe place, but why on earth had he pulled over to somewhere unsafe to call me back? My irritation levels increased further. I was being unreasonable, perhaps, but on the other hand, I knew that I was still emotionally very fragile. Small things could set me back, send me under, and I needed to take care of myself.

Sometimes when I felt like this, desperate to drink to blank it all out, I'd go out for a walk to take my mind off it all. I looked out of the window. The afternoon had become dull and grey, and it looked as though it might rain at any minute. I really didn't want to get caught in it.

Was Charlie cooling off? Had I somehow managed to push him away? Was this yet another male relationship I'd screwed up?

My phone rang again. It was Lynne.

'Hi, Jo,' she said. 'You doing anything this evening? I'm at a loose end as Malcolm's on an early flight for work tomorrow and has decided to stay in an airport hotel. I'd already made a lasagne for two. Fancy sharing it with me?'

'Ooh. Yes, I really do fancy that. When should I come over?'

'Now? If you want to?'

'Thanks. See you very soon, then.'

She was a lifesaver and didn't even know it. Maybe old friends were the best ones. I resolved to tell her my troubles, but maybe not tonight. When the moment was right. Lynne and I had our memories to fall back on, our shared experiences to reminisce about. I didn't want to sully that by burdening her with my more recent past.

I changed my clothes, put some make-up on and brushed my hair. Then I dug a box of posh biscuits out of the cupboard as a gift, and set off in my car to Lynne's.

I felt my mood lifting as soon as I was on my way. This was what I needed – company. The idea of being with someone who'd make no demands of me, whose presence I'd enjoy being with. Maybe I'd pushed it too far too soon with Charlie. And maybe I was speaking without thinking to Ryan and Dad.

Maybe I was blaming myself too much for everything, when actually the men needed to bear some of the responsibility for what happened between us.

Don't brood on it, Jo, I told myself. *Just enjoy this evening with your oldest friend.*

Chapter 18

Jo, 7 August 1976
The Day Of.

'Good holiday?' Rick asked David and me, as we turned up at his place the next morning on our bikes. The general plan had been that we'd go to the farm again.

'Yeah, it was OK,' David said, with a noncommittal shrug. I gave a half-smile and nodded. Neither of us wanted to talk about how our parents had rowed and we'd ended up coming home early.

'It was hot,' I added.

'Hot here too. Shall we go and get Lynne now?' Rick was hauling his bike out of his garage.

'Um,' I said, hanging back a little. 'Can I use your phone, Rick, to call her first?' I should have done this yesterday, I realised. We could have arranged to meet Lynne out somewhere. If we went to her house, it was quite likely Pippa would be there or would see us arriving, and she'd then come and be with us all day. It had been OK playing with her yesterday, when it was just her and me. And I hadn't minded Horace hanging around with us that time. But not every day. This was our first day all together for a week and I wanted it to be just us four.

'Well, yeah. I suppose so. Mum's in the kitchen, ask her.'

I went into Rick's house and asked Aunty Pam if I could use the phone. She said yes but frowned a little. It was morning, peak phone charges, so I knew I needed to be quick.

I dialled Lynne's number and Aunty Margaret answered, passing the phone to Lynne as soon as she knew it was me.

'Hi, Jo. What's up? Thought you were coming round?'

'We are. Just . . . is Pippa there? I saw her yesterday and she said she wanted to play with us all day today.' Behind me, I could feel Aunty Pam listening in.

'She's not here, no, but I saw her mum going out to work.' Lynne's voice then dropped to a whisper, and I guessed her mother was in earshot. 'Are you hoping to give her the slip?'

'Yes.'

'Right. I'll come to your house then.'

'We're at Rick's.'

'I'll come there. If I see her, I'll tell her I'm running an errand for Mum. What? Nothing, Mum. Yeah, just sorting something out with Jo. Sorry, Jo. See you soon.' She hung up. I guessed Aunty Margaret had been asking her something.

'Thanks, Aunty Pam,' I called, as I went back outside quickly, hoping she wouldn't ask what all that had been about.

'Lynne's meeting us here,' I reported to the boys, who were waiting out on the front lawn.

'How come?' David asked.

'If we go there, we'll end up babysitting Pippa Jenkins all day.'

'Who's that?' Rick asked.

'She's eight. Lives near Lynne.' I explained about seeing the little girl yesterday and how she'd more or less invited herself along with our group.

'What will she do instead?' Rick asked.

I shrugged. I hadn't really thought about it. 'Dunno. Stay home or play in the street near her house. But it's not our problem, is it? I looked after her yesterday afternoon, and she's been round at Lynne's quite a lot. So we've done our share already.'

'Also, if we go to the farm, we'll probably have Horace to contend with too,' David said. 'We're not the village babysitters.'

'Exactly.' I was glad David saw it the same way I did.

'Why don't we go somewhere else this morning?' Rick said. 'So there's no chance of being lumped with Horace either? I found this awesome bit of woodland last week when I was out by myself. There's a whole load of trees that are easy to climb, and one with a hollow trunk. It's all nice and shady and cool. We can cycle there, it's about three miles away.'

I'd been looking forward to going back to the farm and checking on where we'd buried the time capsule, but like the boys I didn't want to risk having to deal with Horace. Were we being selfish? I didn't care. It was our summer holiday and we were supposed to relax and enjoy ourselves. Not have to feel responsible for other people. 'Sounds great!'

'We can always go to the farm tomorrow. Or this afternoon, maybe, if we get bored in the woodland.' Rick smiled kindly at me, as if he'd guessed I was slightly disappointed.

'Here's Lynne,' David said, pointing up the road where she was cycling towards us, her bike weighed down with a large bag in her handlebar basket and a rucksack on her back.

'Phew,' she said, pulling on her brakes as she rode up Rick's driveway. 'You guys can carry this stuff now. Mum's done it again, made us all a picnic.'

'I love your mum,' David said, taking the rucksack from her and putting it down by his bike.

'So do I,' Rick agreed. 'Right then, Operation Avoid Unwanted Hangers-On is a go. Troops, follow me!'

Lynne giggled. 'Where are we off to?'

'Some new place. Avoiding Horace, as well as Pippa, we hope.'

We set off cycling, two abreast, the boys in front and Lynne and me behind.

'Hurray. I had Pippa three days last week while you were away. That's why Mum took me out yesterday to get away. Wouldn't have gone if I'd known you were coming back early. How was the holiday, anyway?'

'Usual arguments,' I told her. Once again, I felt tears prick at my eyes as I thought about how our parents couldn't spend more than a few minutes in each other's company. Why they'd thought camping was a good idea when it involved living right on top of each other I had no idea.

'Oh, dear.' Lynne pulled a face, then changed the subject. We'd left the village and were on a lane lined with brambles. 'Look, the blackberries are shrivelling up, as there's been no rain for so long. Remember last summer when we went blackberrying and picked so many berries, and Mum made blackberry jam?'

'I loved that jam,' I said, remembering its sweet but slightly tart taste. Aunty Margaret had given us a couple of jars, and we'd eaten it with crumpets for Sunday night tea until it had all gone.

'Hope we can make more this year. If it rains.'

I glanced at the bushes that lined the lane as we cycled. The leaves were brown and the berries were tiny, hard little things. Unless it rained there'd be no jam this year. I couldn't remember when it last rained. Day after day had been relentlessly hot, sunny, muggy, with no relief. It felt like we were living in a desert. Definitely not a normal English summer.

We cycled in silence for a while, lost in our own thoughts. We followed Rick and David along the lanes, up a hill that made me sweat, then whizzing down the other side. We rode round a corner then along a gravel track that led into the woods, and finally onto a dirt path and into a clearing. It was a beautiful spot, where pollarded oaks and beeches shared space with holly bushes and birch saplings. All the trees were prematurely dropping their leaves due to the drought but there were still enough to provide a canopy. Only the holly leaves were their usual glossy green as if to say 'Drought? What drought?'

We leaned the bikes against trees, and Lynne took a bag of

food out of her basket and put it down. She glanced at the boys. 'What have you done with the rucksack? The bottles of drink are in there and I'm parched after that ride.'

David looked at Rick and Rick looked at David. 'Thought you had it?' Rick said.

'I . . . er . . . I put it down, thought you picked it up?'

'No, mate.'

'Bloody hell.' I couldn't stop myself swearing. 'So we've no drink?'

'We'll have to go back,' Rick said.

'Up that hill?' I couldn't face it. Not immediately. And like Lynne, I was thirsty.

'Well, someone's going to have to go back. I reckon it should be David. He's the one who left the rucksack behind.' Rick looked pointedly at David.

'I-I'm not sure of the way. Wasn't paying attention on the way here. You go.'

Rick swore under his breath. 'We'll both go. Let the girls stay here. We'll be quicker on our own.'

They turned their bikes around and pedalled off, still arguing about whose fault it was. I turned to Lynne, feeling strangely alone without them. 'How long will it take them, do you think?'

She looked at her watch. 'Took us nearly half an hour to get here. So they'll take nearly an hour to go there and back. What shall we do while we wait? Want a sandwich?'

I shook my head. I didn't want to eat without a drink to wash it down. The tree we'd leaned our bikes against looked as though it was one we could climb, so I moved the bikes and hauled myself up to the crown. 'Come on up!'

Lynne grinned and did the same, and soon we were sitting on a branch each, facing each other, about six foot off the ground. We got ourselves comfortable and settled down to wait. 'So, tell me about your holiday?' Lynne said.

And I did. I told it all. There was no one near to overhear, no one to judge, no one to interfere, so I shared everything in a way I don't think I ever had before. There were tears, of course. Talking about how your parents are almost certainly about to announce they are divorcing is so hard. The uncertainties were horrible to bear, and the feeling of being powerless to do anything about the situation was awful. Lynne listened quietly, sympathetically, passing me her handkerchief to mop my tears and occasionally murmuring words of comfort. It helped, I think, talking it all through like that, in such a private place.

The time passed surprisingly quickly. 'They've been gone more than an hour,' Lynne said after glancing at her watch.

'They're taking their time. And to think they said they'd be faster without us!'

We expected the boys back any moment. I didn't want them to appear while I was crying, so we talked of other things. Music, make-up, what life would be like in the new school year; which teachers we liked and which we hated; what Lynne thought of her sister Kate's new boyfriend.

And still the boys didn't arrive. I began to worry. 'Where are they?'

Lynne frowned. 'Don't know. They've been gone nearly two hours.'

'Two hours!' Now I was worried. Visions of them lying injured in the road after being hit by a car passed through my mind.

'One of them has probably had a puncture,' Lynne said. 'And you know what boys are like. Useless at fixing things.'

I forced out a laugh. But actually, David was good at repairing punctures, and I knew he carried a pump and puncture repair kit on his bike at all times. It would only have delayed them by ten minutes or so. No, it wasn't that. 'What should we do? Shall we go back to Rick's and look for them?'

'Do you know the way?'

'Erm, kind of. Left on the lane, then up the hill, down the other side, turn left then right . . .'

'Right then left, I think.'

'OK, yeah, it could be. Anyway, there'll be a signpost. It's only a few miles. We'll follow signs back to the village, go to my house and Rick's, and somewhere along the way we'll find them.'

Lynne smiled, and swung herself down from the tree. 'Just hope we don't bump into Pippa and find ourselves babysitting again.'

'Hmm, yes.' I climbed down, we got on our bikes and set off.

But somehow we took a wrong turn, or missed a turn, and found ourselves cycling along an unfamiliar lane.

'Should we go back?' Lynne said.

I shook my head. 'I can see a church spire over there. Think it's St John's in Hareton Wick. This lane feels as though it's going in the right direction.'

We continued, then a little bit further on we began to recognise where we were. It was the lane that the old farm was on, but we were approaching from the other direction. We spotted the gravel track that led to Horace's home, and as I passed it I thought I saw him, or maybe someone else, in the distance near his house.

It was uphill as we approached the farm and we were puffing hard as we reached it. 'Shall we stop for a minute? Have a little rest?' I suggested.

'Yes, please.' Lynne was already off her bike, leaning it against the gate and sitting on a patch of dried grass. 'Just hope that Mr Willis doesn't come by.'

'We're not in the grounds. We're still on the public road,' I reassured her, as I joined her sitting on the ground.

Just then David and Rick turned up, surprising us. 'Hey, girls,' David said, as he dismounted from his bike. 'We thought we saw you stopping here. Sorry we took so long.'

'What happened?' I asked. I was relieved to see them in one piece, although they looked kind of flustered. Something had happened, I was sure of it.

'Well, we . . . er . . .' David began, then he glanced at Rick as though needing support. David looked flushed and uneasy, and I didn't think it was only due to the heat.

'We've got the drinks,' Rick said, gesturing to the rucksack he was carrying.

'Oh, God, here he is again,' David said. It was Horace, who was running up the hill towards us, flapping his hands about. He was badly out of breath.

'Horace, sit down. Rest. Look, here's some water to drink,' Rick said, taking his elbow and pushing him gently down.

'In there,' Horace said, pointing to the farm with one hand while the other continued flapping.

'You'd best not go in there,' Rick said. 'If Mr Willis sees you, he'll be cross.'

But that only set Horace off even more.

'Ssh, it's all right. He's nowhere near,' I said. It was often difficult to understand Horace, but he was behaving very strangely today.

'What's upset him?' Lynne asked, in an urgent whisper. Horace gave no sign of having heard or understood that she was asking about him.

'Don't know. We passed this way earlier,' said David. 'Because Rick thought it might be a quicker way back to the woods, and we saw Horace climbing over the gate. We took him back to his home. But then he followed us back here. Horace, mate, you've got to go home. It'll be better for you at your home.'

'No . . . no . . .' Horace shook his head fiercely. 'In there!' He pointed to the farm again.

David glanced at the farmhouse and shook his head. 'Not in there, mate,' he said. He was sweating and somehow looked pale under his sunburn. 'You need to go home, Horace.'

Horace nodded and then shook his head, flapping his hands harder than ever. 'Bad thing, bad . . . bad!'

'What bad thing?'

But it was clear we would get no answer. All he could do was shake his head. 'I think we should take him back to his mum,' I said, and the others agreed.

'One of us should stay here with the bikes and bags, and the other three walk him home,' Lynne suggested, and everyone nodded. We decided I should stay, so the others persuaded Horace to his feet. Rick and David gently took an arm each and led him away, down the hill towards his home. Lynne walked alongside, talking kindly to Horace to keep him calm. I stood in the lane and watched until they were out of sight, then I turned away and leaned on the top rail of the gate, staring into the farmyard.

Something was different. I know I hadn't been there in over a week, but it looked as though someone had. There was a scuff mark on the ground as though the gate had been pushed open. I looked at the padlock but couldn't tell if it had been unlocked since we'd last been there. Then I spotted a window in the farmhouse that stood a little way open. The windows had definitely all been closed whenever we'd played there before our holiday. But now that one, on the ground floor, was open.

A part of me wanted to climb over the gate and have a better look. I could pull open the window and look inside. But . . . what if someone was in there? Maybe that's what had got Horace so agitated. Or maybe it was Horace who'd opened the window and been told off by Mr Willis. Or was he just scared of being told off by him?

In any case, I didn't want to leave all the bikes out on the lane. It'd be too much like hard work for me to get them all through the gap in the hedge and into the farmyard by myself. I just needed to wait until the others got back. I pulled a bottle of drink out of the rucksack, took a long swig then sat in the shade of a tree to wait.

They weren't too long. I heard them chattering as they walked back up the lane, and I stood up to meet them. Lynne took the bottle of drink from me and gulped at it gratefully.

'Horace's sister and mum were there,' she said, 'and they took care of him. He gets like this sometimes. Apparently, he struggles to explain what it is that's upset him.'

'Right, then,' David said, his voice sounding a little shaky. 'The day hasn't quite panned out how we thought. It's already two o'clock and I'm starving.'

We decided there was no point cycling back to the woodland. We could always go back there another day. Instead, we hauled the bikes through the hedge into the farmyard, stowing them out of sight from the lane, just in case Mr Willis drove past. We took the bags into the barn and ate the picnic in our usual spot. I told them about the open window I'd noticed.

'Well, that is just crying out to be investigated,' David said, slapping his hands on his thighs as he stood up and strode out of the barn, closely followed by Rick.

I looked at Lynne who shrugged, and then the two of us followed the boys across the yard.

'Reckon we could climb in there,' Rick said, as David tugged the window wide open.

'Yes, but *should* we?' I asked.

David laughed. 'Of course we shouldn't, but then we also shouldn't even be in the farmyard or barn. Come on, let's go inside, have a nose around. We won't touch anything. No one will know we've been in. Give us a leg up, Rick.'

And so, in we went. Rick helped David climb in, then me, then Lynne. Finally, with David's help from inside, Rick climbed in too. The window belonged to a small downstairs room that was off the kitchen. 'A pantry?' Lynne suggested.

'What's that?' Rick asked.

'Kind of a large food storage area,' I replied. 'Old-fashioned, from before they had fridges.' Rick obviously hadn't read the kinds of books I'd read growing up.

A door leading to the kitchen stood open, so we went through. The kitchen had no fitted cupboards but a large, battered table stood in the middle, and there was a filthy old cooker and a deep, cracked sink. The flooring was lino, peeling up around the edges and, like the cooker, it was filthy. Opposite the pantry, there was a door, held closed by a padlock.

'I bet that leads to the cellar,' David said. 'Shame we can't go down and check it out.'

I shuddered. I didn't think it was a shame at all. There was something about the house I didn't like. Its air of utter neglect, I supposed. It had been empty for years, since Mr Willis's parents had died, according to Horace. It looked as though most of the personal or valuable items had been removed, there were just a few tatty pieces of furniture, like the kitchen table, and bags of rubbish here and there. Beside the cellar door there was a hessian sack, tied closed at the top.

'What do you think that is?' Rick asked, touching it with his foot.

'Just rubbish,' David replied.

We went through a hallway to the 'good' rooms at the front of the house. One must have been a sitting room and the other a dining room. Both had peeling wallpaper with mould growing in the corners and ancient, worn carpets. There was a rotten-looking staircase between them leading to the upper floor, but we decided it didn't look safe or enticing enough to go up.

'This place is depressing,' Lynne said, and I had to agree. It smelt damp and mouldy; it was dark and rather spooky; and was altogether an unpleasant place to be.

'Let's go outside again.' I led the way back to the kitchen and was pleased that the boys followed. 'Shall we open the back door and go out that way?' I'd noticed it was closed by a bolt on the inside.

'No, because we won't be able to re-bolt the door again. Then if Mr Willis comes in through the front door he'd know someone's been in.' David pointed towards the pantry. 'We have to go out the same way we came in.'

It was easier climbing out. Soon we'd all jumped down, and we made sure the window was left exactly as we found it.

'Ugh. That place gives me the creeps,' Lynne said, and I noticed even the boys nodded. They'd been trying to pretend the atmosphere in the house hadn't bothered them but I knew it had.

'Let's just go home,' David suggested, and we all quickly agreed. Anything to get away from the farmhouse.

Chapter 19

Jo, 2024

I did have a great evening with Lynne. Almost as soon as I arrived I felt better. Her lasagne and salad were scrumptious, and she had a bottle of zero-alcohol fizzy wine to go with it.

'I thought this might be a good idea, as Ryan said you don't often drink these days,' she said as she showed me the bottle. Behind her words I heard the unspoken question: *What are the problems Ryan alluded to?*

'It's perfect,' I told her. 'Actually, I don't drink alcohol at all, these days.'

'I'm cutting back,' she said, nodding. I loved her for not asking more about why I don't drink. She just accepted me for how I am, now.

After we'd eaten, I helped her clear up. She had the radio playing in the kitchen, and a news bulletin came on. It mentioned one of the Voyager spacecrafts that was now beyond the edge of the solar system. The reporter said that scientists expected that we would soon lose contact with it, but that for the moment it was still sending back information.

'Incredible, isn't it,' Lynne said, 'that something built on Earth fifty years ago could be so far away and still going strong.'

'I remember Dad talking about them and being excited when they launched.' I could picture him now, pointing at some article or other in his *New Scientist* magazine, taking the opportunity to give us kids an impromptu astronomy lesson.

A memory surfaced – of Dad telling us that the Voyager spacecraft carried details of life on Earth. I recalled that had given me the idea for the time capsule we'd buried. 'Hey, remember that day we buried a box of bits and pieces at Four Oaks Farm?'

'We were planning to dig it up five years later, weren't we?' Lynne said, with a laugh. 'I recall remembering about it sometime in the mid-nineties, but none of you were around to try to find it with. Even Rick was living abroad in the US.'

'What a shame we didn't go back and dig it up. I suppose as David and I moved away it wouldn't have been as easy as we'd imagined.' I sighed. 'Well, it's too late now. Developers have moved in at Four Oaks. Where did we bury it anyway?'

'In the ditch by the hedge,' Lynne said. 'Not deeply, as I recall.'

'No. The ground was rock solid. We'd have needed a pneumatic drill to get through it after that long spell with no rain.'

'Still, maybe you and I should take a walk up there sometime soon, just to see if we can find it. It was so near the boundary it probably hasn't been disturbed by the developers yet.' Lynne looked wistful. 'Those memories. That was a good summer. We were so young, so innocent.'

I smiled. 'Yes. And I thought nothing would ever change. That when the summer ended, I'd go up into the second year at Brookhill with you. And David, Rick, you and I would be best friends forever.'

'Any chance of your brother coming for a visit any time soon?' Lynne asked. 'I have contact details for Rick. We could try for a reunion.'

'I haven't heard from David. I know Dad wants him to come.

He's . . . setting his affairs in order.' I felt a lump in my throat as I said the words, remembering our little spat earlier today. How could I have allowed that to happen, when my days of still having a living father were dwindling fast?

'Aw, that's hard.' Lynne looked at me with sympathy. 'David ought to come sooner rather than later, oughtn't he?'

'I think so. But who knows whether he will at all.' I sighed. 'I miss those days, you know. When David and I were so close. Some brothers and sisters would fight but we hardly ever did. We were a team.'

'Shame we can't go back to our favourite parts of our lives, isn't it? I liked being twenty-something. Young, free, my life ahead of me, opportunities around every corner.'

I thought back. That was the period when I was dating and then married Colin. Nursing Mum through her final days. Trying for years to have a baby and ending up with just one. They were good years in some ways but not the best of my life. In many ways, it was that last summer living in Hareton Wick that I liked the most. But I wasn't sure I should admit to that. It all seemed a bit sad. 'I know what you mean,' I said. 'Back to those days when my knees didn't ache every time I go up or down steps. To when my back wasn't always hurting when I get out of bed in the morning. When I had no lines on my face, luscious deep brown hair and a firm tummy.'

Lynne raised the remainder of her glass of bubbles. 'I'll drink to that! Mind you, I'd like to keep the wisdom and security that's come with age, to go with the freedom, looks and body I had in my twenties.'

'Security and freedom at the same time?' I laughed.

'Hmm. Maybe not, then. Wouldn't give up Malcolm for anything. What about you, has there been anyone in your life since Colin?'

I shrugged. 'Well, I dated a few, in the first years after we divorced. But never for more than a couple of months. I got very used to being alone. And I've seen someone a couple of times since moving here. But he seems to be cooling off. He's supposed to be calling me back but . . .'

'I'm sure he will, Jo.' Lynne smiled at me kindly. 'Give him time, then call him again.'

'Yes. Perhaps I should get another dog.'

'You had a dog? What kind?'

'A spaniel. Called Goldie. She was such a great companion. I really missed her when she went.' That was the understatement of the century.

'When did you lose her?'

'About three or four years ago now.' God, it still hurt when I thought of her, and of the spiral of despair I descended into.

'You should definitely get another. Ask down at Marsh Farm. I think Natasha's dog is having puppies soon. Maybe you could have one of those?'

'What breed?' I imagined black-and-white sheepdogs, working dogs, that wouldn't be right for me in my little bungalow.

'Something small and fluffy. Couldn't really tell you – I'm not much of a dog person.'

'Sounds perfect! I'll ask her.'

I left Lynne's at around ten o'clock. We'd had a good chat and a giggle, and we'd put the world to rights, as Dad often used to say. I felt so much better. Even though I still hadn't told Lynne everything, I had talked about Ryan, and the missing child from his school, and how we'd fallen out.

'It's so hard sometimes to say the right thing. I imagine it was the stress. He'll come round. As long as he knows you're always there for him, what more can you do? And I'm sure he does know that.' She'd patted my shoulder. 'You seem happier than when you arrived. I think coming here has done you good, somehow.'

'It certainly has,' I'd replied. 'Thank you.'

'Any time. We're old mates, aren't we?'

Driving home, I found myself singing along to the radio. Yes, going to see Lynne had been the right thing to do. And she was right about Ryan. I was sure we'd make up soon. Same with Dad. As for Charlie – well who knew? He'd said he would call. I'd wait to see if he did.

When I got home, I checked my phone, which had been on silent the whole time I was with Lynne. I expected to see a missed call from Charlie but instead there was a voicemail from Dad. 'Call me, love, when you get this, please,' he'd said. He sounded upbeat, so I wasn't worried. But it was quarter past ten – was it too late to call him? I was just debating this when my phone rang – Dad again.

'Hey, Dad. What's up? I'm just in, was just wondering if it's too late to call you.'

'Not too late, no. I'm staying up. Got a visitor due here – arriving about midnight I expect.'

'That's late! Who on earth—' I began, before Dad cut in.

'David! Your long-lost brother! He called earlier from Heathrow. He'd just landed, and he was going to sort out a hire car and then drive here. Can you believe it?'

'David! Well – wow!' I was speechless. On the one hand I was pleased he was coming to see Dad, at last, while Dad was still well enough to enjoy his company. On the other hand, I was furious – it was just like him to simply turn up, rather than let us know so we could plan things properly.

'Yes! Anyway he's going to stay in my spare room. I'm so excited, Jo. He and I have got an awful lot of catching up to do.'

'Yes, of course.' So did David and I . . . but there'd be time for that later, I hoped. If David wanted. He knew my number and my address. And if he'd lost them, he could ask Dad.

'So . . . I thought you should know.'

'Thank you. Are you going to be OK, staying up so late?'

'Of course. I'm not a child. Even if I went to bed, I'd be unable to sleep until he gets here. David will help me get ready for bed later. I sent the carer home when she came, though she did help me make sure the spare room was ready.'

'That's good. OK, well, don't stay up too late chatting after he arrives. He'll be jet-lagged. Save it for tomorrow. And . . . tell him I said hi.'

'Will do. You'll come over and see him?'

'Yes . . . if he wants to see me.'

'I'm sure he will.'

I wasn't so sure. But I didn't want to risk upsetting Dad again by saying that, so I let it go. 'Right then, you go and sit down with a cup of hot chocolate until he arrives, eh, Dad? And don't overdo it.'

'I won't. Talk to you tomorrow then.'

'Night, Dad.'

I didn't have to wait very long to hear from David. He called me the next morning. I was working, but happy to break off for a bit to have a chat with my brother. Other than brief, dutiful Christmas calls when we'd had to work around the time difference, I'd barely spoken to him for decades.

'Hey, Sis. How are you?'

'David! I'm fine. Pleasant flight?'

'Long. But smooth enough.'

'That's good. I'm glad you've come. Dad was hoping to see you again.'

'Yes. That's why I came?' David had picked up that Australian habit of using a rising tone at the end of a sentence, making everything he said sound like a question.

There was a pause. We'd been so close as kids. Now we could barely summon up small talk. 'Why didn't you tell us you were coming over?'

I could almost hear his shrug. 'It was a spur of the moment decision. Something Giselle said the other day. Her own father died, you know – just last year? Very sudden.'

'Sorry to hear that.' I hadn't known. I'd never met Giselle, David's wife. Or their kids. Or grandkids – I vaguely remembered David listing their names on a Christmas card a couple of years back.

'Anyway, she said something about wishing she'd spent more time with her dad at the end. And I thought about my dad and decided to come over. Before he . . . you know?'

'Our dad. He's mine, too.'

'I know that.'

'It's just – you said *my* dad. And yet . . . you're the one who's spent the last forty years on the other side of the world without visiting.'

'Thirty-eight years. And I've been back to visit heaps of times.'

'Not that I remember.'

'Two years after I first went to Australia I came back. And then Giselle and I came in 1995. You were away somewhere with Colin, so we didn't see you. Then I was back for Mum's funeral. And at least once since.'

'Hmm.' I was trying to recall meeting him on any of those occasions.

'You never once came to Australia to visit. I used to keep inviting you, but you never came.'

'Couldn't afford to, David. And Colin wasn't a good flier.'

'Yes, there was always some excuse or other. Anyway. Here I am. Will we meet up? I've been busy doing heaps of jobs for Dad this morning, but I could bring him over to you this afternoon?'

'I'm working today, David. Can't just drop it all because you've come visiting with no notice.'

'Can't you tell your boss . . . something? Get a half day off? Make up the hours? Dad says you work from home. Everyone who works from home takes time off when they need it.'

'Let's make a date for later in the week. I have a tight deadline for something that I need to finish today.'

'Oh, OK. I suppose it'll give me time to sort some stuff out with Dad. He's all upset about his financial paperwork. Wants everything in order, to make it easier . . . later.'

'I did all that with him the other day! We went through everything and got it all sorted. You shouldn't need to do anything.' I felt irritated with him. Swanning over here, acting as though he needed to deal with it all. 'David, I've been caring for Dad for ages. Doing everything he needs. I'm on top of it all. I did the same for Mum. You've just stayed away, kept out of everything. You're here now, which is good, but all you need to do is keep Dad company. Let him talk. Tell him about your kids and grandkids. About your life. There's nothing else you need to do.'

'But his finances . . .'

'Are all under control. When the time comes, I'll be the one applying for probate, won't I? I'll be the one informing the companies he uses that he's passed on, closing his accounts, selling his flat, transferring his assets into our names. Because I'm the one who's *here*. Because I'm the one who's been helping him with his affairs for years now. And I'll continue to do so, after your flying visit is over.' I snapped at him, expecting him to apologise, to explain, to thank me or at the very least sound contrite. But David said nothing.

I suddenly realised I had no idea how long he was planning to stay. 'How long is your visit, anyway?'

'I don't know. Couple of weeks, I suppose?'

'Not long, then. So don't use it all up on stuff you don't need to do. Spend time with him. Take him out. Let him enjoy your company.' I felt my resentment building further, at this brother who'd kept away and only now, near the end of Dad's life, had come to visit. And yet I knew that Dad would enjoy having David around. It would do him good. And I would not stand in the way. Let them bond again, while there was time. I'd still be here when David had gone back home.

'All right. I'll do that, then. Maybe I'll see you later in the week?'

'Yes.' I took a deep breath. 'There's something I want to talk to you about. From long ago.'

'You've still not put that behind you then.' He said it as a statement, and he was right. I hadn't. I couldn't.

'No,' I replied.

He sighed. 'I'll call you later.'

And with that we said our goodbyes.

Chapter 20

Pippa, 7 August 1976
The Day Of.

'You'll be all right on your own for the morning, won't you? You could go to Lynne's if you like. If so, make sure you're back here before two o'clock when your dad's coming to collect you.' Mrs Jenkins pulled a face. 'Assuming he turns up on time. Right then, Pippa. I'm off to work. Be good.' She turned to go.

'Bye, Mum.' Pippa forced herself to smile and look happy, although she didn't feel it.

Mrs Jenkins turned back. 'Oh, and have a lovely time with your dad. I'll see you in two days.' She gave Pippa a squeeze and a kiss, and then she was gone, hurrying out through the back door and along the street to the bus stop.

Pippa closed the door behind her mum and leaned back against it, staring at the ceiling. There were five hours to get through before Dad was due to pick her up. Five long, boring hours with nothing to do. Again. She knew Mum had to go to work – it was the only way she could pay the bills. Dad was supposed to give them more money than he did. Pippa had heard Mum yelling at him on the phone, saying she'd 'take him to court', whatever that meant, if he didn't pay up. But Pippa didn't think Dad had much money either. She saw him about once every two weeks when he came to take her out, and he always seemed to be wearing old, dirty clothes. His flat was horrible, too. The carpet was stained, the sofa faded and worn out, and everything felt dirty. Pippa always wanted a bath after staying overnight there.

She looked around the kitchen – it was clean and tidy as always. Mum always made a point of washing the breakfast dishes, drying them and putting them away, and wiping the counter before she went to work. Sometimes Pippa wished she'd just leave it. Pippa could do it, while Mum was out. It would be something to do. She'd be able to make the job stretch at least half an hour.

'I bet no other person my age wishes they had washing-up to do,' Pippa said to the empty room. Right then. What was she going to do with the morning? She needed to put a few things in a bag to take to Dad's – clean knickers, a pair of pyjamas, her toothbrush, the book she was reading. That would take about five minutes to put together.

She wandered off around the house, searching for inspiration. It was only nine o'clock; too early to go round to Lynne's. She knew the older girls got fed up with her if she hung around with them for too long. Yesterday afternoon had been a good day. She'd met Lynne's friend Jo, and Jo had taught her a skipping game and bought her a Freddo Frog. Then they'd climbed a tree.

'I like coffee, I like tea, I like Jo to play with me,' Pippa chanted as she went upstairs, pleased with herself at the adaptation of the rhyme. She'd like to do that skipping game again, but you needed two people for it. She couldn't imagine she'd be lucky enough to find Jo again. Jo had been free yesterday only because Lynne was out with her mum.

Pippa slumped down on the floor of her bedroom and pulled out a jigsaw puzzle. She'd already done it about ten times since the school holidays started, but she might as well do it again, before it became too hot to be indoors. Mum kept the curtains closed to keep the sun out, but that made it feel dark and hot, so Pippa had got into the habit of going out to play at about ten o'clock each day.

She glanced at her ballerina watch. 'Twenty past nine,' she announced. In forty minutes, she'd go round to Lynne's. It would be ten o'clock then and only four hours until Dad arrived.

She made the puzzle, and two others, and read a chapter of her book. By then it was stifling in her bedroom. There was no point opening the window, Mum said, because the air outside was just as hot as inside. But the time had crept forward to ten, so Pippa went back downstairs, had a gulp of water from the jug Mum had left out for her before the water went off. Then she went out of the back door, down the side passage and through the gate and the little front garden onto the street. Lynne lived just a few doors along, but Pippa always tried to make the walk from her house to Lynne's last as long as possible, just in case Lynne wasn't at home. And all the time Pippa was walking, there was still the possibility that she *would* be home, and would invite Pippa in. And they'd have a lovely time in the garden like that day when she'd played in Lynne's swimming pool and gone on a hunt for Lynne's old Barbie doll.

It was 267 steps today, from her garden gate to Lynne's front door. Sometimes it was more, sometimes less. Sometimes she lost count. She pressed on the front doorbell, wishing that Lynne or her mum would one day tell her to just come round to the back door and let herself in. Because when they did that, she'd know she was welcome any time.

Inside, she could hear the sound of a Hoover going. She pressed on the doorbell again. This time the Hoover stopped and a moment later Lynne's mum, Mrs Richards, answered the door.

'Oh, hello, Pippa,' she said. She smiled, but it didn't look like a 'pleased to see you' smile. It looked more like a slightly annoyed 'I've got to get on with the housework and don't have time to look after an 8-year-old, but I'm trying to be kind' smile. 'I'm afraid Lynne isn't here. She's gone out with Jo. They're on their bikes.'

'Oh. Do you know where they've gone, Mrs Richards?'

'Sorry, love, I'm not sure. I think they're out for the whole day though.'

Mrs Richards looked as though she was torn between wanting to ask her in, to wait for the girls, and wanting her to go away so she could get on with the hoovering. Hanging around at Lynne's without Lynne there would be even more boring than being in her own house, Pippa thought.

'Thanks anyway. Bye,' Pippa said. As she headed back down the garden path, she heard the front door close behind her and the Hoover start up again.

Pippa looked at her watch. The ballerina's legs were pointing to ten and one. Five past ten. The girls couldn't have gone far. Maybe they were at the climbing tree, or in the rec. Or in the High Street, buying Freddo Frogs or ice creams. She made a snap decision, and ran back to her own house, not counting the steps this time. In the shed in the back garden was her bike. It was a bit small for her these days, but Mum said she couldn't afford a new one yet. Maybe Dad would buy her one for her next birthday. But that was ages off. Anyway, it was all she had. She'd used it a few times already this summer, but only going up and down the road. Today she'd be venturing further.

She wheeled it out to the street and climbed on, deciding to check the rec and the High Street first, as those were the closest possibilities. At the rec there was only a group of women with pushchairs, sitting on a bench in the shade of an oak tree while their little kids played on a picnic blanket. There weren't even any boys playing football. It was too hot. She pushed her bike through the cut that led to the High Street and looked up and down it. They were most likely to be in any shop that sold sweets or ice creams, she thought. So she checked in the newsagent's, but they weren't there.

Perhaps they'd gone to Jo's house. Pippa knew Jo lived on Heather Avenue, but she wasn't sure which house. In any case, she'd heard Jo say she hated being at home because of all the fights, so she was planning to spend the whole of the summer holidays outside. So they wouldn't be there.

Where else could she check? She thought back to the afternoon she'd spent with Lynne and Jo in Lynne's pool. Hadn't they said something about playing in an old barn? It had sounded like fun, Pippa thought. She was fairly certain she knew which farmyard it was – just out of the village and up a little hill. Dad drove past it every time they started the journey to his house, and she knew it wasn't too far.

She jumped on her bike and went back through the rec to her estate, then up to the end of her road. Turning left from there would take her onto the lane that led to the old farm. She might as well go there, she thought. Even if the other children weren't there, she'd at least feel like she'd done something interesting today. There were high hedgerows on both sides of the lane after the rows of houses ended, but you didn't get any shade on you because the sun was too high. Pippa pedalled hard. It was a little bit uphill and she was panting for breath, sweating in the hot sun. The air was dusty as though it needed washing. She passed gateways to fields where wheat was ripening or where cattle huddled beneath whatever shade they could find. An old bathtub in one field was half filled with dirty water for them to drink. The sight of it made Pippa immediately feel thirsty. She wished she'd had another glass of water before she'd come out. Too late now.

The hill levelled out and then there was a bend in the lane that looked familiar. If she remembered it right, she'd be able to see the farmhouse when she went around the bend. With a burst of speed, yes, there it was, down a little slope, which meant she reached it in no time and had to brake hard so she didn't whizz past it.

She wasn't alone. Up the road in the opposite direction she'd come from she could see two people on bikes, riding away from her. They looked like the boys – Jo's brother and the other one. But she wasn't looking for them. She was looking for Lynne and Jo.

And walking up the road towards the farm was that big boy, Horace. She'd seen him before – shopping with his mum in the village. He was a bit different, and she was never quite sure about him. Mum said he was harmless, but Pippa always felt a little bit wary of him.

She leaned her bike against the locked gate and squeezed through the gap in the hedge before any of the boys saw her. Even though there was no sign of Lynne's or Jo's bikes, they might still be there. Maybe they got their bikes through the gap somehow.

'Lynne! Jo? Are you here?' she called out, but her voice sounded small and lost. No one answered.

Chapter 21

Jo, 2024

Lynne phoned me at lunch time, just a couple of hours after my phone call with David.

'Hey, if you're free after you finish work today, I was wondering if we might go up to Four Oaks Farm, see if we can find that time capsule? Worth a try, isn't it? If we arrive around six o'clock the workmen will have finished for the day. We could have dinner in a pub somewhere afterwards.'

'You already missing Malcolm?' I said with a laugh.

'Am I that transparent?' She laughed too. 'Yes, I suppose I am. Anyway, the forecast is for a lovely sunny afternoon and evening, so what do you say?'

'I think it's a great idea.'

'Then I'll collect you at five-thirty, if that's OK?'

'Perfect. And guess what? David came over. He's staying with Dad. Took us both completely by surprise – we only found out when he called Dad from Heathrow while he was sorting out car hire.'

'David came over from Australia?'

'Yes. To see Dad. I'm pleased he did. Dad was longing to see him.'

'Well then, let's get him to come to Four Oaks too! And I could call Rick . . . we could get the band back together!'

I laughed at *The Blues Brothers* reference. 'It'd be nice to see Rick again.'

Something in my tone must have alerted her to a problem. 'And David? Was it good to see him too?'

'I haven't, yet. Spoke to him on the phone this morning.' I sighed. 'I'm afraid I let my frustration with him show. All these years when he's hardly been in touch. And he had the gall to say he was going to help Dad get on top of his finances. What does he think *I've* been doing?'

'I'm sure he didn't mean it. But will you ask him to come to the farm? I just think time's running out. Last time I passed, the demolition crew were in and getting started. It's possible we won't be able to get access.'

'OK, let's try, and all right, I'll call David, if you call Rick.'

'Will do. See you later.'

I'd wanted to wait for David to call me as he'd promised, but there was an urgency to us speaking again now. I wanted to get it out of the way before we all met up again. Judging the moment when Dad was likely to be having his afternoon nap, I phoned David.

'Hey, Jo. Dad's asleep. I was going to call.'

'Good. Listen, remember that time capsule we buried way back?'

'Wait, what? I thought you wanted to talk about—'

'I do. But first, do you remember it? Lynne wants us all to go to the farm and dig it up. Since you're here.'

'Yeah. But Jo, there'll be nothing left. Just a mouldy old plastic ice-cream box, and that's if we can even find it.'

'But will you come? Lynne's going to phone Rick and see if he's free. We thought we'd go out for a pub dinner after.'

'It'll be nice to see them again. Bit short notice though, Sis?

Why the hurry; I'm here for a couple of weeks yet?'

'I forgot to tell you – the farm's been sold to developers. They've already begun clearing the site. So, it's kind of now or never.'

'Right. Well, let me see if I can sort something out for Dad to eat this evening. When are you going?'

'Lynne's picking me up at five-thirty. You could meet us here?'

'I'll go straight to the farm. Think I remember where it is.'

'I'll see you later, then.'

There was a moment's silence while I struggled to find the right words to have the conversation I knew we needed. He waited for me to say something.

'And the other thing?' he said.

'I want you to go and talk to Horace. To apologise.'

'Oh. He's still around, then?'

'He spent ten years locked away, David. He was considered dangerous to society. And it was your fault. He deserves an apology.'

'Don't you think talking to me would be difficult for him? Bringing it all back? Isn't it better to leave it all in the past? Anyway, he won't even know who I am.'

'He remembered me. He remembers playing with us.'

'Wow. Wouldn't have thought he would.'

'So, you'll talk to him?'

David was quiet for a minute, considering. 'Jo, I think you want this more for you than for him. But I'll admit I've felt kind of guilty about what I did. They never did find anything. So . . . yes.'

'Thank you. You've never said before that you felt guilty about it.'

'I've never . . . wanted to admit to it. I guess I buried it.'

'What's changed?'

'Age. And . . . Dad's talked to me about Stephanie. He thinks you felt you could have done more. It got me thinking about that summer. I guess we all need closure, don't we?'

'Yes.' I took a deep breath, and voiced a thought I'd been having, one I'd barely been able to admit even to myself. 'Maybe, just maybe, as his memory's so good, talking to you might trigger something in him.'

'You mean . . .'

'He might remember something about that day. Something that could help . . .'

'. . . resolve the mystery of what happened to that little girl fifty years ago?'

'Yes.'

'I think,' he said in a quiet voice, 'that would be good for all of us. All right, I'll talk to him.'

He'd agreed. That boded well for our chance at reconnecting. It would feel so strange, I thought, as I hung up. Seeing David for the first time in I don't know how many years, at that old farmyard of all places.

Lynne rang my doorbell at five-thirty on the dot. She was dressed in a smart pair of jeans and sparkling white trainers. 'Only ones I have,' she said, noticing me glancing at them. 'I'll just have to try not to get them muddy. I've brought some garden spades and trowels. Don't think we buried it very deeply though, did we?'

'No. I called David. He'll meet us there.'

'Ah, good. Rick's meeting us there too, but he can't make the pub afterwards. He's got to do a shift in his own restaurant.'

'Ah, shame, but I'm glad he can come to the Grand Digging Up.'

Lynne laughed. I was also glad Rick would be there in case it was awkward being with David. Rick's presence would defuse any awkwardness.

I climbed into Lynne's smart Mercedes and she drove the short distance to Four Oaks Farm, parking just off the lane in the turning to the farmyard. We'd got the timing just right – there were no workmen. The old gate had been torn down and a site office installed where one of the barns used to be. There was some heavy machinery in the yard, ready for demolition work, but so far only one barn had been taken down. The other barn, where we used to play, and the farmhouse were still standing. There were no other cars around – we were the first to arrive.

We got out of the car and walked into the yard. 'It was over here, I think,' I said, turning to the right of where the gate used to be. 'Under the hedge.'

'Bit further along, I thought,' Lynne said.

As we walked beside the hedge, another car pulled up behind Lynne's. I felt my heart race as I watched the driver climb out. It felt like a flashback to that time Crispin Willis had caught us playing here and shouted at us. But this time the man who climbed out of the car was all too familiar. Older, with a paunch and thinning grey hair, but still most definitely my brother.

'David!' I ran over to him then stopped just in front of him. We stood a metre apart, regarding each other for a moment. Then he smiled, and the smile was the same as it had always been.

'Hey, Sis.' He held out his arms and I went to him, wrapping mine around him and letting him squeeze me in return. We'd lost a lot of years, but here we were, and that meant so much.

He leaned back, lifting me off my feet, and I squealed. 'Put me down!'

'You never did like it when I did that! Hi, Lynne. You're looking good!'

It flitted through my mind that he hadn't complimented me at all, but then, he was my brother.

'David!' She kissed his cheeks. 'So glad you've come. Rick's on his way too.'

'Fantastic! Can't wait to see him again. Must be twenty years since I last caught up with him, though we do exchange messages now and again.'

Rick and David exchange messages? I felt a pang of jealousy. That was more than Lynne and I had for many years. More than David and I did.

I had no time to dwell on this thought because just then another car pulled up behind David's. Out stepped a silver fox of a man, slim and handsome, and instantly recognisable as Rick. I had no hesitation this time – I rushed over and hugged him tight. 'Rick! So good to see you!'

'Jo! You're looking amazing! Lynne says you're back living in the village?'

'I am, yes.'

'Excellent! I hope to see you at our bistro sometime. Half price for you, of course. Hey, David! Good to see you. And Lynne!' He hugged everyone, then looked at us all expectantly. 'Have you found it yet?'

'No, we only just got here too. We think it's somewhere over there.' I pointed to the hedge.

'We marked one of the beeches,' David said, walking over to the hedge and hunkering down.

'Did we? I don't remember.' Lynne, Rick and I went over to join him and help look.

'Can't see anything,' David said. 'Of course we were expecting to go back to it five years later. We were expecting to all be still living in the area, then Mum and Dad dropped their bombshell on us.'

I nodded. Yes, it had all gone wrong at the end of that summer. I began searching the trunks of the beeches, one by one from where the gate used to be. 'Wait, is this it?' There was a notch on one trunk.

David came over to look. 'Could be. So, how are we going to dig?'

'This'll help.' Lynne had fetched the spade from her car.

'Ever prepared, as always,' David said, smiling at Lynne. She blushed, and I recalled how she'd admitted to having had a crush on him when we were kids.

'I brought one too,' Rick said, fetching his.

'Couldn't get mine in my suitcase,' David said with a laugh. 'I've come all the way from Australia for this.'

I smiled. It was just the sort of joke he'd have made fifty years ago. Some things never changed.

Rick used one spade and I took the other, while Lynne stood to one side in her white trainers. We tried a few places beside that marked beech trunk, racking our memories to recall exactly where we'd buried it.

David hunkered down and began pulling back the undergrowth. 'It wasn't deep, as I recall, was it?' he said. 'The ground was rock solid. I thought we just covered it with leaves.'

'In which case it's probably long gone,' I said.

But at that moment David gasped and scrabbled at the earth with his hands. 'I think I've found it!' A moment later he tugged on a piece of plastic bag which shredded in his hands, and beneath it I spotted a filthy old plastic ice-cream box. 'Good job they made these things that won't decompose for centuries, eh?' David joked, as he pulled it out.

He prised open the lid. Inside were rotting papers and an awful lot of insects. I made out the shape of the Wombles pencil topper I'd donated.

'Ugh,' Lynne said, glancing into the box. 'Well, I'm glad we dug it up but there doesn't seem to be anything left of our stuff.'

'Oh, I don't know. Look at this.' I reached in and took out the Womble figure. 'Orinoco. Remember him?'

'I had the full set,' Lynne said, smiling. 'But I didn't want to give any up for the time capsule. Funny how things like that were so important back then, but I have no idea what I did with them in the end. I probably threw them out when my parents moved and wanted me to clear out all my old stuff that I'd stored in their attic.'

I smiled at her but said nothing. David and I had never had the chance to hang onto stuff that long. We'd moved much more frequently after we'd left Hareton Wick. Then he'd gone to Australia and Mum had died. I'd cleared her house before selling it and binned most of my childhood memorabilia while consumed with grief.

'My trading cards!' Rick said, pulling out a soggy clump of card held together with a decomposing rubber band. 'I should have kept them. Some are quite valuable these days.'

'Well,' David said, pushing aside the mulch at the bottom of the box and flicking insects off his fingers. 'I don't think there's anything else in here that's survived. All those newspapers and copies of *Top Hits* magazine have become food for woodlice. At least we found it.'

I took the box off him and from a corner pulled out a rusty metal dome.

'What's that?' David said.

But I knew immediately what it was, even though until that moment I'd forgotten I'd put it in. I glanced at Lynne.

'Pippa Jenkins' bicycle bell,' she said. 'It fell off her bike at my house.'

'I was going to give her an old one of mine.' It was all coming back to me now. 'But I never did.'

'The police looked for that, didn't they?' Rick said. 'When she went missing and they found her bike with no bell on it.'

'We should have owned up to having it,' Lynne said, 'but we were too scared.'

I shared a glance with David. The others didn't know everything he'd done back then.

'Anyway, it wouldn't have made any difference,' Rick said. 'They just wanted to find it to give them more clues about where she'd been that day.'

We stood in silence for a moment, each lost in our own thoughts. I glanced over towards the house. The developers had cleared some of the land around it, so now it stood alone, a sad and lonely relic. I nodded towards it. 'Wonder what that place is like inside now?'

'Unsafe,' Rick said. He gave a shudder. 'Full of mould.'

'And ghosts,' David added.

'Of whom?' Lynne asked with a smile.

'Who knows! The place is sure to hold some secrets. Anyway, what pub are we going to? I need to wash my hands.'

'I have wet wipes in the car,' Lynne said, hurrying off to fetch them.

'Might have known. She always was the organised one. All those picnics she provided,' Rick said.

'I think that was more her mum,' I said.

We headed off shortly after. We hugged Rick goodbye and promised to all come to his bistro soon. He drove off, then David followed Lynne and me in her car. We went to a traditional New Forest pub tucked away on a small lane and spent the next couple of hours eating and reminiscing. David was surprised to find I didn't drink alcohol.

'Abstaining for health reasons?'

'Kind of. Mental health. I sort of . . . became dependent on it for a while.'

He looked worried. 'Aw, Sis, I wouldn't have thought it of you. What triggered it?'

Lynne was listening carefully. I realised I hadn't told her, either. It was time. I took a deep breath and recounted that awful day, finding Stephanie and losing Goldie, and how I'd spiralled downwards until I hit the bottom of the bottle.

'Jo, you never said!' Lynne exclaimed, when I'd finished. 'I'd have done anything I could to help, you must know that.'

'We weren't really in touch at that point though, beyond Christmas cards.' I smiled at her to let her know I appreciated what she'd said.

'You never told me, either. I only found out from Dad last night. I remember getting a note on a Christmas email that said it hadn't been a great year for you, but that's all.' David looked hurt that I hadn't confided in him.

'I was trying to deal with it myself. Badly, it seemed.'

'But Dad and Ryan, did they . . .?' David said.

'They knew, though I kept the worst of it from Dad.'

'Was Ryan supportive?'

'Yes, but I don't think he really understood why it had all affected me so much.'

Lynne was looking at me oddly. 'You're connecting it with Pippa, aren't you?'

David stared at me. 'Why would you connect the two?'

'Because . . . in both cases I wondered if there was anything I might have done that would have led to a different outcome,' I said, not looking at either of them. 'I was in therapy for a couple of years. I know, I really do know, that neither tragedy is my fault and there's nothing I could have done. I know that now. But it took a long time to work through it all.'

Lynne nodded. 'I get it. I've tormented myself over Pippa too. And so did Mum. She wished she'd offered full-time childcare to Mrs Jenkins that summer, instead of the ad hoc arrangement we had, expecting an eight-year-old to just come round whenever she felt like it.'

David had been sipping his pint while he listened. Now he slammed the glass down on the table. 'The only person who's at fault is whoever took Pippa. God, ladies. It's so long ago. Jo, I'm sorry about all the trouble you had. I'm glad you had therapy. You must never blame yourself. And I wish you'd told me about it.'

I blinked back tears. 'Yes, I probably should have. Just . . . we'd let ourselves drift apart, hadn't we? And it's not like I could just call round and see you.'

'These days, with WhatsApp, video-calls, mobile phones and all, there's absolutely no reason why me living in Australia should stop us communicating. It's as much my fault as yours that we haven't, and I'm truly sorry.' David patted my shoulder, a little awkwardly. 'Now we're back in touch, let's not let it slip again, eh?'

I smiled at him. 'All right. Let's not.'

'Hurray! I'm so glad for you two,' Lynne said. 'How long are you staying, David?'

'I'm not sure,' he said. 'Kind of depends on Dad.'

'Dad will want you to stay for as long as you can,' I said. 'And you can stay some of the time with me, if you're worried it's too much for him.' I surprised myself by offering. But we were reconciling, and that was a good thing. Long overdue.

He smiled. 'Thanks, Smudge.'

Chapter 22

Jo, 8 August 1976
One day after.

I really didn't want to go back to the farm the next day. I wanted to lounge around Lynne's garden again, eating ice pops in her pool, even if it meant we ended up babysitting Pippa. But I was outvoted. In any case, Lynne's mum was hosting a coffee morning, and her ladies were going to sit in the garden, so we had to go somewhere else. Rick's place was no good as his garden had no shade. Our place was no good with both parents at home today. Even though lately Dad seemed to be constantly out of the house, disappearing for hours on end. Mum grumbled she had no idea what he was up to. He'd come back with a furrowed brow as though he was plotting something, though when questioned he just shrugged and turned away.

So we set off on our bikes. Without really discussing it we ended up going towards the farm. As we reached the gate Rick pulled over and stopped. 'Window's closed,' he said, nodding at it.

He was right. The pantry window was firmly closed today.

'Someone's been here since yesterday afternoon,' David said, as he climbed over the gate and went over to the window. He cupped his hands around his eyes and peered through. 'That sack of rubbish has been moved. I can see the door to the cellar but the sack that was beside it has gone.'

'Are we going in?' Lynne asked.

'I don't think we should.' If someone had been here and closed that window between us leaving yesterday and coming back today, who was to say they wouldn't come again? Presumably it was Mr Willis who'd been here, as he'd be the only person with a key. We'd already been shouted at by him once. I didn't want to risk it again. 'David, come back. Let's go somewhere else,' I called to him.

He jogged back to the gate and vaulted over. 'Think you're right, Jo. Let's go back to the woods. We never did get to spend any time there.'

We got back on our bikes and set off, but we'd barely got going before we spotted a familiar figure shuffling up the hill towards us.

'Uh, oh. Horace ahead,' David muttered, as he cycled beside me. 'Let's speed up. He won't catch us.'

We were going downhill so it was easy to speed up and shoot past him. I caught a glimpse of his face – he looked anguished. It was clear there was something wrong, but he wasn't our responsibility, was he? No more than little Pippa was.

'Ha! We gave him the slip!' David shouted once we were round the corner, past the turn to Horace's farm. 'He can't catch us now and he doesn't know where we're going.'

'And no Pippa either!' Lynne said, echoing my thoughts. 'Just the four of us. Come on, let's have some fun!'

And we did have fun that day. We found a spot where someone had tied a piece of rope over a tree branch and added a stout stick to the end, to make a swing. We spent ages taking turns on it, with the others pushing.

We went to the stream, which was little more than a trickle, and paddled. Rick refilled a water bottle from it, but the rest of us refused to drink it. 'You don't know what might be upstream,' I said.

'Could be a dead rabbit or a sheep or a pony,' David added. Dad had always warned us about drinking water where you couldn't be sure of the source.

'Or even a human!' I don't know what made me add that, but it made the others laugh, so I was pleased. Although the thought of someone's remains being in the stream made me shiver.

Then Rick wanted to light a bonfire to burn some of the dead leaves. David talked him out of it. 'It'd soon get out of control. Haven't you heard on the local news, about all the forest fires there's been lately? We don't want to add to that problem!'

Instead, we came up with a game of 999-In where you had to climb a tree, getting your feet off the ground, to avoid being caught. Only the person who was 'It' was not allowed up the trees. We ran around madly, we hauled ourselves into trees and leaped out of them. We laughed, we giggled, we shouted and squealed.

Looking back, it was perhaps the best day, the most fun, of the whole summer.

Eventually, exhausted, we lay on our backs under the canopy of trees and chatted. We'd become a tight-knit little group. I never again felt so much a part of something as I did then. I wanted us to go on forever, meeting up most days, doing everything together, enjoying ourselves without a care in the world.

'Do you feel guilty at all?' Lynne asked, as we lay there looking up at the patterns of leaves against the sky. 'About Horace, I mean. And Pippa.'

'You mean, guilty about avoiding them?' David asked. 'Not really.'

'In any case, we didn't see Pippa today. Not as if we saw her and cycled away fast,' I said.

'We did do that to Horace though.' Lynne sounded thoughtful.

'Yeah. We did. But he's probably used to it.'

'We wouldn't have done that to Pippa. She'd have been hurt.'

David's tone was gentle, and I loved my brother for it. He barely knew the little girl – it was Lynne and me who always ended up looking after her.

'We might have,' Rick said, 'if we saw her from a distance and she hadn't spotted us. And yesterday, we actively avoided her.'

'See, that's what I feel guilty about,' Lynne said, propping herself up on her elbow so she could look down at the rest of us. 'I don't know where she goes when her mum's at work, if she's not round our house.'

'Plays in the street. At least that's what she was doing two days ago when I found her,' I said.

'What if something happened to her? We'd feel guilty then,' Lynne went on.

'No, we wouldn't,' David said firmly. 'Her mother would. She's not our responsibility. Neither's Horace. Stop thinking like that. Hey. What do you think about going to the beach one day? I reckon we could cycle to Lepe beach, if you fancy?'

'That's miles!' I gasped.

'About ten. And then same again to get home. But I reckon we can do it, take a picnic, bring our swimming things . . . Up to you girls, if you think you're up for it? I mean, I think we've exhausted the possibilities of the farm and the woodland.'

'Yeah, I'll do it,' Lynne said, and I agreed.

'Why not? Tomorrow?'

'Can't do tomorrow,' Rick said. 'I promised Mum I'd spend some time helping her sort out the cupboard in the spare room. She says it's mostly my stuff from when I was a baby.' He pulled a face. 'It won't take long, but we'll need all day to make it worthwhile cycling all the way to Lepe.'

'Some other time, then.' David sounded disappointed. I was vaguely relieved; it sounded like a long way to cycle. We'd always driven in the car as a family to Lepe in summers gone by and parked up in the beach car park. Not this year though. Not after our trip to Devon.

'Let's just hang out in the village,' Rick suggested. 'At the rec, perhaps? Buy ice creams in the shop? Honestly, I could do with a rest after the last two days.'

'All right. Then we could always go in my pool to cool off in the afternoon,' Lynne added, and we all decided that was a very good idea.

When would this heatwave ever end? Summers in England were usually a mix of good days, rainy days, cold days and boring grey days. But to have endless sunshine, day after day, extreme heat and no rain since April was unheard of. I had the feeling, even then, when we were still in the middle of it, that we'd never forget that year.

We headed back to Lynne's soon after. We'd drunk all our drinks and eaten all the food, and we were hot and sweaty. It was late enough that Aunty Margaret's coffee morning would have finished, and Lynne said she had stocked up on ice pops so we had that to look forward to. I didn't have my swimsuit with me, but Lynne said I could put an old one of hers on, and the boys decided they'd just go in wearing their shorts. 'They'll dry before we get home, so Mum doesn't need to know, all right, Jo?' David said and I nodded.

I was relieved to reach Lynne's house, but Aunty Margaret came straight out to the garden when we got there and told us we couldn't use the pool.

'I'm afraid the water's too dirty, kids. Lynne's father normally changes it every few weeks, but with the water shortage and the hose pipe ban we've not been able to do it this year. And look, it's pretty uninviting now. I'd be scared you'd catch something nasty from it.'

I had to admit it did look a bit manky. Bits of leaves and twigs from the tree that overhung it had fallen in, and there was a layer of scum over the top. It had been all right the last time I'd been in, but that was a couple of weeks ago now.

'What if we don't go underwater and keep our mouths closed?' David said, hopefully.

Aunty Margaret shook her head. 'I'm sorry, love. I'll talk to Barry this evening. Maybe we'll be able to skim off the top and make it a bit better. Proper swimming pools have filtration systems to get rid of any dirt but this one's a bit basic.'

'Wish there was a proper swimming pool near here,' Rick said. 'Nearer than Southampton, I mean.'

'Anyway, can we have an ice pop each?' Lynne asked.

'Of course.' Aunty Margaret smiled. 'I'll fetch them.' She bustled away to her freezer.

'Shame,' Rick said. 'Think I'll go home soon. My room's usually quite cool. Want to come?' He looked at David as he asked this, and it was clear the invitation was boys only.

David shrugged. 'Think I'll head home too. You coming, Jo?'

I paused, expecting Lynne to ask me to stay, but she didn't. We'd had a great day, but we were all tired and I guessed it was over. I thought of the book I'd begun reading on holiday, and the idea of lying on my bed reading it for the rest of the day appealed. As long as Mum and Dad didn't start arguing again.

'Yeah. Soon as we get our ice pops.'

Right on cue Aunty Margaret appeared with four ice pops and a pair of scissors to snip the tops off. Better than tearing them open with your teeth. Mine was lime flavoured. We thanked her and headed back out to where we'd left our bikes on the driveway.

'See you, then,' Rick said, as he got on his bike, steering it with one hand while he held the ice pop in the other.

'Yeah, see ya,' David replied. We'd made no new arrangement. Maybe we needed a rest from each other. David climbed on his bike, and I got on mine, wobbling a bit until I clamped the ice pop between my teeth and put both hands on the handlebars.

'I'll ring you, Jo,' Lynne called out, as we set off to cycle home, and I waved a hand in response.

Something felt different. We'd had such a good day, but it had all fallen flat, ending with a whimper rather than a bang.

Chapter 23

Jo, 2024

Back home, the evening after we'd dug up the time capsule, I reflected on all that had happened. So our time capsule had been a disaster, but it had managed to bring David and me together again. Somehow the closeness we'd had as children had been bundled up in that old ice-cream box hidden under a mulch of autumn leaves, and now we'd released it again. I made myself a cup of chamomile tea to drink before bedtime and smiled. So that was one of my menfolk I'd made it up with. Dad was never cross at me for long, either. So just Ryan and Charlie to go.

I picked up my phone to message them both. To Charlie I simply wrote: *Sorry to have called at a bad time. Hope we can chat again on happier topics soon.*

He replied almost immediately. *Sorry. I meant to call you back. Life's been a bit hectic. I'm tied up at the moment but will call tomorrow. Speak soon. Xx*

OK, well, he put a couple of kisses . . . that has to be a good thing, right? I told myself, as I sent Ryan a message. *Darling, I'm missing you. Please tell me you're all right and forgive me.*

And to my utter joy he rang me back almost immediately. 'Hey, Mum. I'm sorry I didn't answer your calls or ring you back. Been a weird week, you know.'

'I know. Any more news on the missing boy?'

'Not officially, but I was told off the record that there may well be a happy ending to the whole thing.'

'Oh, that's good news! You mean they're expecting to find him?'

'The police officer I spoke to wouldn't say any more than that. All a bit delicate still, he said. But yes.' Ryan took a deep breath. 'Mum, I'm sorry for the way I behaved, taking what you said the wrong way. I was just so stressed by it all, I lashed out. And you were only trying to show solidarity with me.'

'It's all right, love. Let's put it all behind us. I'm sorry too for being insensitive. Friends again?'

'We never weren't friends, Mum. Love you.'

'Love you, too, darling.' I quietly pulled a tissue from a nearby box and dabbed at my eyes.

He took a deep breath. 'Listen, Mum, weird though it sounds, this really helped me understand how finding that girl in the woods affected you. I mean, I knew how traumatic it must have been, but I never really got why you kept thinking it was somehow your fault, and why you ended up . . . you know, drinking.'

'Yes, it seems to be the way I react to stress. Darling, I . . . almost slipped again, the other day. I was *this* close to buying two bottles of wine and downing them, to block it all out.'

'Oh, Mum! But you didn't, right?'

'No, I didn't. Somehow, I managed to stop myself before I paid for them.'

'Well done.' He paused a moment. 'Back then, when I was doing my teaching course and you were at your worst, all I thought about was how badly your drinking was affecting me. Like, I couldn't bring anyone back home in case you were passed out on the sofa. I never knew what was going to confront me when

I came home each day. I wanted to help, but didn't know how to, and it was easier to just keep out of your way.'

'Oh, sweetie. I hadn't really thought of how it affected you, seeing me like that. I'm so sorry.' I'd been so caught up in my own woes back then. I hadn't spared a thought for how it had been for Ryan, living with me while I spiralled out of control.

'So please, *please*, don't go down that road again, eh, Mum? If you ever feel tempted, call me, or Lynne, or anyone else who understands. Promise?'

'Thank you, my darling. Yes. I promise.'

'Good. I'm glad we had this talk. Feels like we understand each other better now.'

'Yes, it does. Listen, Ryan, your Uncle David's come over for a surprise visit. Mainly to see Granddad but if you can spare another weekend to come down here it'd be nice for you two to meet up.'

'Wow. I haven't seen Uncle David for years. Actually, it's half term starting next week so yes, I can definitely come, if you can put me up again?'

'Of course I can.'

'Right, well let me sort out dates and get back to you. I have a few things in my diary I'll need to work around. It's getting late. Better let you get your beauty sleep.'

'Thanks, love. OK, I'll wait to hear from you, then I'll arrange something. Perhaps if Dad's up to it the four of us could go for a day out and a meal somewhere.'

'Good plan. I'll message you tomorrow, when I've checked my diary. Which I left in the classroom today.'

'Ha! Sounds like something I'd do.'

'Yeah, thanks for passing on your disorganised forgetful genes, eh, Mum?'

We both laughed, then ended the call. I went to bed feeling much more positive than I had for ages. Back on good terms with David and Ryan; Dad on good form; Charlie – well, at least he'd apologised and promised again to call. If I surrounded myself with people I loved and who loved me back, with whom I could talk openly, I could get myself on to a more even keel and finally move on.

The following day, I found myself at a loose end for a couple of hours. I was thinking of Charlie, and with still no word from him, I made a sudden decision to visit his father, Crispin, in the care home. I'd promised I'd go again, and I rather liked the frail old man with his disjointed memories. I was certain Charlie would approve, but I messaged him anyway to say I was going and got a thumbs-up reply.

I changed into a pretty blue dress and tidied my hair, then drove out to the care home. If he was too confused, I'd leave, I decided. The last thing I wanted to do was inadvertently upset him.

'Barbara! My Barbara!' he said, as I walked in. Today he was sitting in a corner of the communal lounge. Other residents were sitting in groups, chatting, knitting, watching TV, or piecing together a jigsaw, but no one was talking to Crispin. I felt sorry for him.

'Crispin! It's good to see you again. You're looking well.' He wasn't – if anything he was looking frailer than the last time I'd seen him. But his eyes lit up at my words.

'You always were a flatterer, my Barbara. I know I'm not long for this world. But there's still good to be found when you come. The snooker was on the telly yesterday. In colour! We had the first colour telly, didn't we?'

'We did, Crispin, yes.'

'It was Ray Reardon who won. Beating old Hurricane Higgins.' Crispin chuckled. 'You like old Hurricane Higgins, don't you, Barbara? You always said he was a nice-looking chap.' He winked at me.

'He was.' I wasn't sure if either of those snooker players were still alive, and wondered what year Crispin's mind had alighted on. Somewhere in the seventies.

'Better looking than me, eh? Now that I'm getting long in the tooth. You're still beautiful, Barbara. You got a portrait in the attic, have you?'

I laughed. 'Perhaps I have! Shall we have some tea, Crispin? I can make it.'

He looked confused for a moment. 'Didn't we just have a cup? Or has Charles gone off to the kitchen to make one? He'll be back soon with it. Don't you bother yourself.' He reached out and took my hand. 'You just sit here with me looking pretty. That's a new dress you have on. You already have a blue one. What do you want another blue one for? Ah, never mind. We've got the money, may as well spend it, eh?'

'We may as well,' I agreed.

'She was in blue that day as well,' Crispin said, his eyes misting as he stared into the middle distance at something only he could see.

'I like blue.' I smiled at him, but he was still in the past, his brow furrowed as he relived some past experience.

'Blue. Five points,' he said, suddenly turning back to look at me.

'I'm sorry, what?' I couldn't follow him.

'In snooker. Blue's worth five points. Where's that boy with our tea?'

'I'll get it,' I said, feeling mildly grateful for the opportunity to slip away for a few minutes.

I made the tea quickly, adding plenty of milk so it wasn't too hot, then returned to Crispin with two cups. He'd fallen asleep, and a member of staff was tucking a blanket around his legs.

'Oh, sorry,' she said, 'but he won't be wanting that now. He'll be sleeping for a couple of hours.' She smiled kindly at me. 'Maybe come again another day? I can see he enjoys your visits.'

'All right, I will.'

I perched on a chair in the reception area to quickly drink the tea I'd made, then left. It was nice to feel I was doing some good by visiting Crispin, but maybe it'd be better to only come with Charlie in future.

Chapter 24

Jo, 9 August 1976
Two days after.

Next morning our phone rang while I was still sitting at the breakfast table, shovelling cornflakes in my mouth while reading the back of the cereal packet. It was a new box, so I hadn't already read it a dozen times.

Mum answered using her posh 'telephone voice', which she soon dropped when she realised it was someone she knew well. Aunty Margaret by the sound of things.

'Who? I can't imagine she knows her . . . Oh. Well, she's right here, I'll ask her.' Mum turned to me with a concerned expression on her face, her hand over the mouthpiece of the phone. 'It's Lynne's mummy. She's asking when you last saw a girl called Pippa Jenkins. I think she lives near Lynne. Mrs Richards says you know Pippa from when she's played round there with you and Lynne.'

I nodded and swallowed a mouthful of cornflakes. 'Yes, I know her.'

'When did you last see her?'

I thought back. We'd spent the last two days making sure we *didn't* see her, though I wasn't going to admit to that. 'Um, we haven't seen her the last two days. But before that, um, the day we came home from the holiday, I saw her.'

'Where, Jo? What was she doing?' There was an urgency to Mum's voice that frightened me.

'Playing in the street. Skipping. I taught her a game.'

'And then what?'

'Then her mum came home from work and thanked me for looking after her.'

Mum smiled. 'Right. That does sound as though you were being kind.' She removed her hand from the phone mouthpiece. 'Margaret, I've spoken to her. She saw Pippa three days ago but left her with her mother. She says she didn't see her the last two days.' She paused, listening. 'Uh, huh. I see. Well, if I hear anything more, I'll let you know. Hmm. It's worrying. I wonder what's happened?'

She hung up soon after, and stood for a moment beside the phone, biting her lip.

'Mum? What's happened? Why are you asking about Pippa?'

'It seems . . . she's gone missing. Her father was supposed to be having her for a couple of days, but he hasn't brought her back. Her mother hasn't seen her for more than a day. Margaret says Mrs Jenkins often left Pippa alone when she went to work, and the little girl would often end up at their house. Margaret felt sorry for her. I don't know how old she is?'

'Eight, I think.' I felt a pang of guilt.

'That's very young to be left all day. Anyway, I'm sure she'll turn up soon. You don't know where she liked to go to play?'

I shrugged. 'Lynne's house. Her own house. In the street. The rec, maybe?'

'Well, I'm sure the police will be searching all those areas.'

'The police!' It hit me then, how serious this was. If Mrs Jenkins had called the police to search for Pippa then it wasn't a game of hide-and-seek. It was bad.

The phone rang again. Mum answered but quickly passed it to me. 'It's Lynne, for you. Don't talk too long. It's expensive at this time of day.'

'Jo, have you heard? About Pippa?' Lynne sounded breathless and also a little tearful.

'Yes. Where do you reckon she is?'

'No idea. Apparently her dad's been seen in the village. They're looking for him. Hopefully she's safe with him still.'

'And if she's not with her dad?'

Lynne made an odd sound, as though she was gulping back a sob. 'If not . . . then who knows? She's only eight. She can't have gone far.'

Mum made me go shopping with her in the village that day. All the parents were worried because Pippa had gone missing, so I had no choice. In that heat the last thing I wanted to do was trail around after her from butcher to greengrocer to the little Spar supermarket, but Mum wouldn't listen to any arguments. 'I need someone to help carry everything. And it's your turn. David came with me the day we came back from our camping trip.'

She handed me two shopping bags and we set off walking up to the village. Why we couldn't use the car I didn't know. On the way, she chattered on, asking me how I was enjoying the holidays, what we were getting up to when we went out on our bikes. I told her about playing in the woodland but didn't mention the farm. We'd been told off once for being there, and I didn't want to be told off again.

As we approached the village we noticed a number of policemen in the High Street. You'd often see one constable patrolling or sometimes on a bicycle, but there were at least three that I could see. They were stopping everyone and asking questions. I saw people shake their heads, or maybe say a few words that the constable wrote down before they were allowed to go on their way.

'I bet they're asking about that little girl,' Mum said. 'Whether anyone's seen her or not.'

And sure enough, as we approached the Spar supermarket we were stopped by a constable. He looked very hot in his dark uniform and helmet, and there was sweat running down his face. He was holding a notebook and pencil.

'Good morning, madam,' he said to Mum. He nodded at me. 'I need to ask you a few questions. I won't keep you long. Do you know an eight-year-old girl named Philippa Jenkins?'

'I don't,' Mum said, 'but . . .' She looked at me.

'Do you know her, young lady?' There was a drip of sweat on the end of his nose, and I wanted to hand him the handkerchief from my pocket to mop it up.

'A bit. Not very well. She's a lot younger than me.'

'Of course. Now then, can you remember when and where you last saw her? Have you seen her recently?'

I glanced at Mum. 'Tell the policeman everything, Jo,' she said, and I noticed the constable lean in a little more, his eyes opening wider as if he thought that he was going to get some important clue that would mean he'd be the one to crack the case of the missing child.

'Well, it was three days ago,' I said. 'We came back early from our camping trip because . . . um. Well, then I went round to my friend Lynne's but she was out, and then I saw her . . .'

'Saw your friend?'

'No, I mean Pippa. That's what everyone called her, not Philippa.'

'And where was Pippa?'

'In the street, playing skipping. I taught her a new game.'

'Which street?'

'Beechwood Road.'

'And then?'

'I took her to the shop and bought her a Freddo Frog.'

'I see. Which shop?'

I told him. All these details, which had nothing to do with Pippa's disappearance, were being noted carefully in his little notebook.

'Where did you leave her?'

'Back in Beechwood Road. Her mum had just come home from work. She said thank you to me for looking after Pippa.'

The policeman nodded. 'And have you seen her since?'

'Er, no.'

'Are you absolutely sure? Not even a glimpse of her in the last two days?'

'No.'

'What about Pippa's father? Have you seen him?'

'I don't know what he looks like.'

'Neither do I,' added Mum.

The policeman made a note. 'Do you know anywhere Pippa likes to go to play?'

'Just at Lynne's sometimes. I've seen her there but not since before our camping trip.'

'Lynne . . .?'

'Lynne Richards,' Mum said, before I had a chance to. 'Jo's best friend.'

And then we had to give Lynne's address, and our names, and it all went down in his notebook. At last, he flipped the notebook closed and thanked us, and we were free to go.

'Well. That's the first time I've ever been questioned by police,' Mum said. 'They're taking this very seriously. They must be very worried.'

'That's good that they're taking it seriously, isn't it?' I asked. 'She's only eight.'

'Yes. Only eight. What her mother's doing letting her roam the streets alone at that age I really don't know.'

We went into the Spar and were soon out again, now carrying heavy bags. But I was happy as Mum had picked up a packet of ice pops to put in the freezer compartment at home. Normally we weren't allowed them as she said there were more important things to put in the freezer compartment. It was only people like Aunty Margaret with her big chest freezer in the garage who could keep a stock at all times.

As we came out, I noticed a group of people gathering in the street. Mum walked over to see what was happening, and I followed. We stood at the back of the crowd and listened to a man who was standing on a box and talking loudly – organising search parties to look for Pippa. 'Everyone pair up with a partner, then see me to be allocated an area to search. If you find anything, *anything at all* that might belong to Pippa, or please, God, the girl herself, one of the pair is to get himself to the nearest telephone and call the police, while the other stays put with the evidence. Everyone got that?' There were murmurs and nods from the men present.

I recognised one man: Mr Willis was among the searchers, his face taut with worry as he listened to the instructions. I moved so that Mum hid me from his sight. Last thing I wanted was him spotting me and coming over to tell Mum I'd been trespassing in his farmyard. Mr Willis's son Charlie was nearby too, but he ducked into a shop, looking like he was trying to keep out of the way of the search parties.

Despite me trying to hide, Mr Willis spotted Mum anyway and came over. 'Bad business, this,' he said.

'Yes. I hope to God she's found soon, the poor little thing.'

'Indeed. Tell Alan we could do with him joining the search party.'

'I will,' Mum said. 'He'll want to help.'

'I'll hope to see him later, then. Bye, Mary. Jo.' Mr Willis smiled down at me then, and ruffled my hair. He seemed to have forgotten he'd told me off the last time I saw him.

Walking up the street, holding hands with an older woman, was another face I recognised. As they approached the crowd the woman said something to Horace. He nodded, joining the edge of the crowd while she – I guessed his mother – went into a nearby shop.

Horace stood listening to the men around him as they organised themselves and set off to search different areas around the village. He began shuffling from foot to foot, and seemed upset. Mum had noticed him too. 'That's the Thompson boy,' she said, nodding in his direction. 'He looks agitated. Wonder if he knows something?'

Other members of the crowd must have spotted him too. One or two people frowned in his general direction and muttered to each other, in much the same way Mum had muttered to me.

I overheard one woman say to her husband, 'Bet it was him. He's not right in the head. Bet it's him who's hurt that little girl.'

Her husband nodded. 'Ought to be locked away, people like that. Before they harm anyone else.' They glared at Horace but then walked away. Horace's mum was coming out of the shop, her face creased with worry when she saw his flapping hands.

'What's wrong, love?' she asked. I wondered if someone would confront them with their suspicions but no one did. They all backed away.

Mum took my arm. 'Come on. Let's get on with our shopping.'

'Aren't we going to help search for Pippa?'

'No. We'll leave it to the men. Maybe your father will stir himself and help. Let's get away from . . .' She tailed off, but I knew she meant get away from Horace.

'He's all right, really,' I said, half to myself.

'Who is?'

'Horace. Remember, he played 999-In with us one time. Wasn't very good at it but we let him win.' I was staring at the ground as I spoke. I had a feeling Mum was going to tell me off.

'I thought I told you to stay away from that lad,' Mum said angrily.

'It was only once.' I shuffled my feet. I didn't want to say we'd actively avoided him since, just like we'd avoided Pippa, and now look what had happened to her.

'You keep away from him, you hear? He's not safe. People like that . . .'

'He's just a kid,' I muttered. I wasn't sure why I was defending him, but somehow I felt sure that whatever had happened to Pippa hadn't been down to Horace. Or had it? I remembered when we'd seen him in the lane a few days ago looking disturbed. Was that the day Pippa had gone missing? Had Horace known something about it after all? I turned and stared back up the road where Mrs Thompson was sitting on a bench, her arms wrapped around Horace, as she tried to calm him down. There was a small crowd watching, keeping their distance, as though it'd be dangerous to stand too close to him.

Despite my misgivings, I felt sorry for him. I needed to see Lynne and the boys, and discuss it all with them.

Pippa's disappearance was all we talked about over dinner that evening.

'The most likely explanation,' Dad said, 'is that Mr Jenkins has got her. It's probably just a big mix-up – he thought he was supposed to have her for a few days but the mother thought he wasn't.'

'She said to me her dad was taking her to see HMS *Victory*. He lives in Gosport,' I said.

'Then that's where she'll be,' Dad said.

Mum scoffed. 'Doubt it. If it was just a big mix-up why can't the police find the father? If he's got her, he'll have taken her away somewhere. But I don't think it's him. Far more likely to be that Thompson lad.' She shot me a look.

'Mum, it's not—' I began, but she shut me down. Her mind was made up about what had happened to poor Pippa, and all I could do was hope and pray that she was wrong.

I didn't sleep much that night. I remembered Horace in the lane; Dad's frequent disappearances to 'take care of something' and coming back looking stressed; David and Rick cycling off to fetch the rucksack of drinks and taking ages. So many horrible possibilities of what had happened to Pippa: none of which I wanted to believe for even a moment could be the truth.

Chapter 25

Jo, 2024

The rest of the day passed with no word from Charlie despite his promise. I was wondering if perhaps he'd call in the evening, when my doorbell rang. It was Charlie himself, standing on my doorstep, but looking anguished, drawn. Something bad had happened – it was written all over his face.

'Charlie! Come in. What's wrong?' I asked.

He shook his head, and pushed past me, into my sitting room, where he sat on the sofa, his head in his hands. I sat on the edge of the sofa beside him. The look on his face – it was a look I recognised. One I'd seen in the mirror far too many times, after finding Stephanie. I tentatively put a hand on his arm. He clasped it tightly, and took a shuddering breath.

'Jo, God, I'm so sorry to turn up here like this. You were . . . the person I wanted to be with, to talk to.'

'I'm here. You can talk to me. God knows I've unburdened myself on you often enough,' I said. 'What's happened? Is it your dad? He was sleeping when I left him this afternoon.'

'No, no. Dad's fine. No, it's . . .'

'Go on.'

'The farm. Four Oaks. The developers found . . . something.'

'Found what?' I felt cold. We'd been there only the day before. Had we left something behind?

'They've been demolishing the main house. Today they were clearing away the rubble and they . . .'

'What?' I knew what it would be. I knew before he said it, exactly what they'd found. It could only be one thing. I put my other hand on top of his, hoping to lend strength.

He took another of those long, shuddering breaths. 'Hu-human remains. A child.'

'Oh, my God. Where?' Although I'd been expecting this answer, it was still a shock to hear the words spoken aloud.

'They think, in the cellar. Hard to be sure, because the house had already been knocked down.'

'Who was it?' I whispered.

He looked at me. 'Yet to be identified. The remains are pretty old, though.'

The words were unsaid but of course we were both thinking, expecting, that it would be Pippa Jenkins who'd turned up at last.

'Jo, I've had to spend the afternoon with the police. They questioned me about the farm – how long it had been empty, when did anyone last go inside and that sort of thing. I answered to the best of my knowledge, but the truth is I don't really know. I never had anything to do with that place. They want to speak with Dad. But they won't get much out of him. You've seen what he's like.'

'Oh, Charlie. It must have been so stressful.' I knew, all too well, how it felt.

'It was. And I felt so helpless, knowing so little. The child's remains are going to a lab where I suppose they'll try to work out how she – or he – died, and when. Then I guess they'll look at records of missing children . . .'

'It could be Pippa . . .' I said, gently.

He nodded. 'I think that's what everyone will assume. Everyone who remembers.' He took in a long, shuddering breath.

We sat in silence for a while, still clutching each other's hands. We didn't even know yet if it was Pippa. It could be some other child. In all those years that the farm had stood empty, anyone could have got in.

'They're going to talk to Dad tomorrow. They've said I can be there, but I'm not to prompt him.'

'I'm glad you can be there with him,' I said. Charlie sounded so downbeat. This had really hit him hard. My heart went out to him. And to Crispin, who wouldn't understand why he was being questioned.

'I don't understand. What do they think they might get from him? I mean, just because he happened to own the place. It was boarded up for decades.'

'I don't know, Charlie. I suppose they have to talk to him, in case there's anything he remembers, anything that might spark ideas for directions of inquiry . . .'

'There's nothing he can tell them that I haven't already. My grandparents left the farm in 1972. It then stood empty. Dad boarded the house up a few years later and replaced the boarding once or twice over the years when it wore out. Other than kids getting in and playing in the barns, no one's been there.'

I remembered then that once we'd been inside the farmhouse. We'd seen an open window and climbed in for a look around. The doors and windows hadn't been boarded up then, Mr Willis must have done it later.

If we'd got in, maybe others had too? Horace, for example? I hated myself for even allowing the thought to cross my mind. Back then I'd never thought for a moment he had anything to do with Pippa's disappearance, not even when he was taken away and locked up. But now it seemed likely Pippa's body had been dumped at the farm, where he used to hang around, or that she might even have been killed there. I couldn't help but wonder if Horace had had something to do with it, after all. I'd never seen anyone else at the farm. Only him and us.

After she'd gone missing, I'd even briefly wondered whether David and Rick, or Dad, might have somehow been involved. Just like with Ryan's missing pupil, something like this made you suspect everyone, even those closest to you.

'I'll go,' Charlie said, letting go of my hands. 'It's helped, talking to you. Thank you.'

'You can stay longer if you want to. I've nothing on this evening.'

'Thanks, but I think I need to be on my own now. Probably I'll have a drink, and I don't want to do that around you.' He gave a small smile, and I was touched by his thoughtfulness.

'All right. I understand. Look, keep in touch, OK? And if there's anything I can do, just listening, whatever, tell me.'

He smiled. 'I'm glad I met you.' And then he leaned towards me and gently kissed the corner of my mouth. It was somewhere between a friendly peck on the cheek and a romantic kiss on the mouth. It was a kiss that said, *now's not the right moment, but here's a promise for the future.* And I liked what it promised.

An hour after Charlie left, while I was cooking myself some dinner, my phone rang. It was Ryan. 'Two calls in two days!' I joked, as I answered it. 'I'm honoured!'

'I said I'd let you know about when I could visit and see Uncle David.'

'You did. I was expecting just a text, but it's nice to hear your voice.'

'Ah, thank you, Mum. Anyway, I'll be able to visit end of next week, if that's any good? Got something on this coming weekend, then I have a few things I can't get out of during the week. I'll come down Thursday. Hope Uncle David will still be around then.'

'I think he will be. Thanks, love.'

'Uh-huh.' There was a silence, and I had the impression there was something else he needed to say. 'Seen the news?'

'No. I've had a visitor.'

'It's Ben Byatt. They've found him. Turns out his dad had him all along.'

'His father!'

'Yes. His parents are divorced and estranged. Ben's dad had picked him up and taken him to an Airbnb cottage in Scotland he'd rented under a different name.'

'Didn't they question the father?'

'They did, right at the start. But he claimed he knew nothing, of course. And all the time Ben was safely hidden away.'

'Why didn't Ben let his mother know where he was? Surely he had a phone?' These days all kids had phones.

'Apparently the cottage has no Wi-Fi and no mobile coverage. And no TV. It's advertised as "off-grid". So Ben didn't even know anyone was looking for him. His father had told him it was all arranged with his mum – some quality father–son time riding bikes, going for walks, fishing, etc. Ben was left alone for the first day, while his father met with the police.'

'I can't believe he'd have been happy with no internet connection!'

'No, and that's how it all ended. His dad went off food shopping one day leaving Ben alone. Ben decided to walk to a nearby village. Once there he managed to find a mobile signal, then called his mum to say he was getting bored, and realised for the first time that he'd been reported missing.'

'Oh, my God.' I imagined Ben's mother receiving that phone call. The relief she must have felt!

'The police, of course, have been criticised. Surely they should have looked more deeply into the father. But he'd planned this for a while. He was making a point, he said, to his ex-wife. Saying he wanted more contact with his son, and he'd have that contact whether she agreed to it or not.'

'He's not going to get much contact with him from prison,' I said, wryly.

'No. I don't think he properly thought it all through, really. But

I am so glad the boy is safe and well, back home, reconnecting with his friends. He's not coming back to school this week though. He's going to wait until after the half-term holidays. Think the idea is he lies low, away from reporters, until the whole thing becomes yesterday's news. He and his mother are staying in a hotel somewhere for the moment.'

'Good idea.' I considered telling Ryan about the grisly discovery the developers had made at Four Oaks Farm. That hadn't yet made the news, so I decided to wait. 'I'll watch the news later this evening, see what they say.'

'Think I've told you it all anyway.'

'Thank you. I'm so pleased he's been found well.'

'So am I, Mum. Wouldn't want to lose a kid from any of my classes. I'd feel . . . guilty, even though—'

'—Even though it's not your fault and there was nothing you could do. I know.'

'Of course you do. I understand now, Mum, why what happened to you hit you so hard. I'm sorry I didn't really get it before.'

'It's all right. I think, unless you've been through it, it's difficult to understand.'

'You're all right now, though, aren't you, Mum?'

'I'm getting better and better. I'm not drinking, and I'm loving living here, despite—' I'd been about to say something about Pippa, '—worrying about you and Dad.'

'I'm sorry to be the cause of some of your worry.'

'It wasn't your fault. It was that boy's father's fault. Taking him away like that. It was reckless.'

'And yet, he did it for the love of his child.'

'Yes.'

'Anyway, how is Granddad?'

'Pretty good, considering. But every time I see him he looks a little smaller and frailer.'

'I'm glad Uncle David's come to see him.'

'So am I.'

'How are you getting on with your brother? Last I heard you had no time for him.'

'Actually . . . we kind of made up.' I told Ryan then about the time capsule and how David had turned up for its opening.

'Wow. You were proper 1970s kids, weren't you?'

'Well, yes!'

'I'm trying to imagine the kids I teach doing something like that. Actually, I might suggest they do it as a half-term activity. I reckon maybe two or three in the class might be inspired by the idea.'

'Passing it on. I like it.'

'I will suggest that they don't wait fifty years to dig it up again, though.'

'Well, we'd meant to go back to it after five years! But David and I had moved away by then so it just didn't happen.'

'Glad you've done it now, and it's helped you with David. Anyway, I'd better go. Thanks for the chat, Mum.'

'Thanks for calling. And it's such good news about Ben.'

As I put the phone down, I couldn't help but think, if only that had been the outcome for Pippa. I vaguely remembered her parents had been divorced, and her dad couldn't be found after she disappeared. But if that child in Four Oaks Farm did turn out to be Pippa, it couldn't possibly have been her father who killed her, could it?

That evening the news bulletins carried the good news story of Ben being found alive and well, but spent more time on the story of the discovery of a child's remains in a derelict farm. The early evening news did not name the child, but the late-night news confirmed it was Pippa Jenkins.

And even though I'd been pretty certain it would turn out to be her, the news threw me. Lynne was on the phone in minutes.

'Did you see? It's her, oh, God, after all these years they've found her!'

'Yes. Isn't it awful?'

'They searched the farm back then, though, didn't they? I remember your dad was out with the search parties.'

'I don't remember where they searched, but yes, Dad helped out.'

'And we were questioned. But Pippa never came to the farm with us, did she?'

'Not that I remember. It was either just us four, or sometimes Horace tagged along.'

Lynne gasped. 'Horace! Oh, yes. Oh, the poor man. This news will bring it all back for him. He was hounded back then, wasn't he? Everyone assumed that because he was different, he must be guilty of whatever had happened to her. And then he was locked up, deemed a danger to the public.'

'I'm worried that'll happen again. Because of where she was found, and it being near his home.'

'But it wasn't him,' Lynne said firmly. 'I would stake everything I own on that. He doesn't have – never had – the mental capacity to kill someone and hide a body. I never understood why the police went after him. In any case, he's a gentle soul. Always was. I've known him nearly all my life. Have you spoken to David since the news came out?'

'No. To be fair, you rang me within about five seconds of Pippa's identification being announced.'

'He's probably trying to ring you. I'll let you go. Hope you're OK, and it's not . . . you know . . . bringing back too many difficult feelings.'

'I'm fine. Bit shaken by the news, same as you, but I'm all right.'

We said goodbye. I found myself, once more, feeling that if there was a bottle of wine in the house I'd be opening it now. But there wasn't, and I wasn't going down that path again. *Don't be alone, Jo*, I told myself.

I called David.

'Seen the news?'

'Oh, my God, yes. I was going to call you, once I'd finished getting Dad settled.'

'Has he seen it?'

'Yes. He's sad about it of course. He said he always harboured a tiny hope that she'd eventually be found alive. Even now, when Pippa would have been in her fifties.' He sighed. 'But he didn't have the connection to Four Oaks that we had. You OK, Sis?'

'Yes. You?' Was I OK? I wasn't sure, but it definitely felt good having Lynne and David at the end of phone lines to talk things through.

'Yes. Feels . . . I dunno . . . a bit strange. Her being found there, where we played. I think we might even have been there on the day she was reported missing.'

'Were we?' That sent a shiver down my spine.

'Yeah. Think it was the day we got in through that window and looked around the house. Or maybe that was the day before. I'm not sure, to be honest. I'm trying to remember.'

'It was a long time ago.'

'I wish we'd seen something. Something concrete, that we could have reported, that might have resolved the mystery, even if it hadn't saved Pippa.'

'But you *did* report something,' I reminded him.

'And I wish I hadn't.' There was genuine remorse in his tone. 'I mean, though, if we'd seen something at the farm, that could have helped the police find her.'

'I don't think that would have done any of us any good. Not me, anyway. I'd have been traumatized.'

'I suppose. Well, now she's found, it's closure for her mother at last.'

'Yes, that's something.'

David caught his breath. 'Jo, this isn't going to . . . you know. Make you want to start drinking again? Because if so, if you feel you might, I'll come right over and be with you.'

'Thank you. But I'm all right, I think. I nearly relapsed over that thing with Ryan but I was able to stop myself. I'd been alone, I'd so nearly bought that wine, but in the end I was saved by a toddler playing peekaboo. And now I was saved by knowing that David, Lynne, Charlie and Ryan were all at the end of phone lines. All of them had my back. I wasn't alone anymore.

Chapter 26

Jo, 10 August 1976
Three days after.

The next day was horrible. Dad was out with the search parties, looking for Pippa. Mum kept me busy all day with stupid jobs – putting away shopping, dusting the house, watering houseplants, which were all suffering from the heat. Then worst of all she wanted me to get the Hoover out. In that heat! 'Well, how do you think I feel when I have to do it every week?' she said, when I complained. 'Just this once you can help me out. Every other day you've gone out with your friends and today you're helping me. Just do the downstairs. I'll ask David to do upstairs.'

At least my brother was having to do some as well. If he made one comment about it being 'girl's work' I'd thump him, I decided. In this age it was only right that boys did housework too. Not that Dad ever did anything. No wonder Mum got fed up with him.

I worked my way through the jobs and was finished by two o'clock. I was also hot and sweaty, but the water was off so there was no chance to have a wash.

'Thanks, love,' Mum said with a smile, as I put the Hoover

back in the hall cupboard. 'Those ice pops should be frozen by now. Would you like one to cool you down?'

'Yes, please!' I chose a green lime one and went to sit in the garden on a deckchair under the shade of our ash tree. Mum came to join me with a cup of tea. Why grown-ups liked hot drinks in hot weather I would never understand. Dad was still out, and David was in his bedroom, claiming to be working on his summer holiday English homework. I knew he wasn't. He was lying on his bed reading.

'Can we go out later?' I asked Mum.

'Who, you and me?' She looked pleased to be asked, but her smile vanished as I shook my head.

'I meant me and David.' I wanted to find Lynne and Rick and hear their thoughts on what might have happened to Pippa.

'Ah. No. I don't want you kids wandering the streets alone after . . . what's happened. Not until they've found that little girl.'

'But what if . . .' I couldn't say it. I couldn't say *what if they never find her?* An image flashed through my mind of her little face smiling at me as she ate her Freddo Frog. She was a sweet kid.

'We must hope for the best, Jo. Pray that she's found safe and well, and soon. And if the worst has happened, let's hope the police catch the man responsible.'

'What if it's not a man?'

'It's always a man. Or an . . . older boy. That Thompson boy must be about, what, nineteen by now? Almost a man.'

'More like a kid, though.'

'A child with the strength of an adult. He won't understand his own strength or how easily he can hurt someone a lot smaller than him. He probably doesn't even realise he's done anything wrong.'

'Mum, perhaps he *hasn't* done anything wrong.'

'You saw the way he was so upset when he heard people talking about searching for the child? He knows something, that's for certain. I just hope the police can get the truth out of him.'

I couldn't argue. Horace had certainly been acting strangely.

'Anyway. Enough of that. Look, I'll telephone Margaret and suggest Lynne comes round here for the afternoon, if you like?'

'Yeah!'

'And David could ask Rick to come too, if you want all of your little gang together. As long as you stay in the garden. Not in our lovely clean house.' She winked at me and I had to agree, I didn't want all the gang traipsing through the house I'd just spent hours dusting and hoovering.

But it was a good plan, and half an hour later we were all there, in the garden, sprawled on the parched grass under the ash tree and slurping ice pops.

'So, is she gone for good, do you think?' David asked the group.

I shrugged. 'Hope not.'

'Police are questioning everyone, I heard,' Rick said.

I sat up straighter. 'Yeah, they are. Me and Mum were questioned when we went shopping. They asked when I last saw Pippa, where she plays, and all that.'

Lynne nodded. 'They came round our house asking the same things. Her mum had told the police Pippa often came to ours, so we all had to answer the same things.'

'Police found her bike,' Rick told everyone.

'Really? Where?' This was news to me.

'In the New Forest. If you go up that track past the Thompson farm and continue on for a couple of miles there's some woodland. They found it dumped there. Her mum's confirmed it was hers. So the police are searching that area. Though it's too far for her to have cycled, so she must have been taken there by someone.' Rick rolled up the plastic sleeve from his finished ice pop and flicked it at David.

'They're saying her dad was seen around. They're looking for him,' Lynne said. 'He's disappeared.'

'Couldn't her mum just phone him and ask if he has Pippa?'

'They don't get on. Her mum never talks to him.'

'Not even to arrange when Pippa's going to stay with him?' I was confused. Surely if your parents split up you still got to see both of them? I thought you'd spend the week with your mum and the weekend with your dad. I'd tried not to think too hard about such arrangements, but when I had, lying awake in the middle of the night, too hot to sleep, that's what I'd imagined would happen.

'Don't think she often stayed with him,' Lynne replied. 'He moved away when they divorced. Mum said he found another woman and didn't care anymore about Pippa.'

'That's very sad.'

'I passed the rec on the way here,' Rick said. 'There was a load of people walking across it in a line, looking at every blade of grass for clues.'

'What sort of clues?' I asked.

'Might be a spot of blood, or something small like, I dunno, a hair toggle that belonged to Pippa.' David tried to sound knowledgeable, but I suspected he had no real idea either.

Rick nodded. 'Apparently the bell's missing off the bicycle, and the police want to find it because it might give a clue as to where she was snatched.'

Lynne and I stared at each other.

'What?' David said, catching the look.

'That bicycle bell I put in the time capsule – it was Pippa's,' I whispered. 'We should tell the police.'

'We'll get in trouble,' Lynne said. 'And it won't help them find her.'

'But it's pointless them looking for it,' I went on.

'They need to search anyway,' Rick reassured me.

'Yeah.' I nodded, though I thought I should own up about the bell. 'Me and Mum saw lots of people in the High Street, getting themselves organised to go searching. Dad went and helped. Some man was standing on a box putting everyone in pairs.' I remembered Horace then. 'And Horace was there. Looking all agitated, just like he did that day when we had to take him home.'

They all stared at me. 'Why's he so upset about it? He knows something, doesn't he?' David said.

'I think he does,' I said, carefully. 'But . . . I can't believe he would do anything to Pippa. He's a gentle person, really.'

'Yes, gentle but not very clever,' Lynne added.

'You're right, Jo. He wouldn't have harmed her. But maybe he knows who did. Maybe he saw something. That day, when we found him in the lane. That's the day she went missing, isn't it?' Rick was sitting up, excited, alert.

'Yes, he was upset, and what was he saying? "Bad thing. Bad thing." Maybe he was referring to Pippa and what he'd seen?'

'Or what he'd done. Her bike was found up his lane,' David said. I glared at him.

'I don't mean . . . anyway, we should find him. We should ask him what he saw,' David backtracked.

'I think it'd upset him even more.' I felt so sorry for Horace. I recalled the last view of him I'd had that morning, as he'd sat on the bench with his mum, her arms wrapped tightly around him as she tried to calm him down. 'I reckon if he knows anything he'll tell his family, and they can tell the police. Not really our job, is it?'

'But should we tell the police we saw him that day?' Lynne asked, frowning. I guessed she was thinking of the possible consequences if we said anything to the police – they might decide Horace was a suspect, and he wouldn't cope too well with that.

We all stared at each other, wondering what the right thing to do was. Tell the police what we'd seen that day – which of course meant confessing to trespassing on the old farm, as well as potentially pointing the finger at Horace, who was most likely completely innocent – or keep quiet, even though our information might be crucial to the police finding Pippa?

'No, we don't tell them.' Rick spoke with authority. 'For all we know, he was upset about something completely different that day. Maybe his mum had told him off. And now he's upset for the same reason everyone else is – because a small girl has gone missing. We know he can't be to blame for whatever's happened to her. Telling the police he was acting oddly that day would only make things bad for him.'

'What about the bell? I still think I should tell them,' I said.

Rick looked at me. 'Say nothing. Because if you start telling the police that, they'll ask more and more questions, and you might end up talking about Horace without meaning to.'

'And we *know* he's innocent,' Lynne concluded, her voice also carrying authority. She was always the most compassionate of the four of us.

'All right,' I said. 'I'll keep quiet.'

David nodded. 'Agreed. I wouldn't want them to know we've been hanging around that farm anyway. We were in enough trouble when Mr Willis spotted us that day. Don't want any more. We'd be kept at home for the rest of the summer!'

'Ugh. That'd drive me mad.' I spoke quietly, in case Mum was anywhere within earshot.

'So, we keep quiet. And we don't tell anyone we've played at the farm. I don't think we should go there again either.' Rick was once more becoming our leader, telling us what to do. For once David seemed to be accepting it. He nodded slowly.

'A pact, then. To never speak of this again.' David held out his hand.

The rest of us put ours on top of his. It all felt very serious and sombre. I was glad when a moment later Rick changed the mood and began telling jokes.

'Hey, did you hear the one about the wooden car with the wooden engine and the wooden wheels?'

'No?' Lynne played along.

'It wooden go. Geddit? Wooden, wouldn't!'

David let out a huge groan and gave Rick a play-punch on the arm. 'I've a better one. What's brown and sticky?'

'A stick!' the three of us yelled at once. We dissolved into fits of giggles, rolling around on the grass. It was good to defuse the moment, to be kids again and stop thinking about the awfulness of an eight-year-old who'd gone missing, right here in our village, practically from under our noses.

We had a good afternoon, in the end, even though it was not as exciting as the days out on our bikes. But that evening, when I was getting ready for bed, David tapped on my bedroom door. When he came in, he looked anxious.

'What is it, David?' I asked.

'Been thinking. About our pact not to speak of . . . it again.'

'She'll be found, I hope,' I said. I tried to speak in a reassuring tone.

'It's Horace. I can't get him out of my mind. The way he was when we saw him in the lane.' I stayed quiet, watching him carefully. He screwed up his face trying to find the right way to say whatever it was he needed to get out. 'He knows something. He either saw something or did something.'

'Just coincidence that he was upset the same day,' I said. It was what we'd decided.

But David shook his head. 'I don't think it was. I want to . . . talk to the police. Tell them I saw him and how he was behaving. And let them decide whether that's important or not.'

'David, you can't! We decided!'

'I won't mention the rest of you. I'll just say I was cycling past on my own when I saw him.'

'David, no!' I tried to say 'no' in the same way Mum or Dad did when they really meant it. The tone of voice that always stopped us in our tracks. But it came out shrill.

'I've got to. If I don't speak up and it turns out it was him, I could never live with myself.'

'But it wasn't him!'

'Smudge, we don't know that for sure.'

'It just doesn't feel right.'

'Let the police decide. I've made up my mind, I'm going to . . .'
'Break our pact.'
He nodded, looking close to tears, and left the room.
I was left alone, facing a sleepless night. I wavered between thinking that maybe David was right and then believing there was no way Horace could have harmed anyone. Somehow, I needed to talk David out of his plan. He was right that we should let the police decide. We needed to let them do their job and keep our noses out of it.

Chapter 27

Jo, 2024

'Will you come with me? To see Dad, and to prepare him, for when the police talk to him?' Charlie was on the phone the next morning, sounding distressed.

'Of course I'll come, if you want me to,' I replied. 'But I'm not sure how I can help.'

'He liked you last time. And he's . . . sometimes better if there's someone else there besides me. It kind of opens him up a little.'

'Well then, yes. When do you want to go?'

'As soon as possible. The police are asking when they can see him. But when's convenient for you?'

'Charlie, I work from home, flexible hours. I can take time off whenever I like.'

'Thank you. Can I pick you up in half an hour?'

'I'll be ready.'

Charlie seemed distracted as we drove the short distance to the care home. I wasn't surprised. He had a lot on his mind.

A member of staff signed us in at the entrance. 'He's not so good today,' she said. 'Got another chest infection, the doctor says.'

'Oh, dear. Another round of antibiotics, then?' Charlie asked.

'Yes. That'll soon clear it up.' She gave us both a reassuring smile.

'Has he seen the news recently?' Charlie asked.

'No. He tends to get upset over news stories. Thinks any disaster anywhere in the world will affect him personally. So we usually leave the TV on a nature channel. He seems to like that.'

'OK. Thanks. We'll go and see him now.'

Charlie led the way to Crispin's room, where we found him sitting in the same place as he'd been the first time I visited. He looked a little greyer and was coughing now and again into a handkerchief he was clutching.

'Hey, Dad,' Charlie said, crossing the room to kiss his father on the cheek. 'Sorry to hear you're not so well.'

'Only a cold, son. Be gone in no time.'

'Good, I hope so. Look, Jo's come with me to see you again.'

Crispin refocused on me and smiled. 'Why he calls you Jo I'll never know. My Barbara.'

'Hello, Crispin.' I sat beside him and let him take my hand. 'Good to see you again.'

'Lovely girl. You light up the room, you do.'

'Dad, listen,' Charlie said. 'There's something very important I need to tell you.'

The old man turned his gaze to his son and looked as though he was making an effort to concentrate. Charlie seemed encouraged by this and leaned forward. 'It's about Four Oaks Farm.'

'Four Oaks,' repeated Crispin. 'I grew up there.' He turned his face away and coughed into his handkerchief in one hand, while keeping hold of my hand with the other.

'Yes, you did. But then it sat empty for years after Granny and Granddad died, didn't it?'

'I'll sell it one day.' Crispin looked at me. 'It's worth a bit, you know.'

Charlie glanced at me. I noticed the warning in his eyes to

say nothing about the fact the farm had already been sold. But I'd already decided to keep quiet. This was Charlie's conversation to have with his dad. I was just there to . . . well, I didn't really know. To hold Crispin's hand and support Charlie, because he'd asked me to.

'Yes, Dad. Anyway, in the farm, they've found something.'

'In the farm?'

'Yes. They've found the remains of a child.'

'Children? Children were always playing in the farm. Always breaking in and running round, making a mess of everything. Damned children.'

I kept my face straight and somehow managed not to look at Charlie as Crispin went on his rant.

'No, Dad. Not those children. A dead child. They think she was in the cellar.'

'In the cellar? There's nothing in the cellar, maybe just a sack. Nothing there.'

'The thing is, Dad, the police might want to talk to you.'

'About the speeding?' He coughed again. 'Wasn't me driving. I told them that. Told them it was Barbara, not me. So she got the points, see.' He turned to me. 'I need to drive for my business, see, so you got the points and I didn't.' He squeezed my hand. 'You always had my back, didn't you, Barbara?'

'I tried to, Crispin,' I replied, and he smiled fondly at me.

'It's not about your driving, Dad. The police want to talk to you about Four Oaks Farm.'

'Nothing in the cellar,' Crispin said again. I noticed his face was reddening and he was beginning to fidget. Something was bothering him.

Something was bothering me too, from his ramblings. Something niggled at the back of my mind – a memory trying to surface from fifty years ago. I couldn't put my finger on it. I pulled my hand out from under his. Crispin moaned softly, and clutched at the blanket that was over his knees, twisting it on his lap.

'It's all right, Dad.' Charlie turned to me. 'We probably better leave. When he gets like this it only gets worse if people stay.'

'Oh, dear. Should I go and let you sit with him a bit longer? I can wait in the reception area.'

'Would you? Just two minutes.'

'No problem. It's been nice to see you again, Mr Willis, but I must go now.' I stood up.

'Who are you?' Crispin stared up at me uncomprehending. 'You aren't my Barbara, are you?'

I looked at Charlie who nodded for me to leave. As I left the room the old man called out once more. 'Who are you? Who is she? Don't believe anything she tells you!' I could hear Charlie trying to quieten him down, telling him I was a friend and a good person.

The whole episode had unsettled me. Not because of Crispin's dementia and being incoherent, not because he'd suddenly switched from being sweet and harmless to shouting at me, but because of that niggle. Something he'd said had triggered a memory. That day we went inside the house. No, not then. The next day. When we didn't go in but looked through the window. A sack. By the entrance to the cellar. No, it was the previous day – the sack was there when we went inside. The next day, when we looked in, it had gone.

Crispin had mentioned a sack. And he'd been insistent there was nothing in the cellar.

As I made my way back to the reception area, I felt myself break out in a cold sweat. I couldn't help but feel rising suspicion. What to *do*? I had no idea. But for now, at least, I decided to say nothing to Charlie. What could I say? Our relationship was barely beginning. If I said anything, it'd ruin what we had. But if I was right, then surely I had a duty to say something?

Charlie was out in two minutes, as he'd said. 'Well. Not sure he understood anything I was trying to tell him, but I've had a go. I'm sorry he turned so unpleasant at the end. He's very unpredictable – you never know what'll trigger him.' He sighed and shook his head sadly. 'I'll drop you off at home, then I need to speak to the police again.'

'OK.' I followed him out to the car. 'What do you need to talk to the police about?' Was it possible Charlie had suspicions too?

'I said I'd tell them what form Dad was in, and whether I thought they'd get any sense from him. I think the answer's no.' He gave a wry smile. 'Poor old Dad. Horrible to see a once proud, articulate, intelligent man reduced so much.'

'Yes.'

'Not sure how I kept a straight face when he ranted about children breaking into the farm.' He grinned at me. 'I don't think he was referring to just your lot, though. I suspect children were always playing there, all through the years.' Then the grin suddenly fell from his face. 'And now we know that all along Pippa's body was hidden there. Oh, God. Not funny.'

'No.' Another one-word answer from me, but there was nothing I could say. I needed to process what I'd heard.

We drove back to my house largely in silence, and Charlie declined the offer of a coffee. 'No, I need to go to the police station and get that over and done with. Thanks, anyway. And thanks for coming with me. I really appreciate it, and I'm sorry he . . . I'll be in touch soon. Time we had another proper date, eh?'

'Yes. I'd like that. See you soon.'

He kissed my cheek then was gone, leaving me alone with my terrible thoughts. I was glad that I had a dinner invitation to Dad's that evening. Spending time with Dad and David would take my mind off it.

By the time I arrived at Dad's I'd decided to talk things through with him and David. David might have better memories of exactly what we'd seen. And Dad, though physically frail, was intellectually as sharp as ever. He'd taken part in the searches for Pippa, and I knew he remembered every detail of that terrible time.

David answered the door. 'Hey, Sis. Glad you could come. God, the news about little Pippa Jenkins, eh?'

'Terrible. Does Dad know?'

'Yes, we've discussed it.'

'Good. Because I've more to say on it. Something I want to ask you about. But it can wait until after dinner.'

'Good, because I've made your favourite.'

I grinned, knowing he'd have made spaghetti bolognese, my favourite meal when I was in my teens, just as it had been Ryan's. As far as David was concerned, I was still that kid. And I suppose I was, just with a few more layers built over the top. Peel them away and you'd find the same young Jo at my core.

It was indeed a bolognese sauce, though with penne pasta, and baked in the oven with a cheesy topping. It was absolutely scrummy, and even Dad ate every morsel of his portion, I was pleased to see. He needed feeding up.

'Thank you, David. That was a splendid meal,' Dad said, as he put down his cutlery neatly on his plate.

'You're very welcome. Jo, you get to clear up.'

'No problem, of course I will.' Dad had a dishwasher, so it took no time to clear the table and load it, then I returned to the dining table where the men were still drinking wine. I had a glass of sparkling water.

'So,' David said, 'you wanted to talk about Four Oaks Farm.'

'Yes. So, a while ago I met a man in a coffee shop . . .'

'Oh, yes?' David waggled his eyebrows suggestively at me. I glared at him. This was a serious conversation.

'And it was Charlie Willis. The son of Crispin Willis, who owned Four Oaks Farm. You remember them?'

'I do. Didn't Crispin Willis once—' David began, with a glance at Dad. It was as though we were those kids again, scared we'd be told off if our parent found out what had happened.

'Shout at us for playing in the farmyard? Yes.'

Dad tutted and shook his head but looked more amused than annoyed.

'Anyway, Crispin Willis now has dementia and is in a care home. Charlie has power of attorney, and he decided to sell the farm to developers to help pay Crispin's care costs.'

'Ah. That makes sense,' Dad said. 'Wonder why Crispin never sold it himself. All those years it stood gradually decaying.'

'So, as you know, they found the body of Pippa Jenkins at last, when they were demolishing the farmhouse. She'd probably been hidden in the cellar.'

David was frowning. 'I don't remember them saying that detail on the news.'

'No, I don't think they did. Charlie told me.'

'I've been trying to piece together in my mind exactly which days we were there. I seem to remember we went inside the house around that time, didn't we?' David was still frowning, trying to remember.

'Yes. A window was open and we climbed in. Next day the window was closed, but we looked in, I think.'

'That's right.'

'David, when we went in, was there a sack, tied up at the top, just dumped, by the entrance to the cellar? Can you remember?'

'We didn't go in the cellar. You girls were too frightened.'

Dad was looking from one to the other of us as we spoke.

'No, we didn't go down. I think it might have been padlocked anyway. But do you remember a sack?'

David closed his eyes, fingertips to his temple, in an effort to remember. 'There was something there. Meant that we couldn't have got the door open without moving it. And then . . .' He opened his eyes and stared at me, 'when we were back the next day and looked in through the window, that sack wasn't there. And that was the day—'

'—that Pippa was reported missing.' I finished for him.

Dad leaned forward in his seat. 'Kids, are you saying what I think you're saying?'

'That sack . . . Oh, God, that might have been her!' David clapped a hand to his mouth, horrified by the thought.

'Yes. And we went right past her.'

'She'd already have been dead by then. Nothing we could have done, but God, it turns your stomach, doesn't it? Are they any closer to finding who did it?'

'That's the other thing.' I took a gulp of my water and then a deep breath before continuing. 'Charlie took me to see his dad this morning, in the care home. He wanted to warn his dad that the police wanted to talk to him. And . . . Crispin's got severe dementia. Gets very confused at times. Makes little sense. But when Charlie mentioned that a child's remains had been found at the farm Crispin said something about a sack, then kept repeating that there was nothing in the cellar.'

'So, you suspect . . .?' Dad said, looking at me intently.

'That Crispin Willis was the killer. Yes.' There was silence. I looked from Dad to David. Both were open-mouthed.

'Willis helped search,' Dad said at last. 'He was on the same team as me.'

'At the farm?'

'We searched part of the village first. Then later our group went to that farm. Made sense for Willis to help search there, he said, because he had keys to open it up.' Dad screwed up his face in an effort to remember. 'There were four of us in that team. Two went into the barns, and Willis and I went into the house.'

'Did you check the cellar?'

Dad put the heel of his hand to his forehead. 'Crispin sent me to search the upstairs rooms. He did the downstairs. I *think* he did the cellars as well.'

There was a moment's silence again as we all processed this.

'Good God,' Dad said. 'He seemed as keen to help look for the little girl as the rest of us.'

'To avert suspicion,' David said.

Dad shook his head slowly from side to side. 'If I'd checked more thoroughly; if I'd insisted on searching the whole house myself . . . I might have . . .'

David put his hand on Dad's shoulder. 'Dad, there was no reason to check any particular place more than any other. There was no reason to think she'd be at Four Oaks.'

'Still, I can't help but feel a bit guilty. If only I'd done more . . .'

Oh, God, I knew that feeling. An image of Stephanie's body came to the forefront of my mind. Her corpse, still warm, the crushed undergrowth beneath her, her hair across her face. Goldie sniffing at her and whining plaintively. If only I'd been in the woods at my usual time. If only. I got up and went to stand behind Dad, wrapping my arms around him. 'It's not your fault, Dad. Not your fault.' Or mine, I silently added.

'No, you're right,' he said. 'I mustn't start thinking like that. Thank you, both of you.'

Another memory floated up. 'Dad, around that time I remember you going out some evenings and being kind of cagey about where you'd been?'

'Probably at the library,' he replied. 'Researching how one went about getting a divorce.' He shrugged and smiled sheepishly up at me. 'Did a lot of that, during that last summer.'

I smiled back at him, and squeezed him tightly, kissing his cheek. It must have been a tough period for him and Mum, just as it was for David and me.

'So, the question is,' I said, as I returned to my chair, 'what do I do? Do I go to the police and tell them what Crispin said, and about seeing that sack? Do I talk to Charlie?'

'Hmm.' David rubbed his chin.

Dad coughed. 'I think you must talk to Charlie first. It'll be difficult, I know.'

'It'll be a horrible conversation to have. And then . . . what then? Crispin Willis is so far gone with dementia. They won't be able to try him in court.'

'But there may be some evidence. You know, some DNA or something. The police might well want to swab Crispin anyway. And Pippa Jenkins' family deserves to know the truth.' Dad's tone was forceful, and I was reminded of the man he used to be, the head of the family, the one we all looked to for guidance.

'You're right, Dad. I'll find a way to talk to him. I'm wondering if all Crispin's mutterings about there being "nothing in the cellar" might have made Charlie suspicious anyway. He barely said a word as he drove me home.'

'Charlie will be in denial. No one would want to think their parent might be a killer,' David said.

'I know. All right. I'll find a gentle way to bring up the topic.' I gulped down the rest of my water, wishing it was wine, wishing I could drown it all out. David must have guessed how I was feeling. He picked up the near-empty bottle of wine and took it to the kitchen. Out of my sight, out of my reach, just in case. I smiled at him gratefully.

'I am glad they found her,' Dad was saying. 'She won't end up entombed in concrete under a housing estate. She can be properly and respectfully buried now. Put to rest, the poor thing.'

'I'm glad of that too.'

I recalled the last time I'd seen her, the day we'd played skipping games in the street together, and I'd bought her a chocolate Freddo Frog. She'd been so grateful. I felt a wave of regret, again, that we hadn't been kinder to her.

'It's not our fault, Jo.' David once more seemed to be reading my mind. 'Nothing we could have done.'

'What scares me,' Dad put in, 'is that you kids were at the farm, right when Willis was in the process of hiding the sack. He might have been there that day.'

'He wasn't. No car, no sign of anyone. We wouldn't have gone in if there was.'

'Except the open window could have been a sign someone was there? The one you say you climbed through?'

'Yes.' Dad had a point. But it didn't bear thinking about too deeply. Had we been in danger fifty years ago? There were four of us. We'd have fought him off.

We talked around the subject a little more, until Dad began looking tired. David gave me a meaningful look. I glanced at my watch. 'Oh, is that the time? I should probably get going. Need me to do anything first?'

'No, thanks, Smudge. I've got this.' David stood up to see me out. I kissed Dad and picked up my bag.

'Good luck, Jo,' Dad said, as I left.

At the door David hugged me goodbye. 'You were right all along. It wasn't Horace. Which means it's even more important that I go and apologise to him.'

Chapter 28

Jo, 14 August 1976
Seven days after.

Over the next few days I did something I wasn't much in the habit of doing. I prayed. I pleaded with God to help the police find Pippa alive and well, and wondering what all the fuss was about. I bargained with God to make it happen soon. If only Pippa would turn up, I promised I'd study hard when school restarted, and I'd help Mum around the house every week. I pictured her having been taken on a lovely surprise holiday to the seaside by her dad. Her being missing was put down to a lack of communication between her parents. That had to be the most obvious answer to the mystery.

But day after day passed and there was no news. The local people who'd stepped forward to form search parties began to give up when all the nearby places had been searched. 'She could be anywhere,' Dad said, after he came back from an afternoon searching an area of woodland outside the village. 'She could have been taken by car to another part of the country.'

I kept wondering if they'd search the old farm. There was no reason to think she'd ever been there, though. She'd never been there with us, and it was quite a way out of the village. Too far for a little girl to wander by herself. I couldn't ask Dad, though. He'd wonder why I was so interested in that old place, and we'd get in trouble again.

I asked David one evening whether he'd heard of that area being searched. He nodded. 'Yeah, I think it was. Think it might even have been one of the places Dad's team searched. She's not there.'

His words brought me some relief. I didn't know why but I still had a vague feeling of unease about it all. As though we had something to do with Pippa's disappearance, as though there was something we might have done to prevent it, or to help the police find her. They were still looking for her bicycle bell, and that made me guilty that they were wasting their time and it was all our fault. More than once, I pictured everything we'd done between coming home from our camping trip to hearing that Pippa was missing. But other than Horace acting strangely there was nothing I could remember that was in any way suspicious. At least David hadn't followed up on his plan to tell the police about Horace's behaviour that day.

We were still not allowed to go off on our bikes, and I was beginning to wonder what would happen if Pippa was never found. It was a horrible thought, but what if that came true? Would we never be allowed to go out alone again? Even in September when the new term started? No going round each other's houses after school without an adult chaperone?

I kept my promise to God and offered to help Mum with the shopping again. She looked surprised but quickly agreed. I didn't need to tell her I'd offered because I thought it might help Pippa be found, or because I was simply bored.

It was a hot but not sunny day. There were some clouds in the sky, but it was the type of cloud that just acted as a blanket, making the air feel sticky and stuffy. Worse, really, than the relentless sun. Mum and I were both pretty sweaty by the time we reached the High Street.

We lingered around the freezers in the Spar supermarket, even though we weren't buying any frozen food. I wished for the hundredth time we had a chest freezer in the garage like Lynne's family had and could fill it with ice creams. Or just open it now and again and let the cool air rush out and envelop me. Mum kept up a running commentary on all the frozen food that was available, as though she was checking it out, and I wondered if perhaps she was going to suggest to Dad that we bought a freezer.

When we headed back out into the street there was, once again, a bit of a crowd gathered outside the newsagents. But unlike the last time when the crowd had a sense of urgency, this crowd seemed hostile. As we passed, I realised Horace was there, sitting on a bench with his head bowed and his hands flapping. The crowd around him was jeering, taunting him, accusing him of having done away with little Pippa.

'Was you, wasn't it?' one man said, poking a finger at Horace's chest. 'C'mon. Own up, be a man!'

'He can't. He's not a man, he's a moron,' another man said.

'Where's his mum?' I asked.

'How should I know?' Mum replied. Her tone was harsh. I thought she was cross at the crowd for being abusive towards Horace, but when I glanced at her I saw her face was twisted and ugly. She stepped towards the group of people, who were now chanting, 'Lock him up! Lock him up!' To my horror, she joined in with the chant.

Horace was rocking back and forward on the bench, his hands over his ears. But there was no way he'd be able to block the sound of the angry mob. Yes, that's what they'd become, my mum among them – a mob.

Suddenly he got to his feet, pushed through the crowd, fending off those who tried to grab at him. I stood aside to give him space, and he ran, sprinting up the street. Some of the men ran after him, waving their fists in the air, and I feared what would happen if they caught him. I grabbed Mum's arm.

'It's not fair! He didn't do anything!'

'We don't know that, Jo. He might have. He's dangerous.'

As she spoke, I saw Horace's mum, emerging at last from a shop further down the road. As she hurried up towards the remnants of the crowd one or two people began shouting at her too. Telling her she should keep her son locked up so he couldn't harm anyone else, saying she'd brought up a murderer.

'Where is he? What've you done to him? My poor boy!' she was saying.

'He went up there,' I said, pointing up the street.

Mum tried to shush me, pulling my arm down, but Mrs Thompson had heard and set off quickly the way I'd pointed.

'Should someone call the police?' I asked Mum.

'What for?'

'To make sure Horace is safe,' I replied.

'Nothing to do with us. Come on. We're finished here.' She grabbed my arm and pulled me away, back in the direction of our home.

I took a final glance up the street. Mrs Thompson was still hurrying after Horace. But it looked like the men who'd begun chasing him had quickly given up and were walking back down the road. I was glad of that at least.

It was awful. Poor Horace. What I'd seen made me even more sure that we shouldn't say anything about Horace's behaviour on the day Pippa had gone missing. I resolved to talk to David again, to make sure he wasn't going to do that. People were accusing Horace of being a murderer without even the slightest bit of evidence. Just because he was different.

Mum and Dad were talking about Horace over teatime that day.

'We searched everywhere,' Dad said, shaking his head sadly. 'What happened to her I have no idea. I thought we'd find her in a ditch or something.'

'Ssh, not in front of the children,' Mum hissed at him.

'They're old enough. And it's not as if we can shield them from what's going on. It's been on the local news every day, on the radio, in the papers.'

He was right. There'd been endless speculation about what had happened on every news outlet. Some papers had mentioned Horace but not all.

'I don't think the police believe it's Horace,' Dad said.

Mum glared at him. 'What makes you think that?'

'I heard the police spoke to Horace's mother and that they've ruled him out. Apparently, they were happy he'd had nothing to do with it.'

'Why don't they talk to him directly?' I said, but no one seemed to hear. David, I noticed, was keeping his head down, focusing intently on what he was eating. I hadn't had chance to talk to him yet.

'There's rumours his family left their home this afternoon,' Mum said. 'They've taken him away somewhere, Mrs Lewis told me. That's an indication he's got something to hide and the family are covering for him, in my book.' She pursed her lips together and nodded to underline her point.

'Maybe they took him away so he doesn't get chased up the street by people calling him a murderer,' I said, surprising myself by how passionately I felt about it. Mum may not have run up the street after him, but she'd joined in with the chants of 'lock him up', hadn't she?

'Maybe he *is* a murderer, Jo. We don't know, do we?' But Mum sounded less sure of herself. I wondered if she was feeling ashamed that she'd briefly been part of that ugly mob. 'Anyway. That's quite enough talk of it all.'

'Well, no, it isn't,' Dad said, glaring at Mum. 'I'm interested to hear the lad's family have taken him away. I wonder where?'

'What's it matter? I suppose they want some peace and quiet. And maybe they want to coach him to get his story straight.'

'Mary, if the police don't think he did it perhaps there's no story to get straight?'

'Well, if it's not that lad, then who did it? The little girl didn't just vanish into thin air, now, did she?' Mum sounded defiant, and I recognised the old signs of a pointless argument brewing between the two of them.

'Perhaps we'll never know.'

'Dad, when can we start going out on our bikes again?' David asked.

'I said, not until they've found whoever did it, and if it's not that Thompson lad then . . .' Mum jumped in, but Dad held up a hand to cut her off.

'We can't keep the kids at home all summer, Mary. As long as they're together, or with their friends, they'll be safe enough.'

'Safe enough, Alan? Safe *enough*? I want them to be completely safe, not just safe enough! I'm not sure I want—'

Dad cut her off again. 'Mary, they're thirteen and eleven. They're—'

'Twelve.' I wasn't letting him knock a year off my age. And David was nearer fourteen.

'Twelve. Whatever.' He waved a dismissive hand in my direction. 'They're old enough, Mary. What if the police never find the child, never find out what happened to her? You want us to keep our kids in for the rest of their lives?'

'They haven't been in all day. Jo was out with me shopping this morning.'

'You know what I mean, woman. Don't be so pedantic. We have to let them grow up. And that means letting them go out and about with their friends.'

'With a killer on the loose?'

'We don't know that!' Dad slapped his hands on the table and stood up. 'I've had enough of this argument. I'll be in the garage, if anyone needs me. Need to look at fixing that . . .'

Whatever it was he was going to fix was lost in the sound of the kitchen door banging on his way out.

'Oh. Well, I'd best clear up, then,' Mum said, getting to her feet with a sigh.

I felt a pang of pity for her. 'I'll help.'

'Thank you, love.' She gave me a small smile. David was already beginning to stack the dirty plates. We cleared up in silence, the three of us, each lost in our own thoughts. Selfish though it seemed, my mind was more on my parents' relationship than Pippa's fate. I wondered if David and I would end up taking sides, and if so would we take Mum's side over Dad's? I'd always thought Mum was more often the one picking the fights but maybe that was unfair. They were each as bad as the other. But only with each other – they were both good, fair, loving parents towards David and me. They just seemed to bring out the worst in each other. And that was the elephant in the room, the big issue that none of us ever spoke about. David and I had never talked about what might happen if they split up. I didn't even allow myself to dwell on the thought too often.

Because if I did, I'd end up sobbing.

When we'd finished the washing-up and all the dishes had been dried and put away, I went up to my room. At least if I started crying there, on my own, no one else needed to know. David followed Mum into the lounge. I heard snippets of an urgent conversation between them drifting up the stairs. Only odd words, but enough to get the gist of what they were talking about.

Horace. Upset. That day, yes. I'm sure. He might have . . . Police. I want . . . You need . . . Parent. Tomorrow.

I lay down on my bed and stared at the ceiling. So he'd told Mum. And he was going to break our pact and go to the police after all.

I hated my brother right then. He was wrong, I was sure of it. But I felt utterly powerless to do anything about it.

Chapter 29

Jo, 2024

I decided to discuss the situation with Lynne before talking to Charlie. Maybe I was simply putting it off, but I felt I needed more input. From someone else who'd been there, back in 1976. It was pretty late when I got home from dinner at Dad's, but not too late to send a message. *Are you still up? Can I give you a call, to talk something through?*

The answer came immediately – Lynne called me. 'What's up, Jo? Of course I'm always here for you, day or night. It's the news about Pippa, isn't it? Has it upset you?'

'No, well, I mean, yes. It's awful. And we were there, right around the time she went missing.'

'Yes. I've been trying to remember; I was going to call you tomorrow about it. Did we go in the house before or after she disappeared?'

'Before. I mean, before we knew she'd gone. But listen . . .' I updated her quickly on what I'd heard from Crispin Willis, and my suspicions.

'Oh, my God, Jo. I get why you're suspicious. I really do. But

I don't remember any sack. I can barely remember going in the house, but I know we did – you and David mentioned it the other day. God, that seems so long ago. When the farm was still just the innocent place where we liked to play. Not the graveyard of a poor little girl, one whom we knew. Makes me shudder.'

'Me too. I was with Dad and David earlier tonight, and I was asking them what they thought I should do about my suspicions. They think, and I guess I do too, that I should talk to Charlie first. That maybe he'll also have suspicions, what with his dad going on about there being "nothing in the cellar". But . . .'

'But you think it'll ruin any chances you have with him?'

'It will, won't it? It'll be the end. Before it's even got going.'

'It might not. Anyway, if you don't say anything, and he doesn't say anything, and . . . well, it'll hang between you and ruin any relationship you might have regardless.'

'You're right. I couldn't live with myself if I said nothing, and they never found Pippa's killer . . . I mean, it might not be anything to do with Crispin but the police need to look into it, don't they?'

'Of course they do. But I agree with your dad and David. Talk to Charlie first. Tell him about what you remember seeing. Let him put two and two together. It'll be hard, I know, but you have to do it.'

'I know, I do. First thing tomorrow I'll call him.' It had been fifty years. Another day wouldn't make any difference.

'Good luck. Here for you after, if you need me.'

'Thanks.'

It'd be a restless night, I thought, as I hung up. I knew I'd spend all night tossing and turning, and rehearsing what I was going to say to Charlie.

In the morning, I made myself a cup of tea as I watched the clock tick on towards eight o'clock, the hour I'd decided would be a reasonable time to call Charlie. But just before eight, my doorbell rang. I was still wearing my pyjamas and dressing gown, with bed hair completing the look, so I smoothed my hair as best I could and tightened my dressing gown belt as I answered the door. I half expected it to be Lynne, or David, or the postman, but it was Charlie himself. And he looked anguished. Worse than when he'd turned up here to tell me about the police finding Pippa's remains.

'Jo, sorry, I know it's early but . . .' He ran his hands through his hair, apparently unable to complete the sentence.

'Come in. Tea or coffee?' I pushed him through to the kitchen and put the kettle on.

'Tea. Yeah, um, tea. Thank you.' He sat down and put his head in his hands.

I said nothing as I busied myself making him the drink. He needed time, I could see. And so did I. I'd prepared myself to talk to him, to tell him about the sack, and remind him of what his father had said yesterday – how could it be only yesterday! But I'd expected to be calling him, to be having this most awkward of conversations over the telephone, at a distance. Yet here he was.

As I put the tea in front of him, retrieved my own part-drunk cup and sat opposite him, he looked up at me. I was horrified to see tears in his eyes, and reached across to him. 'Charlie?'

He took a long, shuddering breath. 'Yesterday, after I dropped you off, the police went to see Dad. They weren't with him long, but they took a DNA sample from him. And they've fast-tracked processing it.'

I still said nothing, watching his face closely.

'When he went on about "nothing in the cellar", he was so adamant about it, I began wondering. Why was he saying that? No one had said anything to him about Pippa's remains being found in the cellar. But I couldn't . . . even begin to wonder if . . . And then half an hour ago, the police called me. They said Dad's now the prime suspect in Pippa's death.'

'Oh, my God.' Even though I suspected him myself, hearing that the police thought so too was shocking.

'Pippa's remains were found in a sack. There was a bloodstain on it, and it wasn't her blood. They managed to extract some DNA from it, and it was Dad's.'

'Your dad muttered something about a sack yesterday,' I said, quietly.

'Did he?'

'Yes. And it struck me because . . .'

'Because?'

'We saw a sack. Beside the entrance to the cellar. That day we'd got into the house and had a look around.'

'That was her. You were there, when she was there.' He seemed as shocked by this as David and I had been when we'd worked it out.

'Yes.'

'I first thought there could be an explanation for the blood on the sack. The killer might have found it in the house, and Dad's blood could have been on it from years before. But then they said there was the same blood on the remains of Pippa's clothing.' Charlie put his head in his hands. 'My dad's a child-killer.'

All I could do was reach for him again, take his hand, hold it, while he sobbed. Grieving for the father he'd thought he had, trying and failing to come to terms with the father he now knew he had – a man who'd done such a terrible thing to such a young child, and got away with it for fifty years.

He stayed for a while, drinking a few cups of tea, talking in circles as he tried and failed to come up with some other explanation, some way in which he could still believe his father innocent of such a horrendous crime. Trying to imagine a scenario where the whole thing was a tragic accident, but then failing to work out why his father wouldn't have reported it. I stayed at his side, supporting, but unable to offer anything concrete that could make it all go away. As we sat there, processing it all, I felt the fledgling bond between us deepen. Sharing something like this could either push people apart or bring them closer together. With us, it seemed to be having the latter effect.

At last Charlie declined another tea and said he needed to go. 'I should see Dad, and the police, and . . . I don't know. I don't know what one does in these situations. I don't know how to cope, how to move forward.' He looked at me as though I could tell him what to do.

'You just take it one day, one hour, one minute at a time. Be kind to yourself. And remember, I am always here for you.'

'Thank you, Jo.' His eyes showed my support meant a lot to him.

He left then, promising to keep me informed of any developments by text. He sent a few, as the day wore on. I couldn't concentrate on work and spent half the day playing mindless games on my phone.

That night was another sleepless one, even though I knew there was nothing more I could do in all this, beyond being there for Charlie.

The following morning, I needed a few things from the Marsh Farm shop. The news about Crispin's DNA being found on Pippa had not yet been released. I'd heard from Charlie that the police were waiting until one of Crispin's more lucid days before attempting to question him. They were taking it slowly, but the waiting was agonising for Charlie.

At the shop, Natasha was busy putting out more vegetables, loading the baskets and trays with potatoes, onions and late season parsnips. Her mouth was set in a thin line, as if she was furious with someone or something.

'Hello, Natasha. How are you?' I said, as I entered and picked up a basket.

'Oh, you know. It's been a tough few days. Since the news about . . .' She waved a hand vaguely.

'Yes. It's awful. How is your brother?'

'I've been trying to hide the news from him. It's brought it all back – we had a terrible time, you know, after Pippa first disappeared. Everyone thought Horace must have done it, because he was *different*.' She spat out the last word.

'I remember.' I could still picture how that crowd of people in the village had taunted him and run after him. Hadn't my own mother even joined in with it?

'He spent ten years locked away, deemed a danger to society, even though there was no proof he'd done anything. And you know, we had a couple of old folk in here yesterday. They saw Horace sweeping the floor, and I swear I heard them muttering that they'd always known who did it, and it was awful he wasn't still locked up.'

I was shocked. 'Are you sure they were referring to Horace?'

'Well, they kept looking over at him, so I think they must have been. Honestly, I was *this* close.' She held her hand up, thumb and forefinger half an inch apart. 'From refusing to serve them and throwing them out. But then I'd have to explain it all to Horace, and God knows he doesn't need to—' She broke off and glanced behind me.

I followed her gaze. There was Horace, carrying a box of cabbages through to the shop. He didn't look as though he'd heard what we were talking about.

'Ah, thank you, Horace. Just put it there, will you?' Natasha said with a bright smile. 'Then could you take away these empty bags for me?'

'Yes, I can do all that,' Horace replied, looking pleased to have more jobs to do. He picked up the bags while I began choosing some vegetables and fruit to go in my basket. 'They found her, didn't they?' he said to me.

'Found who?'

'The little girl. I seen it on the news. Tash thinks I don't watch, but I do, sometimes.' He nodded towards his sister who'd returned to the till.

'Yes, they did find her.' I felt there was no point lying or trying to hide it from him.

'They found her in the farm. I knew she were in the farm. I seen him. He didn't think I seen him, but I did.'

'Saw who, Horace?'

He became agitated in that manner I remembered from all those years ago. 'I call him the shouty man. He shouted at you once, didn't he? I seen that too.'

'Horace, what's wrong?' Natasha had returned to the veg section. 'What's wrong, honey?' She glanced at me, accusation in her eyes.

'Natasha, he says he saw the news,' I said. I didn't want her to think I'd upset him. Somehow Horace remembered me from all those years ago and associated me with Pippa and the farm, and all that had happened there. If he remembered me, he'd remember David too.

'You've been watching the news?' she said, incredulously.

'Yes. On my iPad.' He nodded, proudly, calming down.

'Well. I didn't know you liked to watch the news.'

'Now they know I never hurt her. It was him. I never told them, then. I didn't like them police. I was scared of him, too. He shouted at me.' Horace pulled himself upright. 'I'm not scared of him now.'

Natasha frowned. 'Now then. We don't know who it was. We must let the police investigate, eh? Now they've found her they might be able to work out who did it.'

It was all I could do to stop myself from blurting out that Horace was right, it was the shouting man who'd done it, and the police had proof. Somehow, I kept quiet, focusing on picking out a dozen similar-sized potatoes from the display.

'She was your friend,' Horace said to me. A statement not a question.

'Now, come on, Horace. Don't be bothering Jo anymore.' Natasha tried to gently push Horace away to the back room, but he wouldn't move.

'It's all right. Yes, Horace, I played with her sometimes.'

He nodded. 'You played with me too.'

'We did. Yes.'

Natasha looked from him to me and back again. 'You know each other?'

'Yes, from many years ago,' I said.

Horace nodded again. 'They're nice. Jo and her friends. I like them. They were nice to me.'

'Well, that's good, Horace.' Natasha still looked puzzled. I smiled and continued with my shopping.

By the time I went to the till to pay, Horace had gone back into the storeroom again. 'I did know him, back in 1976. Not very well, but we did let him join in with our games a few times. At Four Oaks Farm.'

'I'm amazed he remembers,' Natasha said. She still looked astonished but also pleased, as though she'd learned something new about her brother, and liked what she'd seen.

'So am I, but I also feel rather honoured.'

She glanced up at me as she rang up my shopping. 'Thank you. That's a lovely thing to say.'

'It's the truth. Anyway, let's hope the police find Pippa's killer soon.'

'Whoever it was is probably long gone. I don't know who Horace is talking about – this "shouting man".' She frowned. 'Do you?'

'I have my suspicions. But it's for the police.'

'I just hope they won't want to talk to Horace again, after all these years. He was terrified of them, back then. Their uniforms, the way they spoke to him, sent him into a real tailspin, and they took that as meaning he was probably guilty. Then someone said they'd seen him acting oddly around the time she'd gone missing and that was enough for them.' She rubbed a tear from her cheek. 'They took him away. I missed him so much for those years. They should have sent someone gentle, someone sympathetic to talk to him. Someone who could have got him to talk about what he'd seen. We – my parents and I – should have insisted. We failed him.' She whispered this last part.

I nodded but kept my face sympathetic. 'Don't torture yourself,

Natasha. We were kids back then. There wasn't anything you or I could have done that would have changed things.' As I said it, I felt a pang of guilt. I'd tried to stop David but had failed.

She smiled, but there were tears in her eyes. 'You're right, of course. But even so. My poor, gentle brother who has never hurt a soul, has been considered a murderer by some people for fifty years. It's hard to deal with.'

'I understand. But I reckon they'll soon know who the real murderer is.' I stopped talking. Anything more and I'd give away what I knew.

'I hope you're right. That little girl deserves justice. And my Horace deserves to be exonerated at long last.'

Chapter 30

Jo, 23 August 1976
Sixteen days after.

Mum and David were out early the next morning. They'd gone before I came down for breakfast. Dad was out in the garage tinkering, so I had the house to myself. I wandered from room to room aimlessly. I knew where Mum and David were, and what they were doing, and it was *wrong*. But there was nothing I could do about it.

Except . . . maybe there was. Perhaps I could warn Horace. Maybe I could go and talk to him, find out why he was upset that day, and when it turned out – as I was sure it would – that it was nothing to do with Pippa, I could tell the police and counteract whatever David was telling them.

As soon as I'd had the thought I rushed upstairs, put on my plimsolls, and went to get my bike out of the garage.

'Where are you off to?' Dad said, as I began wheeling it out.

'Just . . . going round to Lynne's.' I hated lying. But if I went to Lynne's after seeing Horace then it wasn't technically a lie.

'You normally just walk there.'

'Yeah . . .' I shrugged, and carried on pushing my bike out into the driveway, hoping Dad wouldn't say anything more.

Thankfully he didn't. I turned in the direction of Lynne's and then by a roundabout route got onto Hawthorn Lane and headed out, past Four Oaks Farm and down to Marsh Farm. It was odd cycling along the familiar lanes by myself. As I approached, I slowed down. What exactly was I going to say to Horace? Why did I think that I, a child, would be able to get him to talk? But maybe I could, if he thought of me as a friend.

He might not even be home, I realised, remembering what Mum had said about the rumours that his family had taken him away. This whole expedition might be a waste of time. But in case he was home, I had to at least try.

As I reached the farm I realised with despair that I was too late. A police car was parked outside. There were raised voices coming from inside. I recognised Horace – he was shouting something incoherent, sounding terribly upset. His mother was screaming, 'No, no, you can't take him away!'

As I watched a young girl, younger than me, came out of a side door of the house. She was sobbing, and on seeing me she turned and ran into the back garden. She was followed by two policemen who were each holding one of Horace's arms, dragging him out to their car. He was struggling, shouting and kicking out at them, and I knew that was making things worse for him.

I wanted to run over and stop them but what would I say? How could I, a twelve-year-old, stop the police taking him? I knew it would be David that had caused this, but I had no real evidence, only my gut feeling, to contradict it.

Horace didn't see me. Neither did the police. I turned and cycled away, back home, as fast as I could.

By the time I reached home, David had returned. Mum had gone shopping and Dad was still in the garage. I threw my bike down on the driveway and marched up to David's room. 'Do you know what you've done?' I screamed at him. 'They've arrested him. And he *didn't do it!*'

David looked deeply unhappy. 'He might have done something. He was acting oddly, and that's all I said to them. Anyway, why do you think they've arrested him? They just said they needed to talk to him.'

'I went there. And I saw the police shoving him out of his house and into their car.'

He stared at me, horrified. 'Oh, my God. I didn't want that.'

'You didn't bloody think, David, what might happen to him. You should *never* have talked to the police!'

'Mum said it was the right thing to do.' His voice was small.

'She was always against Horace. But we made a *pact*, David!'

'I know, I . . .' he began, but there was nothing he could say to justify what he'd done, and he knew it.

I stared at him, hating my brother in that moment. Then I turned my back on him and walked out, slamming his bedroom door behind me.

Nothing would ever be the same between us. It felt like I'd lost him.

The days wore on, each one as hot as the last. Sometimes it was overcast and muggy, sometimes it was clear, hot and bright, but with no rain. The search for Pippa had been wound down, and there was no more news about what had happened, other than news that Horace had been incarcerated in Broadmoor.

'What's Broadmoor?' I asked Dad.

'A secure hospital, for people . . . like him . . . who could be a danger to others,' he replied. I glared at David, who hung his head in shame but said nothing. He hadn't told Rick or Lynne what he'd done, and I knew that already he was regretting it.

I spent most of my time with Lynne, while David went to

Rick's. The days of the four of us going out together were over, and I was glad. I could not bear being in David's company any longer than I absolutely had to.

Lynne's pool was no longer in use – the water shortage was still going on so her father had used the water, bucketful by bucketful, on their garden. There was no chance of refilling the pool with fresh water. But Mum had bought a shower hose attachment for our bath taps, and I'd discovered that if you sat in an empty bath, turned on the cold tap only and sprayed yourself with the shower attachment, it was a fantastic way to cool yourself down. There was a shock of course when the water first hit you, but once you were over that it was bliss. And Dad said it used far less water than filling a bath, so I was allowed to do it every day.

It was funny how something we normally just took for granted had become something so precious that you needed to make the most of every drop.

'There's a change in the weather coming soon,' Dad said over the tea table one night. 'It'll rain before the week is out.' He'd been watching the evening news and weather forecast, and although Mum always dismissed weather forecasts as no more accurate than reading tea leaves, she did perk up at this news.

We all did. Lynne and I had spent an afternoon in her bedroom performing a rain dance a few days before. We'd been to the library and with the help of the librarian who'd seemed to enjoy the challenge, found books on cultures around the world who did rain dances. We'd then spent hours going through them trying to find any details on exactly what a rain dance looked like, with little success. In the end we'd propped up a yard brush with piles of books to make a totem pole, tied scarves around our wrists and pranced around banging on an old child's tambourine Lynne still had. We'd whooped and hollered and made such a din Aunty Margaret had come to tell us off, but when we explained what we were doing she'd smiled. 'Well, I suppose it's worth a try. You keep going, girls.'

So we had, until we were hot and breathless, and collapsed with giggles.

And now rain was indeed forecast. Not before time, as everyone was saying. 'When it rains, will that be the end of the drought?' David asked Dad. 'I mean, will that be the end of the water going off every day?'

Dad shook his head. 'Wouldn't have thought so, son. It'll take ages for the reservoirs to refill. Wouldn't be surprised if the restrictions go on for quite a while yet. Perhaps all through September. Depends how much rain we get over the next few months.'

'Will we get a summer like this next year?' I was in two minds about whether I enjoyed the reliability of day after day with no rain more than I hated the incessant heat.

Dad shrugged. 'Who knows? They say the planet is beginning to warm up. So I suppose summers like this one might become more frequent.'

'Oh, God, please, no,' Mum said, rolling her eyes. Dad darted a look at her. David and I fell silent, concentrating on what we were eating, but both aware that such a tiny remark could lead to a snide comment from Dad, a disagreement from Mum, a rebuttal from Dad and escalation to World War Three before we knew it.

Thankfully not this time.

Lynne and I cycled past the farm the next day – it was still hot and bright with no sign of the promised rain – which looked different. There was a new fence in front of the hedge, preventing us reaching the gap we used to crawl through. The gate had been replaced with a higher, metal one with vertical bars which was impossible to climb over.

I got off my bike and peered through the bars of the gate. 'The house has been boarded up. All the windows and doors – look.'

'Well, that's that, then,' Lynne said. 'We can't get in to check on the time capsule or play in the barn again.'

'We didn't want to anyway,' I said.

We spent a minute staring through the railings, and then Lynne turned away and remounted her bike. 'Come on. Let's go. I hate this place.'

I hated it too. There was something eerie about it, as if it was hiding secrets from us. I could hardly believe we'd spent so long playing in the barn on those earlier visits a few short weeks back. I shuddered. 'Yes, let's go.'

We were soon pedalling fast down the hill and along the lane to our favourite spot in the woods. Aunty Margaret had provided what I suspected would be the last picnic of the summer, and we'd brought a picnic rug to sit on while we ate and chatted, just us two.

There was an air of finality about that day. As though the impending rain was sounding the bell for the end of summer, even though it was still August and we had another few days before the new school year began.

The following day was the August Bank Holiday Monday. And it was also the day when the rain finally came. We woke up to thick grey cloud and by mid-morning it was raining heavily. When the first drops fell, David and I ran into the front garden whooping with delight. Dad came out of the garage where he'd been fiddling with something to do with his telescope, and even Mum came to stand by the front door, smiling. All the way up the street people had come out to see this strange phenomenon of water falling from the sky, precious water that had been restricted for so long, just there for the taking. Some neighbours were putting out buckets to try to catch some of it, but Dad said that was pointless, that you'd get so little in the bucket even if it rained all day.

I was soon wet through, and cold. I'd forgotten how cold rain could be. I went back inside and changed into something dry and warm, putting a long-sleeved top on for the first time in months. It felt odd having my forearms covered and soon I was pushing up the sleeves.

We spent the day indoors, looking with wonder out at the rain, which continued for most of the day. I'd expected it to turn the garden into a muddy quagmire, but the rain seemed to bounce off the hardened earth and run downhill to the lowest point at the bottom of the garden.

But it wasn't only the rain that changed everything that day. In the mid-afternoon Mum and Dad walked into the sitting room where David and I, having called a temporary truce, were sitting on the floor, playing a game of Cluedo. I was winning, at least I thought I probably was, when they came in. Each held a cup of tea and wore a grave expression.

'Kids, sorry to interrupt, but we need to . . . tell you something,' Dad said, as he perched on the edge of the sofa. Mum sat on an armchair and put her tea on a side table. She didn't look at either of us, but I saw her throw a glance in Dad's direction. Whatever it was, she clearly wanted him to tell us.

'The thing is,' he began, then he cleared his throat and looked back at Mum for help.

'We've been talking,' she said, and still, she did not look at us. She just stared at her cup of tea, or her hands that were clasped on her lap.

'Yes, your mother and I have been talking,' Dad repeated, 'and we . . . well . . . we've come to a decision.'

'Now I don't want you two to be upset about this, but . . .' Mum put in, glancing briefly at each of us. We were still on the floor, legs tucked beneath us, as though we were tiny kids. David caught my eye but I looked away. I had a horrible feeling I knew what was coming, and that I definitely would be upset by it.

'Upset by what?' David asked.

'Your mother and I think that it would be better . . . I mean, better for everyone, including you two, if we . . . erm . . . well, if we separated.' Dad looked at each of us in turn as he stuttered his way through this, then watched us to see our reaction.

'You mean, get divorced?' I whispered.

He nodded. 'Eventually, yes.'

I felt strangely detached from it all. Here it was, the news I'd been dreading, the thing I had not wanted to consider might actually happen, the idea I'd been too upset by to imagine coming to pass. And here it was, this was the moment, and I was calm and quiet. No tears. No shouting at them to think about us, to sort out their problems and stay together for the sake of us children. All I felt was a quiet acceptance that this was inevitable, and that there was nothing I could do about it. It was their decision to make.

And perhaps it would be for the best, as Dad said. For so long it had been awful whenever they were in the same room. All those arguments, all those rows – they'd be a thing of the past if they lived in separate houses.

But where would we live? David and I . . . would we stay with Mum? When would we see Dad? Would the house be sold? I sat there with my mouth slightly open as endless questions tumbled through my brain, tripping over each other so that I was unable to voice any of them. David was staring at me, and I had the feeling the same thing was happening to him.

'So, um, any questions, kids?' Dad said, his voice artificially bright.

Oh, so many questions. Too many.

'What . . . I mean, where . . .' David began.

Both parents watched him, waiting for him to find a full question. David looked torn, as though he was about to cry. I was still numb. I hated my parents in that moment. For forcing him to formulate a question, for making us drag the details out of them, rather than laying everything on the table at once.

'Where will we live?' David finally managed to ask in the smallest voice I'd ever heard him use. I realised then that he might never have imagined this happening, not the way I had. We'd never discussed the possibility.

'Well,' Dad gave a huge sigh, 'we will sell this house. I'm going to rent a small flat in Southampton near my work.' He looked at

Mum as though expecting her to continue.

'I want to be near my parents. Your grandparents,' she clarified, as though we might have forgotten who her parents were to us. 'So, I'm going to find a place near them.'

Oh. Neither of them had mentioned us. David and I looked at each other and then at them, waiting. Mum realised what she'd done, belatedly. 'And you two, of course, will come with me. We'll find a nice little place near your grandparents. We'll have to stay with them to start with, so we can go before the start of the school term. Better to start a new school at the beginning of a school year rather than part way through, don't you think? Easier to make new friends and everything. So, it won't be long, not at all, for us. Dad will stay on here until the house is sold.'

She was gabbling, and I was struggling to take it all in. I hadn't expected this. We were going to move, away from Hareton Wick, out of the New Forest, all the way to Northampton. It'd be nice to see more of Nanny and Granddad, but . . . Lynne? Rick? All our other friends from school? This was the only place I'd ever lived. It was home. It was all I knew. The thought of starting again somewhere else . . . I couldn't picture it. I didn't want it.

'No!' The word escaped unbidden, and both parents stared at me in shock.

'Jo, it'll be all right, you'll make new friends in no time,' Dad said.

'And won't it be nice being near your grandparents? You always love going to see them.' Mum's tone was wheedling, pleading with me to accept it.

'Yeah, I love seeing them. I don't want to *live* with them though! And what about Lynne? I'll never see her again! And we're going before the start of term? That's a *week* away! That's madness! Can't we go next year? Or stay here? How are we going to see Dad if he's in Southampton and we're in Northampton? Why can't we stay here and Dad leaves?'

'Because we can't afford that, sweetie,' Dad said. 'We can't pay the mortgage here and my rent. Northampton is a cheaper place to buy property. Once this house sells both your mum and I will have enough to buy a place each. Long term you'll have your own bedrooms again. Don't worry.'

He smiled at me. He actually smiled, and so did Mum. In the way they had when they told us we were going on the camping trip. As though it was all one big adventure and we'd love every minute of it.

'Well, I'm not going. I'm staying here,' I shouted. 'I'll go and live with Lynne, in her sister's old room. I hate you all!' I flounced out and up the stairs to my bedroom. I flung myself down on my bed, and let the tears come. The numb feeling I'd had when they first told me was long gone. Now, I was nothing more than a ball of misery, crying and sobbing into my pillow. I heard David's bedroom door slam – he must have followed me up the stairs.

Any minute now Mum or Dad would come in, sit on the bed, pat me awkwardly on the shoulder and tell me everything was going to be all right. And I would tell them to . . . to . . . *fuck off*. I rarely swore. I'd never sworn at them before. But if ever a swear word was warranted this was that moment. Fuck them. Fuck what they were doing to us, breaking up our family, taking us away from the place we'd always lived, the friends we loved. Screwing up our lives. Fuck them.

I couldn't believe that I'd thought that their splitting up might be a good thing. That there'd be no more arguments, a better atmosphere in the house. Even though it would mean not having Dad around much. But I hadn't for a moment imagined that we'd be moving so far away. I'd thought Dad would move somewhere else in the village or nearby. I'd thought we would stay at Brookhill until we took our O levels. I'd imagined never moving from this house until we were adults.

They'd messed all that up, Mum and Dad had. I felt a sudden

pang of sympathy for little Pippa. This must be how she'd felt when her parents split up. No wonder she was lonely and needed company. We could have done more for her.

And then the tears came again, this time not only for me but for her, for sweet, innocent, lost little Pippa.

Chapter 31

Jo, 2024

Two days later I was watching the evening news, while I ate a snack dinner. A reporter was standing outside Crispin's care home. 'Police have announced the arrest of an eighty-nine-year-old man, in connection with the discovery of the remains of Pippa Jenkins, the eight-year-old child who went missing in the summer of 1976. The man, who has been named as Crispin Willis, was the owner of the farmhouse where Pippa's remains were found. The BBC understands that because Mr Willis has advanced dementia, he is to remain living in this care home where he currently resides. It seems unlikely that the case will ever go to trial. We reached out to Joyce Sanderson, Pippa's mother, for comment, and she had this to say.'

The picture changed to a shot of a neatly dressed woman who looked to be in her seventies standing outside a suburban home. 'I'm so glad that at long last my daughter has been found, and we can lay her properly to rest. It's a shame the police didn't look more closely at that man fifty years ago but at least now he can face justice.'

She said these words as though she'd rehearsed them. A gaggle of reporters around her began shouting questions but she was led away by a man of around her own age. Her husband, I imagined. Lynne had said she'd married again and had another family after losing Pippa.

Well, that was it. The news was out. I called Charlie as soon as it was over. 'Are you OK?' I asked.

'Yes. As well as I can be.' He sounded shaky. 'It's difficult. Dad has no idea what's going on. The police and I have explained it to him, but he just seems to switch off. I can't tell if he understands at all or if he somehow just blanks it out. And because his daily routine and living arrangements are unchanged, it all means nothing to him.'

'Well, what can they do? His . . . dementia is too advanced to . . .' Face the music, I'd been going to say.

'There are some that don't think that,' Charlie said. 'A couple of the staff in the care home don't want him there. They say he should be in prison, regardless.' He sighed. 'Jo, I'm so conflicted. I mean – he's still my dad. He's still the man I looked up to as a kid, as a teenager. More recently I've thought of him as just a sweet old man, losing his mental abilities, sad to see, but he was still someone I love. And now . . . now he's a murderer. A child-killer. And God knows what else he did – I mean, why did he kill her? Maybe he . . . abused her. Why else would he kill her? And were there *others*? Might there be other children he abused but who kept quiet? Others he killed that somehow they haven't found? Is he a monster, after all?'

'Charlie, these trains of thought do you no good.' I knew – all too well – the dark paths his mind was leading him along. He'd start wondering if he should have noticed something, if something his dad had said or done ought to have rung alarm bells. If there was anything he, Charlie, could have done to change what had happened. 'We don't know what happened. Don't torment yourself.'

'I'm sorry, Jo. I know it's wrong for me to think like that. And yet . . . I can't help it. I'm having to . . . re-evaluate everything I thought he was. All that I thought our family was, our history. My kids – the indulgent, kind grandfather they thought he was . . . I felt like a monster myself when I had to tell them.'

'Charlie, it's him not you. You're still the same person. A good person.' He needed to distance himself from his father in his mind.

'There have been reporters outside my house all day. Wanting to get a statement from me. Some are still there now. Police are guarding the care home to stop them getting access to Dad.'

'Do you want to come here? You could stay over in the spare room if you like.' The words were out before I realised what I was offering.

'You mean it? I would love to get away from here.'

'Come, then. Pack a bag for a few days and come. Just don't let any reporters follow you.'

He arrived half an hour later. I was struck by how he seemed to have aged since the last time I saw him. 'Come on in. Sit down. What can I get you?'

'A stiff whiskey,' he answered, then he froze, realizing what he'd said. 'Oh, sorry, of course you don't . . .'

'I don't have any. But I can pop out and buy a bottle of something from the off licence in the village. It'll take me ten minutes, tops. And it's OK. I can handle having drink in the house.' I didn't wait for an answer but went straight out, coming back with a bottle of Jameson. I steered away from wine which had always been my weakness, but I'd never liked whiskey anyway.

And I knew I'd be OK. Somehow helping Charlie through this period was helping me too. Pippa had been found, the mystery surrounding what had become of her resolved at last, and I was becoming able to move on.

Back home, Charlie was where I'd left him, on the sofa, phone in hand, scrolling through news websites. I went straight to the kitchen, poured him a whiskey and added some ice, then brought it back to him.

'God, you are good,' he said, taking a sip of it. 'I don't usually want this, but . . .'

'It's completely understandable. Just don't let it consume you, like I did.'

'I won't. You were on your own. I've got you. It helps.'

We talked for hours that night. Until well after midnight. Charlie drank a couple more whiskies, but he was far from being drunk by the time we called it a night.

And then, at the threshold to the spare room, as I showed him in, there was a moment where he put his arms around me and pulled me close. 'Thank you, Jo,' he whispered. 'I don't know how I'd cope without you.'

I thought he might kiss me. But it didn't feel like the right time to move our relationship on to another level.

He must have thought that too, for he smiled sadly and gently let me go.

'I'll see you in the morning, then,' I said. 'I'll be up by seven-thirty.'

'Me too. Sleep well.'

And I did, dreaming of a time when all this was over, when Charlie and I might see if we had a future together.

The following morning, after breakfast, Charlie told me he needed to see his father. 'They let me see him for twenty minutes at a time, with a policeman standing outside the door,' he said. 'Will you come? I know it's hard, knowing what he did, but he opens up more when you're there. Maybe he'll tell us . . . what happened that day.'

I swallowed. When I'd visited Crispin before it was to see a harmless old man who I'd rather liked when I was a child. But Charlie wanted me there, so for him, I'd do it. 'Of course.'

I wondered, though, if Crispin did talk about what happened, would Charlie really want to hear it?

'And then, after, I want to go to visit Horace Thompson and his sister,' Charlie continued. 'He took the blame all those years ago, for my father's crimes. I'm ashamed to admit that I too thought that Horace was probably the culprit.'

'Let's have breakfast and then make those visits,' I suggested. I was a little nervous at the prospect of going to Marsh Farm. If Horace started talking about having seen 'the shouty man' that day, knowing it was Mr Willis who'd killed Pippa, that might be hard for Charlie to hear.

'All right. Let's do that,' Charlie replied, setting his mouth into a thin line. It was going to be a difficult morning.

At the care home, as Charlie had said there was a policeman stationed outside the door to Crispin's room. 'As if Dad's capable of escaping,' Charlie muttered, as we gave our names and entered the room.

I took a deep breath, half expecting to find Crispin transformed into the monster Charlie feared he was, but no, he was the same frail, confused man I'd seen on previous occasions. The only difference was that he was in bed, propped up on several pillows, his eyes staring at nothing across the room and his hands fiddling constantly with the edge of a blanket.

'Barbara,' he said, his voice weaker than the last time I'd seen him. 'My Barbara. They won't let me out of this room.'

'You need to stay here, Dad,' Charlie said, and I nodded as I sat beside Crispin. I didn't want him holding my hand this time, but he reached for me and somehow, I let him take my hand, even though the idea of this child-killer touching me filled me with revulsion.

'Crispin. Do you understand why they won't let you out? Why the police have been to see you?'

'She was in a blue dress. You always looked so nice in blue, Barbara.'

Beside me, Charlie sighed. 'He's incoherent again.'

But I kept my eyes on Crispin. 'Who was in blue, Crispin?'

'Her. The child.'

I glanced at Charlie, who leaned in closer, frowning. 'You remember her?'

'Course I remember. Wish I didn't. Never meant to hurt her. But they think I did.'

'Dad, what happened?'

Chapter 32

Crispin, 2024

It was all Barbara's fault, Crispin thought. His lovely Barbara. She'd stayed away so long, and then she'd come back to visit him, and now the police were talking to him. They knew something about the child, the child so long ago, the one where it all went wrong. Sometimes Crispin understood that Barbara was long gone, but then hadn't she come back to him; hadn't their boy, what was his name, brought her along to see him? They were here now.

He didn't know what this place was. But they fed him and put the TV on a channel that showed nature programmes, and he'd fall asleep watching penguins in the Antarctic or gorillas in Africa. And those programmes stopped him thinking about anything else, and that was a good thing. Because sometimes his thoughts and memories were dark.

There were days when he remembered and days when he didn't. He preferred the ones when he didn't remember, when there was only the mealtimes and the TV and the penguins and gorillas.

When he did remember, it was bad. Barbara didn't know, and

that was just as well. No one knew. But Barbara was here now and they were asking, and it was one of the days when he remembered.

He hadn't meant any harm. It had all been just a terrible accident. There were kittens, and he'd wanted to show them to the child because she'd looked lonely. He'd taken her up the stairs where they were. One of the stairs had rotted and his foot went through and he fell, on her, on the child. She tumbled all the way down, landing in a heap at the bottom.

He picked himself up, cursing at the gash on his ankle, then went down to see to the child. But she was lying there, not breathing, all crumpled and broken at the foot of the stairs.

He panicked. His heart was racing, and he was sweating. What should he do? There was no telephone at the farm. If he reported it, they'd think he'd hurt her on purpose. They'd ask why he'd brought her into the old house, what he'd intended doing with her. He'd be accused, he'd be assumed guilty, he'd be locked away. And Barbara, his darling Barbara, would never forgive him for hurting a child. Even though it was an accident, he couldn't have anyone think he'd had anything to do with the death of an innocent child.

Suddenly he couldn't bear to look at the girl, her lifeless face staring at him, accusing him. He fetched an old potato sack from a pile in the scullery. It was musty and dark in that room. He opened a window to let in air and light, then put her in it. Now she was no longer staring at him. He tied the top. Best thing to do was to put it in the cellar. No one ever came in the house. There were places in the cellar where he could hide the sack and no one would ever find it. No one need ever know. And in time the memories would fade and he would forget all about it.

He took the sack into the kitchen, to the cellar door. But it was padlocked and he realised he didn't have the key with him. It was at home, in his desk drawer. He left the sack by the cellar door and went out to his car.

The child's bike was leaning against the fence. He cursed and threw it in the back of his car. He'd need to dump it somewhere, far from the farm. That idiot boy from the next farm was in the lane, staring at him. He shouted at him to go away, go home, then drove quickly back home to fetch the key, so he could hide the sack properly.

All that was such a long time ago. Even though time seemed to have no meaning anymore, he knew it must have been many years ago. They'd never found the child. But now the police knew, or they thought they knew. Barbara must have led them to her. And now she knew that it was an accident. A terrible, horrible accident, followed by bad decisions that he'd had to live with all his life.

It didn't matter. None of it mattered anymore. He could feel death's hand on his shoulder. It wouldn't be long, now. Charlie – that was his name, his son's name – Charlie would see to it that he had a good send-off. The whole village would turn out for him. He was an important person in these parts. Parish councillor, chair of the school Board of Governors. If the village had a mayor, it would have been him. Everyone loved him, and they'd all mourn him when he went. He'd done everything he could, he'd done good things for the community. All in an attempt to make amends for that one moment, that horrible accident, that moment of madness when he'd decided to hide the child rather than face police suspicion.

Charlie would put an announcement in the broadsheets – the *Telegraph*, the *Times*. All his old colleagues and business rivals would attend his burial. There'd be a granite headstone for his grave that would last for centuries. *Here lies Crispin Willis, beloved benefactor of this parish.*

And as a coughing fit overtook him, Crispin drifted off to sleep dreaming of the thousands who'd attend his final send-off, the glowing obituaries that would be published, the mass outpouring of grief as his remains were lowered into the ground. It was a shame he couldn't attend his own funeral. But Barbara would be there waiting for him, in her blue dress, with her sunny smile, and all would be well.

Chapter 33

Jo, 2024

As we walked slowly out of the care home towards my car, I took Charlie's hand. 'So now we know.'

Charlie nodded. 'An accident. That he never reported.'

'He panicked. And he's regretted it ever since.'

'That's the gist of it. Or at least, that's the story he's told himself all these years.'

'Do you think he'll repeat all that to the police?' After Crispin had fallen asleep, we'd left his room and told the policeman on duty what we'd gleaned from Crispin's ramblings. He'd looked at us sceptically as if we were making it up but promised to pass it on to the detective in charge of the case.

'I doubt it. I think he's at his best when he thinks he's talking to Mum. He'll clam up and say nothing when the police are with him.' Charlie took a long, shuddering breath. 'I don't think it matters. I don't think he'll be around much longer.'

'His reputation.'

Charlie stopped walking and spun to face me. 'I know now he's not a murderer. I can truthfully assure my children he's not.

You know too. That's all that matters to me.' He took another deep breath. 'I do feel so much better for knowing it. Thank you for coming.'

'That's OK. I'm glad I could help.' I was glad for myself, too, that I finally knew what had happened to Pippa.

'And now, I need to see Horace,' Charlie said. We got into my car, and I drove off in the direction of Marsh Farm shop.

When we reached Marsh Farm Natasha seemed pleased to see me again. 'Jo! More potatoes already?' I was ahead of Charlie as we entered the shop.

'No, I've still got plenty. You've heard the news?'

'Yes. We used to know the older Willis's quite well, being near neighbours. Though I was only very young when they died, and the farm was boarded up. Couldn't believe it was . . . oh!' She broke off as Charlie entered. 'Charlie Willis, isn't it? I haven't seen you for a very long time.'

'Hello, Natasha. 'Yes, it's been a long while. I'm sorry I've not been a customer of your shop but looking at all this wonderful produce I think that has to change.'

She nodded but said nothing. Her expression was guarded.

'Listen, Natasha, I wanted to come by to say sorry. Sorry for what my father did, and what it put your brother through. I had no idea, none at all, that my father was involved in any way with Pippa's disappearance. He helped search for her, back then, so of course I never . . .' Charlie shrugged and spread his hands. His face showed grief and confusion, horror at how things had turned out. 'From what my father says, it was an accident, but he covered it up.'

'Thank you.' Natasha reached out and placed her hand on his arm. Her touch seemed to help Charlie compose himself a little. 'I'm just glad that they've finally solved the mystery, even if . . . I'm sorry for how it all turned out. I can't imagine how you must feel.'

'Just as I can't imagine how you felt for all those years when people were blaming Horace,' Charlie said, and there was genuine compassion in his voice.

'It was very difficult at times. Nothing will bring back those lost years.' There was a hint of bitterness in Natasha's tone, though I could see she was trying to keep it out.

'How is he?' Charlie asked. 'Does he know the news?'

'Yes. And it was strange . . . when I told him, he just nodded as though he'd known all along. I think . . . he might have seen something or suspected something. But no one would listen to him or treat anything he said seriously.'

'Things would be different now,' I said. 'I think people like your brother are treated with more respect.'

'Perhaps.' She shrugged. 'What is going to happen to your father, Charlie?'

'I don't know. I think he's just going to stay where he is for now. He's pretty unwell.'

'Oh, I'm—' Natasha broke off. 'I was going to say I'm sorry, but I don't know if I am.'

'I know,' Charlie said, unhappily. He gulped.

Natasha and I looked at each other, neither of us able to find any words to express sympathy for Charlie yet none for his father.

'Hello.' Horace emerged from the back storeroom. He was grinning broadly. 'Hello, Jo. They got him, the police did.'

'I know.' I glanced at Charlie, wondering what he would say to Horace.

'Now they're building houses there.'

'Yes, they are.'

'For people to live in.'

'That's right.'

'That's better than it all just falling down on top of her.' Horace turned away then and picked up a broom. 'I've got work to do.'

'Before you start,' Charlie said, stepping forward, 'I just want to say it's good to meet you, Horace.'

Horace nodded. 'We met before. When we were little, you

were brought here to play. My mum looked after us both. Three times. Before Tash was born.'

'You know me, then?'

'Your dad was the shouty man. But it's OK. You're not shouty.' This was all said as a matter of fact, and then Horace turned away and began sweeping.

'He remembered me too. He never forgets anyone,' I said.

Natasha smiled. 'Thank you for coming round, Charlie. It can't have been easy to face us, but I think it's been good. For him.' She nodded towards her brother. 'I had no idea he'd remember you. But I think at last he and I can put it all behind us.' She put out a hand to shake Charlie's. 'I hope you find peace in the end, too. What your father did was not your fault.'

'I know. But thank you.' Charlie's voice broke a little as he spoke. When he'd let go of Natasha's hand I put a hand on his arm.

'Shall we . . .?'

'Yes, sure, Jo.' We said our goodbyes and left the shop. Outside, Charlie gave a huge, shuddering sigh.

'I'm glad I went there. Horace . . . I can't believe he remembered me. I have no memory of playing with him as a child. He's older than me, I think. But I can well believe I was sometimes brought to Marsh Farm by my grandparents.'

'I'm glad you feel good about our visit.'

We were about to get in the car when Natasha came out again. 'Jo, I meant to say. Your brother called here yesterday afternoon. He spoke to Horace. It seems he said something to the police, back then, that he thinks might have pushed them into believing Horace was to blame.'

'He did, yes.' I remembered it all too well.

'Jo, your brother did the right thing back then. He was only a child, and it was right for him to tell the police what he'd seen. I don't blame him for Horace being locked away.'

'I didn't see it that way. I hated him for it.'

'But Jo, Horace doesn't hate him. He was delighted to see him and treated him like an old friend. It was good of your brother to come to see him and apologise for his part in it all, but we must put it in the past now. Especially as we now know the truth.'

My eyes filled with tears at her magnanimity. She squeezed my hand. 'I'll let you get going now. Thank you for bringing Charlie to see us. It's good to have closure.'

The route back to my house took us past Four Oaks Farm. Workmen were back on site, now that the crime was solved, and Pippa's remains removed. Grab lorries were taking away the debris from the demolished farmhouse, and a bulldozer was at work levelling the ground. The site was moving on.

It was time, I thought, that I introduced Charlie to Dad, and to David while he was still in the country. He'd decided to stay another week at least. 'Until after the funeral,' he said when I phoned.

'What do you mean?'

'Pippa Jenkins. I saw in the paper that her remains are going to be buried in Hareton Wick's churchyard, next Monday. Thought I'd like to be there.'

'Oh! Yes, so would I. And I'll let Lynne know — I'm sure she'll want to come too.'

'And Rick. Feels like it should be all four of us.'

'We could go to a pub after.'

'Do you think Charlie will go to the funeral?'

'I-I honestly don't know. Maybe. But I'd like you to meet him before you go home, anyway. I'd like Dad to meet him too.'

'Bring him round here at the weekend? For afternoon tea on Saturday perhaps?'

'Perfect.'

Charlie was still staying with me, and I'd promised him a sausage casserole for dinner that evening. He'd been out all day – he'd had some business to take care of and then was visiting his father. These days, any visits to his father had to be planned in advance, were limited in length and a policeman would be present at all times. 'Though why, I don't know. I'm hardly going to try to break him out of there,' he'd said. 'He's on oxygen now.'

I was expecting him back at about five o'clock, in plenty of time to unwind before dinner. But when six o'clock came and went with no sign of him I sent him a message. *Just wondering what time I should put the oven on – will you be back by seven?*

There was no immediate reply. I decided to put the casserole in the oven anyway – it could be kept warm for hours after it was cooked if necessary.

And then, at half past six, Charlie returned. He looked devastated, and as he stumbled in, he pulled me into his arms and held me tight. I hugged him back – it was clear he needed comforting.

'What's happened?' I whispered.

'Dad.'

Just one word, but I knew what it would be.

'Is he . . . gone?'

'Yes. This afternoon.' Charlie let me go and went through to the sitting room. 'I thought he was asleep when I arrived, but he'd slipped into a coma. I sat with him for a while. His breathing grew more ragged. Then the policeman told me my time was up and tried to make me leave. I pointed out that Dad's time was very nearly up and refused to leave his side. About thirty minutes later it was all over.'

'Oh, Charlie. I'm so sorry.'

'I'm glad I was there at the end. Holding his hand, talking to him, even if he didn't know I was there.'

I reached out and rubbed his shoulder. 'I'm glad you were there, too. He may well have been aware of your presence, on some deep level.'

He gazed at me sadly. 'I hope so. And as everyone's going to tell me, it's probably for the best.'

I gave him a squeeze but said nothing. It *was* for the best, I thought. But it was still Charlie's dad, and his death coming on top of everything else was going to be hard for him to deal with. Gosh, what I'd had to deal with finding Stephanie and losing my dog suddenly felt so small and insignificant compared with what Charlie was going through.

'Charlie, I'm here for you, you know? You can talk to me, stay here as long as you like, let me help you with all the arrangements regarding your dad's funeral and everything.' As I mentioned 'funeral' I remembered about Pippa's, on Monday. I'd planned to ask Charlie this evening if he would go to it. But now wasn't the moment.

'Thank you, Jo. Being with you has been what's got me through these last few days.'

'I'm glad I'm helping.' And as I said the words, I realised that having Charlie around, even during these tumultuous times, had been helping me, too. I felt, well, *normal* again. I felt as though I was healed, at last. I was able to help someone else without feeling as though I would go under myself at any moment. Maybe it was because being there for Charlie had forced me to look outside myself rather than dwell on my own problems. Maybe because I'd reconnected with Lynne, and David, and made up after the little spats with Ryan and Dad. Maybe because with Charlie in my life I could see a future I was excited about, once we were past the present difficult time.

Chapter 34

Jo, 24 August 1976
Seventeen days after.

I was desperate to tell Lynne the news. I needed to talk it all through with someone, someone who understood just how hard it was for me to accept the bombshell my parents had dropped. David must have been feeling the same way, for the day after we were told of Mum and Dad's divorce plans, he announced he was going out with Rick for the day. The way he said it told me he wanted it to be just him and Rick. I understood – I also wanted to be only with Lynne that day. In any case, David and I had had a whispered argument in my room that morning. He'd been blaming Mum for the split, saying she shouldn't have nagged Dad so much and no wonder he was leaving us. I'd pointed out how Dad did hardly any jobs around the house despite being at home all summer, and no wonder Mum was fed up with him. And then David had thrown his hands up in the air and stormed out. I hated it. David and I had always been close, but it felt as though our parents' divorce was going to push us apart too.

I headed to Lynne's house straight after breakfast, which had been awkwardly quiet as David and I brooded. Mum tried to act normally and Dad kept quiet as though scared of what he might say if he opened his mouth.

I was at Lynne's before she'd even finished her own breakfast. It was a grey and overcast day, looking likely to rain again at any moment. But suddenly the weather didn't matter at all. The heatwave and drought could continue, or it could rain until Christmas, for all I cared.

Aunty Margaret opened the door to me. Mum must have phoned her and told her the news because she greeted me with a sympathetic expression. 'Lynne's in the kitchen, Jo,' she said, patting my shoulder as I passed by.

Lynne was just spooning the last of a bowl of cornflakes into her mouth when I entered. She finished quickly and put her bowl into the sink. 'Come up to my room. Mum told me . . .'

I gulped back a sob as I followed her upstairs. We flopped onto her bed, backs against the wall with her pillows behind us as we'd sat so many times over the years. I remembered when we were little and only our feet would overhang the side of the bed. Now as we slouched across the bed our knees were at the edge and our feet dangled towards the floor. I couldn't believe that there wouldn't be many more times that I would sit like this with her.

'You were worried that they'd do this, weren't you?' Lynne gently asked me once we were settled.

'I kind of knew,' I agreed, 'that they'd divorce sooner or later. But I didn't think that we'd be moving away, and at such short notice.'

'Moving?' Lynne gasped. 'Mum only said that your parents were splitting up. Where are you going?'

'Northampton. To stay with my grandparents to begin with.'

'When?' Lynne's question emerged as a whisper.

'This week. So we can start the new term at our new school.'

'Oh, Jo.' Lynne clapped a hand over her mouth, shocked.

'I know. I can't believe it.'

'It's not very fair of them, is it?'

I shook my head, not allowing myself to speak in case I broke down in tears.

'I suppose,' Lynne went on, 'they think it's the best way to do this, for you and David. I mean, I know when kids join the class part way through a school year, they never properly become part of it, do they? It probably will be easier for you to move at the start of the term. Though I don't know why you have to go. Couldn't they split up without you actually moving house? Like, if your dad just moved out?'

'That's what I asked them. But apparently they can't afford Dad renting somewhere and also paying the mortgage on the current house. Houses are cheaper in Northampton. And Mum wants to be near her parents.'

Lynne nodded. 'You'll see more of your grandparents.'

'That's the only good thing.'

'Jo, we'll still be friends. We'll stay in touch. We'll phone each other every week and you can come to stay with me every school holiday. Mum won't mind, I know it. Won't be the same being in school without you but we'll still be best friends. Just at a distance.'

'You'll make a new best friend.'

'Only a local one. And so will you, in Northampton.' She picked up her Friends Forever teddy and rubbed it against my cheek. 'But you and I . . . nothing will ever split us up. Not this. Not anything.'

I loved her for those words, but they also proved the tipping point and for the next few minutes all I could do was sob, my hands over my face. Lynne shuffled over to me and wrapped her arms around me. At some point I was aware that Aunty Margaret looked in on us, then went away to fetch us a glass of squash each. No more ice pops now the weather had changed. It was a small thing, but her kindness, her understanding that I was going through tough times, really helped. Not all parents were like mine.

At last, I calmed down, dried my tears, and determined to make the most of the remaining time I had with my best mate.

We decided to go out for a walk around the village, taking an umbrella in case it rained, calling at a newsagents for bars of chocolate to eat in the rec, passing by all our old haunts, all the places that held endless memories for me, and that I would soon be moving away from. The rec, the climbing tree, the high street, the newsagents, even the school gates. It was hard to wrap my head around the fact that I would never again pass through those gates. What would my new school be like? What kind of friends would I meet there? What would the teachers be like?

I voiced some of this to Lynne and she smiled wistfully at me. 'I'm glad you're thinking about what's ahead now, Jo. You'll be all right, in Northampton. You'll make a new life there, and it'll be a good one. And we'll still be friends.'

'We'll still be friends,' I repeated, and we threw our arms around each other and held each other tightly.

It all happened so quickly after that. We had one more outing on our bikes to the woods, the four of us, with a picnic prepared by Rick's mum. It wasn't as much fun as usual. It was more of a goodbye. Lynne gave me a present of a set of make-up and some glittery hair clips. I felt bad I had nothing for her, but the boys didn't exchange presents either.

We cycled home slowly, as if prolonging the final farewells. David and I had been told we needed to pack our things the next day, and then we were off. As we passed Four Oaks Farm I glanced over the gate. The farmhouse looked as foreboding as ever. I couldn't imagine anyone ever wanting to buy it and live in it. One day, I supposed, it'd be knocked down and something new built in its place. Perhaps by the time we were due to unearth the time capsule, the village would have expanded to here and the whole place would be under tarmac.

'Guys, we must promise to all meet up to dig up our time capsule!' I called to them, as we pedalled along the lane. 'Even though we'll be living far away. We said five years. So, we'll all come back to dig it up?' I felt I needed a promise from everyone that we would definitely all be together again, even if it was at such a distant date in the future.

'Of course we will, Jo,' Lynne said.

'Yes, of course,' Rick agreed.

There was something so final about that day. Our last all together, the last day of that long hot summer, the last day of our childhood. Lynne and I would soon turn thirteen – we'd be teenagers, no longer kids. We wouldn't be passing that milestone together, though. We'd be far apart, living different lives. As would David and Rick.

I'd cry, if I thought about it any longer, and today wasn't the day for crying. It was the day for goodbyes and for plans to find ways to meet up in the future. For awkward hugs, promises we weren't sure we had the power to keep, for reassurances that we'd have weekly phone calls and that no friendships would ever be better than what we'd had. For last comments about what might have happened to poor Pippa Jenkins, and confirmation that none of it was our fault and there was nothing we could have done to prevent what had happened. David kept quiet through all this.

And then we left Rick at his house, Lynne at hers, and David and I cycled in silence slowly, so very slowly, back to the only home we'd ever known, for the last time.

Chapter 35

Jo, 2024

The funeral – Pippa's – was on Monday afternoon, at the village church. Charlie said he would like to attend, as I'd expected he would. He'd been dealing with his own father's death well. I'd accompanied him to the funeral parlour and had sat with him while he made arrangements for a direct cremation at Southampton crematorium. There'd be no service, no memorial stone, no announcement in the papers, and only Charlie and his children would attend. I'd also helped Charlie with clearing his dad's room at the care home.

Despite it all, Charlie had come with me on Sunday to meet Dad and David. We'd stayed only for a cup of tea and a chat, but it had been a happy occasion. David and Charlie seemed to get on well, reminiscing about footballers in the 1970s. 'I was a huge Mick Channon fan,' Charlie told David. 'When Southampton won the FA Cup I was in heaven.'

I smiled, then remembered that had been in 1976. I hoped we wouldn't end up talking about that summer once again.

'So was I,' was all David answered.

And Dad had been on good form too, happy and chatty. I couldn't help but compare my lovely, lively dad with Charlie's. There really was no comparison.

'Your dad's great,' Charlie told me when we left. 'And I liked your brother a lot too.'

'I'm glad,' I'd replied, happy that it looked as though Charlie would slot right into my family. He only had Ryan still to meet, and he was coming down that weekend to stay. I was pretty sure they'd like each other too.

Charlie had moved out of my house, back to his own. 'I've so many of Dad's things to sort out, it's easier being there. And then when we are together, I can concentrate on you and leave all that behind,' he'd said. It suited me. Our relationship was still at the fledgling stage, and I wanted to ensure we didn't rush it. We'd had a lot to deal with, in the few weeks since we'd met.

Even so, on the day of Pippa's funeral, we decided to go together. I'd put on a black dress and jacket and waited for Charlie to arrive. He parked outside my house and we walked together to the church.

David was already there, chatting to Rick.

'Jo!' Rick opened his arms for a hug as I approached. 'Good to see you again so soon, even though the circumstances aren't quite what we'd have chosen. Are you coming along to the pub for a meal after?'

'Absolutely. And I hope you don't mind if I bring Charlie here along as well?'

'No problem. I'm bringing Anton, my better half.'

'Look,' Lynne said. 'Natasha and Horace Thompson are here.' We went over to say hello, and I was delighted to see that Horace recognised us all instantly and seemed delighted that the four of us – five, counting himself – were all together again.

'999-In!' he quipped, and we all laughed.

Natasha shushed him but smiled. 'Horace, this is a serious occasion. Remember what I said about being quiet?'

'You said quiet in the church. Not outside,' he replied.

'Yes, all right smarty, you've got me there,' she said, and Horace looked pleased with himself.

We went into the church then. Soon after, Pippa's coffin – a simple, white painted one topped with pink flowers – was brought in. Behind it walked a neat, upright, elderly woman whom I recognised from the TV as Pippa's mum. She had a middle-aged woman on one side of her, and a man on the other. These were most likely her other children, born some years after their half-sister's death. And behind them was her husband, their father. They looked like a nice family, and I was glad Pippa's mum had found happiness again.

The service was beautiful. Reflective and poignant. The vicar spoke of the sadness of a child dying so young, being denied the opportunity to live life to the full, but also spoke of the courage of the living, of those who'd been affected by Pippa's loss but had managed to move on, to make a new life. Now Pippa was finally at rest, her family could be at peace.

We sang the hymn 'All Things Bright and Beautiful', introduced by the vicar as Pippa's favourite. I remembered singing it with her that day I'd played with her, and was glad her mother had remembered. I wished I'd brought a chocolate Freddo Frog to drop into her grave.

There were no tears. She'd been gone so long that the mourners were there to pay respects but not to cry. At the graveside her mother only smiled sadly as the coffin was lowered into the ground. Now, at last, she had somewhere she could come to remember her first daughter. Now, at last, she knew what had happened to her, fifty years before.

Afterwards we spent a little time mingling with other mourners in the church yard. It was a fine, bright day, warm for the time of year. It seemed fitting that Pippa should be buried on as sunny a day as those of her last summer.

Mrs Jenkins (or rather, Mrs Sanderson as she was now called) had a brief chat with us. Charlie hung back out of the way.

'Jo?' said Mrs Sanderson, when I introduced myself, 'Jo Salway?'

'Yes, that's me.'

She took my hand and squeezed it. 'One of the last conversations I had with Pippa was her telling me about the lovely afternoon she'd had playing with you. It would have been the day before . . . you know. Didn't you teach her a skipping game? And buy her chocolate?'

'I did, yes.'

'She loved that day. And you know, over the years, it brought me a shred of comfort knowing her last full day on earth was a happy one. Thank you for all you did for her that day. It means a lot.'

'It was a fun afternoon.' I choked up. After all these years wishing I'd done more, that Pippa's mum thought I *had* done something for Pippa, felt as though the final piece of the puzzle to rebuild myself had slotted into place.

It felt like absolution.

'I wish, as you might imagine, that I hadn't left her so much that summer. I should have—'

I held up a hand to cut her off. 'We all wish we'd done things differently. Lynne and I wish we'd taken her under our wing more. But there's really no point thinking that.'

Mrs Sanderson nodded. 'I know, I know. But even so, in the dead of night . . .'

I nodded, too. I knew that feeling. I took her hand and squeezed it. 'It's been nice to see you, Mrs Sanderson.' Her son and daughter were closing in, ready to take her home. She must be, I realised, nearing eighty. Possibly older. And although she looked well, it must have been a difficult time for her, since Pippa's body was found.

'Good to see you too, Jo.' She allowed herself to be led away, and I turned back to Charlie.

'You knew her – Pippa, I mean – more than you let on to me. Playing with her the day before she died?'

'We'd come home early from a holiday, because Mum and Dad

were fighting. Lynne was out, and I came across Pippa in the street. We were both at loose ends so . . . we hung out. Skipped, and yes, I bought her a Freddo Frog.'

'And now I fully understand why you were so affected by her disappearance, for all those years.' He looked at me with compassion. 'I get it. We'll talk more about this, when we've put a bit of distance between it and ourselves, yes?'

'Yes. Might be therapeutic for us both.'

If there was one thing I'd learned over the last few years, since finding Stephanie, it was that we should never bottle things up. Always talk. Find someone sympathetic, someone who has your best interests at heart, and talk to them. Tell them everything. Go round and round, looking at it from all angles, until you understand it and have come to terms with it. Whatever it is.

'I'll write to her,' Charlie said, nodding towards Pippa's mum. 'When a little time has gone by, I'll write and tell her what Dad told us about Pippa's last moments. That it was an accident, and that it was over quickly and she didn't suffer.'

'I think that will help her,' I said.

'You two ready to go?' Lynne had rejoined us, after speaking to Mrs Sanderson. David and Rick were right behind her. 'We thought we'd go to Julio's.'

'Sounds perfect!' I said and glanced at Charlie.

'Jo, I'll go home now, I think. I'll let you catch up with your old friends without me hanging around. But if you're free tomorrow evening, I was thinking about taking you out somewhere special. Just the two of us.' Charlie caught hold of my hands.

'I'd love to.' I smiled, and he smiled back. There was an expression of longing in his eyes. A look that told me that soon our relationship would move on to a new phase. We'd been through a lot together, and it had brought us closer, building us a firm foundation.

'All right then. Enjoy your catch-up.' He said goodbye to everyone and walked away.

'You've found a good one there, Jo,' Lynne said, watching him go.
'Yes. I think I have,' I replied.

Later, at Julio's, with our meals ordered and a round of drinks – lime and soda for me – in front of us, we exchanged thoughts on how Pippa's funeral had gone.

'You know what Pippa's mum told me?' Lynne said. 'She's heard from the developers. They're going to call the development Philippa Close, after Pippa. Something to remember her by.'

'That's nice,' Rick said, and we all nodded agreement.

'Definitely. A new name, a new life.'

'And the area where the old house stood, where Pippa was found, that's going to be left as a communal garden. So no one will live in a house built exactly over the spot,' Lynne went on.

'I'm glad they're being so sympathetic,' I said.

'Good job we dug up the time capsule when we did, eh?' David said. 'It was definitely the last chance we had to do it. Shame there wasn't anything exciting in it.'

'I know.' Rick chuckled. 'A few mouldy magazines and a pencil topper. We could have tried a bit harder back then. It was barely worth the effort digging it up!'

But it *had* been worthwhile, I thought. It was reopening that time capsule that somehow had brought David and me close again. And Four Oaks Farm had brought us all back together, fifty years on. As the conversation moved on to general reminiscences about that last summer, I gazed around at the three people in front of me. We'd all done OK really, over the years. We'd each had our ups and downs, good times and bad, but here we were. We were still those same kids that cycled the lanes during a long hot summer, and at the same time we were the mature, experienced adults sitting around the table now. Scratch the surface and Lynne and I would probably still have an opinion about Donny Osmond versus David Cassidy, and given half a chance the boys would still indulge in one-upmanship. Some things you never grow out of – you just grow another layer around the outside of it. Occasionally those layers were protective, but sometimes you needed to peel them back, expose the bad stuff to the light. Talk about it, understand it, deal with it.

It had taken me fifty-plus years, but I understood that now.

An image of Charlie floated across my mind. I was certainly looking forward to the future for the first time in many years. David laughed at something Rick said, then caught my eye and winked, and I felt as though I was back home, with my friends around me, summer ahead of us and everything to live for.

Author's Note

The idea for this novel first came to me while out cycling with my family on the edge of the New Forest, during one of the Covid lockdowns. We passed a boarded-up, abandoned farmhouse and its outbuildings, and I commented to my son that back when I was a child in the 1970s that place would have been an absolute magnet for kids to play in. And then I got thinking: *what if . . . what if . . .* and this novel was conceived. I remember the long hot summer of 1976 very clearly so that seemed an obvious backdrop to choose for the novel.

It was fun dredging through my memories of that year while writing this novel, reliving my childhood, remembering how it felt to be young and free with the whole school summer holiday stretching before me.

If you enjoyed this novel, please consider leaving a review on your website of choice. To be the first to hear news of my future books and to receive a free ghostly short story, please sign up to my mailing list via my website: https://kathleenmcgurl.net/home

The Girl from Bletchley Park

Will love lead her to a devastating choice?

1942. Three years into the war, Pam turns down her hard-won place at Oxford University to become a codebreaker at Bletchley Park. There, she meets two young men, both keen to impress her, and Pam finds herself falling hard for one of them. But as the country's future becomes more uncertain by the day, a tragic turn of events casts doubt on her choice – and Pam's loyalty is pushed to its limits . . .

Present day. Julia is struggling to juggle her career, two children and a husband increasingly jealous of her success. Her brother presents her with the perfect distraction: forgotten photos of their grandmother as a young woman at Bletchley Park. Why did her grandmother never speak of her time there? The search for answers leads Julia to an incredible tale of betrayal and bravery – one that inspires some huge decisions of her own . . .

Gripping historical fiction perfect for fans of *The Girl from Berlin*, *The Rose Code* and *When We Were Brave*.

The Lost Child

All she wanted was a child of her own . . .

1912. As the steamship *Carpathia* takes the survivors of the *Titanic* to New York, Lucy desperately searches the decks for her baby, thrust into the arms of another woman as a lifeboat left, and now nowhere to be found. Madeleine is helping her journalist husband to interview the survivors, and when she meets Lucy, she promises she will do anything she can to help her find her lost child.

2022. When archivist Jackie finds a notebook containing the stories of women saved by the *Carpathia* amongst an auction lot, she learns the story of the missing baby. Desperate to start a family of her own, she feels compelled to dig further. And her search will lead her to a century-old mystery . . .

Inspired by true events, bestselling author Kathleen McGurl weaves history and fiction together in this captivating, deeply moving story.

Acknowledgements

Many thanks to my editors Priyal Agrawal and Grace Marshall for your input to this book. It's a little bit different to my previous books so thank you very much for steering me in the right direction through the various rounds of edits.

Thank you to my husband Ignatius who patiently endured many a 'plot walk' with me while I talked through ideas, then reworked them all several times.

Thank you also to everyone at HQ – copyeditor Teresa Palmiero, cover designers, proofreaders and the marketing team for all your work getting my books ready for publication and then promoted thereafter. You do a fabulous job and I'm proud to have been an HQ author from the very start.

Finally, thank you to my loyal readers and followers for your continued support and encouragement – it means a lot. I'll keep writing if you keep reading – deal?

Dear Reader,

We hope you enjoyed reading this book. If you did, we'd be so appreciative if you left a review. It really helps us and the author to bring more books like this to you.

Here at HQ Digital we are dedicated to publishing fiction that will keep you turning the pages into the early hours. Don't want to miss a thing? To find out more about our books, promotions, discover exclusive content and enter competitions you can keep in touch in the following ways:

JOIN OUR COMMUNITY:

Sign up to our new email newsletter: http://smarturl.it/SignUpHQ

Read our new blog www.hqstories.co.uk

𝕏: https://twitter.com/HQStories

: www.facebook.com/HQStories

BUDDING WRITER?

We're also looking for authors to join the HQ Digital family! Find out more here:

https://www.hqstories.co.uk/want-to-write-for-us/

Thanks for reading, from the HQ Digital team